Dr. James C. ('Jim') Hendee worked as a scientist for the U.S. Government for 30 years before retiring in September, 2020. He has authored or co-authored 63 scientific publications, written two novels, been a commercial fisherman in Alaska, an aquaculturist in Hawaii and Texas, a snake-hunter and orchid collector in the Florida Everglades, worked on the Trans-Alaska Pipeline, served in the Peace Corps, worked for three universities, and has been a scuba diver in the Pacific, the Indian, the Arctic, and the Atlantic Oceans (Florida and the Caribbean). He currently lives in Pompano Beach, Florida.

Dedicated to the late
Julianne "Jules" Nordby-Milanese

James C. Hendee

STONES

AUSTIN MACAULEY PUBLISHERS
LONDON * CAMBRIDGE * NEW YORK * SHARJAH

Copyright © James C. Hendee 2023

All rights reserved. No part of this publication may be reproduced, distributed, or transmitted in any form or by any means, including photocopying, recording, or other electronic or mechanical methods, without the prior written permission of the publisher, except in the case of brief quotations embodied in critical reviews and certain other non-commercial uses permitted by copyright law. For permission requests, write to the publisher.

Any person who commits any unauthorized act in relation to this publication may be liable to criminal prosecution and civil claims for damages.

This is a work of fiction. Names, characters, businesses, places, events, locales, and incidents are either the products of the author's imagination or used in a fictitious manner. Any resemblance to actual persons, living or dead, or actual events is purely coincidental.

Ordering Information
Quantity sales: Special discounts are available on quantity purchases by corporations, associations, and others. For details, contact the publisher at the address below.

Publisher's Cataloging-in-Publication data
Hendee , James C.
Stones

ISBN 9781638292616 (Paperback)
ISBN 9781638292623 (ePub e-book)

Library of Congress Control Number: 2023901103

www.austinmacauley.com/us

First Published 2023
Austin Macauley Publishers LLC
40 Wall Street, 33rd Floor, Suite 3302
New York, NY 10005
USA

mail-usa@austinmacauley.com
+1 (646) 5125767

There are so many to thank for just being supportive, but I would first like to thank Jeff Sali for his editorial skills on this and my previous novel, *Codon Zero*.

I would also like to thank Linda Pikula, the best librarian I've ever had the great pleasure to meet, formerly, like myself, of the National Oceanic and Atmospheric Administration's Atlantic Oceanographic and Meteorological Laboratory. She graciously offered to help in her off-time, and I greatly appreciate it.

I should also like to thank Marcia King-Gamble, a prolific romance novelist and friend, who has helped me understand the ropes of the publishing business and introduced me to the very informative and helpful, Mystery Writers of America/Florida Chapter.

Without the help of an FBI Special Agent, who prefers to remain anonymous, I certainly would not have gotten some of the great information about guns, agencies, bad guys, and so forth. Thanks, my friend!

I would also like to thank all the members of my immediate family: my brother, Bruce; my adult kids, Kazz, Kiel, and Katy—who showed unwavering support (or were they humoring me?); as well as my ex-wife, Sonja; an extremely intelligent lady friend, Raizha Chiesi, who has put up with yet another pipe dream in the writing of this book.

And finally, though they passed away some years back, I would like to acknowledge the continual support in writing as I grew up, of my mother and father, Keith and Ellen Hendee.

The most precious jewels are not made of stone, but of flesh.

—Robert Ludlum

Chapter One
Pact Over Saba Bank

"This time," said Kostya Chugunkin, "I want you to kidnap the American President's daughter for me." He was a tall handsome man of medium build in his mid-fifties and white hair. He turned to his partner in human trafficking, Zoran Marek—a slightly overweight man in his early fifties with a thick mat of black and gray hair all over his body—and said, "If you can't do that, then I want you to kill her."

Marek, as he preferred to be called, was silent for a moment. "That's a tough one—I don't know if it's worth the heat."

They were walking toward the open afterdeck of Kostya's superyacht, the *Turquoise Lament*, where next to the pool was a large satellite-connected television screen that had the sound turned low. Surrounding the TV were two lushly upholstered and curved bamboo sofas. Behind the TV was the Eastern Caribbean Sea, and as the sun began to set, it imbued the sky with a magnificent fuchsia changing to amaranth. Kostya's barman placed two cold pisco sours with whalebone coasters on the glass table in front of them, then retreated and the two men sat down.

The winds were calm and the surface of the ocean was nearly flat, save the occasional slight heave originating from the North Atlantic thousands of miles to the north. Below them one could see the magnificent tapestry of corals and of fish moving only forty feet below, though the water was so clear it appeared as though you could touch them easily by merely sticking your hand into the warm sea.

Marek looked Kostya directly in the eye. "Are you serious?"

"Deadly."

"You know I'm good at this, and I have a better than fifty-fifty chance of pulling it off, but it would cost you twenty-five million."

Kostya just stared at the sunset and nodded his head slightly. "But only half that if you have to kill her."

Marek said, "All right. May I presume that she is for your own enjoyment?"

"You may, but I will probably sell her to another yacht owner for more. As you know, the President has many enemies who would delight in abusing her, even though they wouldn't be stupid enough to let the President know they had her."

"And may I ask why you picked her in particular?"

"The fucking President's Homeland Security Investigations froze all my assets in Antigua for trade-based money laundering, and I want them back. We're talking about one hundred million American dollars. Take his daughter and I'll demand he let me transfer the funds out of that bank. If he does, I'll let her go on some island with a canteen and a chewy bar."

"To our continuing ventures," said Marek, as he held up his glass for a toast. "I accept your challenge."

"Good, I'm glad," replied Kostya. They toasted and took the first swallow. "Now let's finish up our original business."

Marek wiped the froth from his upper lip and said, "I've inspected all six of the young women you've brought me and they are magnificent. You have chosen well, as usual, my friend. Extremely well. My clients will be overjoyed and appreciative when they see them."

"Exceptionally beautiful women are difficult to find, but it's a great challenge," said Kostya with a broad smile. "Could a man of leisure have anything more enjoyable to do?"

"I think not," said Marek, as he handed Kostya a blue velvet bag. "I trust you will find the payment of equal quality?"

Kostya spilled the contents of the blue bag onto the glass table in front of them; out tumbled three large deep blue sapphires and three light blue diamonds, one of which was easily fifteen carats.

"Magnificent!" said Kostya, his eyes widening. "That is quite generous of you, sir." He picked them up and inspected each one. "We have made each other very rich selling women and children over these last five years, have we not?"

"You started out rich anyway, my friend," said Marek, "but I thank you for giving me the opportunity to enrich myself, so paying you top dollar is my way of saying thank you. I already have buyers for the women too, so they won't be at the mountain for very long."

"Good, very good," said Kostya. "I shall bring you some more as soon as I can return and arrange it." He gathered the resplendent stones into the bag and left it on the table between them.

They sat back to watch the TV, which was showing a benefit for the relatives of the victims of the Covid-19 pandemic that had killed so many people before vaccines were finally developed. They continued to watch and soon they were both drunk and laughing at their own jokes.

Finally, on the big TV screen, there was a beautiful country western singer with long, thick red hair, named Colorado Jacquette, who got up on the stage and sang her heart out and brought the house down with long-lasting applause and shouting.

"Boy, wouldn't I love to get a piece of that," said Kostya quietly.

After a few moments of silence, Marek said, "Well, exactly how much *would* you pay to have a piece of that one, too?"

Kostya bent over laughing and spat out his drink. "Damn, Marek," he said. "What, grabbing the President's daughter isn't a big enough challenge?"

"Well, you'd have to pay me, in loose stones, as usual, but I could try."

Kostya laughed. "You're crazy. You'd never get close enough to either one."

"So you were not serious about the Pearl woman after all?"

"Oh yes I am, *very* serious, but it's not my ass on the line to get caught. It's yours. But I will pay you if you can pull it off."

Marek smiled as he finished his pisco sour. "I shall get you both," he said, putting his glass down hard on the table. "But it's going to cost you forty million in precious stones."

Kostya stared at Marek for long seconds. "You are out of your mind," he scoffed. "There's no way you could even get close to the redhead, never mind kidnap the President's daughter."

"You underestimate my team, Kostya. Forty million for both of them. If I just get the redhead, fifteen million. If I only get Charise Pearl, twenty-five million. If I get both, forty million."

"'Only'. Hah! Marek, you'll be dead or in jail for the rest of your life before you know what happened. I mean, I do believe you're the best man to do this, and I'm willing to pay, but it's just such a long shot." He stopped and was just shaking his head. "I don't know…"

"So, you don't have the forty million, is that it?"

Kostya's face turned red with anger. "Of course, I have the forty million. You know I do. We're floating on many times that much right now. Just make Charise Pearl your priority, and if you can get the other one, excellent."

"What you do with them after you get them is your problem—or pleasure. I'm going to disappear."

"Well, I'd keep them and face-fuck them whenever I damn well felt like it, at least until I've found another yacht owner like I usually do, but you'll probably get busted before you even get close to Pearl."

"You underestimate me, Kostya. Promise me that if I get either one of those women that you'll pay me what I ask. In the meantime, keep the girls coming as you've been doing, and I'll pay you as usual in the best of precious stones."

Kostya motioned to the barman to bring them both another drink. He stood and looked out at the sun going down over a flat sea and laughed out loud again.

"Okay, you crazy bastard, if you can pull that off, I will pay you what you ask, but I'm not going to pay you for trying. The expenses and how you're going to do it are all on you. I want no part of the logistics, and I don't want to know anything about this plan. If you are so unbelievably lucky—"

"Talented," interrupted Marek, his face deadly serious.

"—if you are so unbelievably *talented* as to deliver either or both of those women, I will pay you what you ask."

"In loose stones," said Marek. "Just like we've always done."

"Well, of course. I'll have the weight and worth certified ahead of time, okay?"

"Deal."

The two men leaned forward and shook hands. Kostya laughed loudly yet again, but Marek just looked hard into Kostya's eyes with a cold stare. "You'd better start saving your pennies, my friend," he said. "I'm good at this, and you know it."

Kostya just laughed as he took the drink from the barman. "See you soon," he said, and raised his glass to an already departing Marek, who waved goodbye without looking at him and headed down to his own boat, the *Bloodstone*, docked inside the *Turquoise Lament's* aft tender garage.

Chapter Two
Starry Night

The three women were held captive by the confines of the yacht *Emeraldine* and the expanse of a calm black sea under a cloudless night with a new moon and scintillating stars. The yacht was one hundred one feet long and rested motionless, save the occasional movement by the autopilot to stay on station. They were at an agreed upon spot off the coast of Fort Lauderdale, Florida, to exchange the women for a dazzling and large collection of precious gems.

To the north northwest, in the distance, the skipper could see the expected yacht heading straight for them. He called over his shoulder to the first mate, "Here they come, off the port bow."

The first mate, whose name was Nadav, made ready the rubber fenders and the lines for hoving-to with the oncoming vessel. He then stepped down the companionway to the cabin below where the three women sat glumly and apprehensively on the couches along the bulkheads. "Get ready. We're moving you to another boat."

The women solemnly gathered their purses and things they'd been allowed to keep.

Soon the approaching yacht was but a hundred yards away when it began to slow its engines. Its following wake pushed it gently up and down as it caught up with the boat then the engine was cut to a silent idle speed.

The captain of the *Emeraldine* switched on the searchlight and shone it at the approaching yacht. As the distance closed, he barked through the ship's hailer, "Ahoy! Name your vessel!"

The other skipper blared back on his hailer, "London Blue!"

"Come alongside, then."

The *London Blue* made her way slowly to come abeam of the *Emeraldine*.

One man from each vessel tied lines to their bow, stern and beam cleats, cinching the boats snug against the rubber fenders between them. One other man on each boat held submachine guns and locked eyes on the others, their guns pointing obliquely at no one in particular. The skipper of the *Emeraldine* took quick glances at the men and their activities while the skipper of the *London Blue* stood in the dark of the cabin by the wheel of his boat.

The skipper of the *Emeraldine* stepped to the gunwale and shouted at the other skipper. "Step out here. Let me see the stones."

The skipper of the *London Blue* stepped into the glow of the faint deck lights. His hair was black and peppered with silver, and he had a beer drinker's belly. His lower lip protruded from a grizzled face with puffy cheeks. With little effort, his voice, used to shouting orders over stormy seas and diesel engines, projected very loud and gravelly: "Let me see the women first."

Neither skipper moved for a moment then the skipper of the *Emeraldine* turned and shouted down the companionway, "All right ladies, let's go, everybody up on deck."

The women came up the companionway.

"Right," the skipper of the *Emeraldine* shouted, "now show me the stones!" Everyone on the *Emeraldine* was now facing the skipper and crew of the *London Blue*.

Just then, a man in a wetsuit and still wet from a breath-hold dive below both boats silently and quickly pulled himself up onto the transom of the *Emeraldine* and with a Glock 21 shot its skipper in the back of the head. The man with a submachine gun on the *London Blue* opened fire on the other two men and killed them before they got off a single shot.

The women screamed—all except one who immediately took three quick steps across the after-deck and dove off the starboard quarter of the stern and into the deep black water.

The skipper of the *London Blue* bellowed, "Find her!" He tossed a flashlight to one of his men, then all the men quietly searched the sea around them. The skipper climbed to the flying bridge, turned on the searchlight, and began shining near the stern of the *Emeraldine* looking for her.

The man in the wetsuit stepped quickly back over to the *London Blue* and retrieved an underwater light and fins from the dive bag he'd left on deck. He put on his fins and jumped back in the water to look for the woman.

The two captive women screamed hysterically, looking down as they stepped in the spreading blood from the slain crew of the *Emeraldine*. The skipper lay face up, his eyes open but lifeless. The crew members were twisted and crumpled in death and still bleeding profusely.

* * *

The woman who had jumped into the sea held her breath as she swam back under the two boats and toward the bow of the *London Blue*. She had been on boats before and was a diver and knew it would be hard for them to see her if she were just under the bow. If none of them jumped into the sea to look for her, she had a chance—a slim one, but a chance.

Then she heard the splash and realized the man with the wetsuit had probably jumped into the water to find her. She took a deep breath and dove down as far as she could, her eyes constantly opened. In the pitch black and with no face mask, everything was blurry, but she could see the man's underwater light surveying the area in front of the direction in which he was traveling; he had no scuba gear so he was holding his breath too.

He was moving away from her so she surfaced as silently as she could but bumped her head on the hull of the *London Blue*. She swam underwater toward where she thought the bow was and surfaced again quietly. She was close to the bow but not under it like she was before. She backstroked further away from the boat, keeping a careful eye on the lights flashing from the boat out over the sea, then dove again to see where the skin diver was heading. He was heading toward her, the arc of his light swinging back and forth. She surfaced quietly again, saw there were no lights shining out toward her, then—so there were no splashes from her swimming—quickly swam a breaststroke away from the diver.

She turned and stuck her head under water and noticed by the glow that he was returning toward the boat. She dove down and swam toward him, but not too close, as he swam toward the boat. She pulled up near the bow again, and waited for the diver to return to the boat.

The diver swam up next to a ladder the crew had put down for him and said, "Nothing. I couldn't find her."

She heard the skipper of the *London Blue* roar from the flying bridge down to his men, "Never mind! There's no way she can survive out here without a boat. You women over there, shut the hell up and move over here!"

The women continued whimpering, frozen in fear.

"I said move! Now!"

She heard the two other women struggle mightily to contain their cries as they stepped quietly over to the *London Blue*.

The skipper spoke loudly from the flying bridge to the men scattered about the boat: "We'll just have to make do with the two of them. I'll go ahead and meet Julene at Aruba's on Saturday at noon like we planned and call Marek and tell him what happened. Nothing else we can do. Torch the boat and let's get the hell out of here."

The woman in the sea treaded water in a gathering panic wondering what to do next. She heard the crew scurry around below deck, then peeked around the bow to see them carrying fuel cans back over to the *Emeraldine*. They doused the yacht and its dead crew with the fuel, then stepped back aboard the *London Blue*. The crew untied the lines, then she heard the engine engage with the propeller and saw the boat start to creep forward slowly. The crew threw some flares over onto the *Emeraldine* and in seconds the boat was on fire with flames spreading rapidly.

Just as she took a deep breath and swam as deeply as she could, she heard the engine roar and finally diminish as it sped away from the scene. Her lungs bursting, she shot to the surface and gasped. The *Emeraldine* was ablaze and the heat warmed her face. She turned as she treaded water and saw the *London Blue* speeding away, its white wake shining and undulating under the brilliant moonlight and starry skies, the low roar of the engine fading in the distance.

There were no other boats nearby and the coast was too far away to see clearly, but at least she saw some lights. As she turned again to look at the blazing boat, she could see it begin to sink slowly, then more rapidly, and then it was gone. There was nothing for her to do now but swim for the lights and pray for survival.

Chapter Three
Marathon

Jason Geronimo Stouter was on the last lap of his jog along a trail through the mangrove thicket near his house on Yellowtail Beach, a short distance from the city of Marathon on the island of Key Vaca in the Florida Keys. At six and a half feet tall, with thick jet-black hair and still retaining the high cheek bones and swarthy skin of his half-Apache heritage, his routine dedication to keep the muscle on and the fat off, made for an impressive warrior of a man for being in his early forties.

The day was the typical steamy heat in the high eighties in the Keys, and the woody smell of the mangroves and Geiger trees filled the air yet restrained any possible breeze from cooling Jason in his run.

Jamie Horgood stepped into the path a short distance in front of him. Jason knew her well, every inch of her—every golden-furred curve of her sensuous body and the moist puffiness of her lips. He thought of her often, though they hadn't been lovers since their time together in the Agency just a few years ago.

His pace slowed and he placed his hands on his hips as he slowed to a walk, his breathing labored and sweat pouring into his soaked "Conch Nation" T-shirt.

"Jamie," he said, smiling and shaking his head slowly.

"Hi, Jason," she said quietly.

He loved that big beautiful toothy smile of hers, and the cascade of her lush brown hair over her shoulders enhanced her sunny charm and slim physique. She wore a shiny turquoise blouse and khaki knee-length shorts.

Still breathing heavily from his run, he said, "God you are so beautiful. Still."

"Well, it hasn't been that long," she said with an affected frown.

Jason lifted her and they embraced with a short kiss.

"Is this an official visit, or would I be so lucky as to entertain you for a vacation?"

"I wish," she said. He put her down and they turned and walked slowly with arms around each other toward Jason's home.

"Are you still an Intelligence Analyst in International Operations working for Homeland Security Investigations?" asked Jason.

"I am that, and HSI just received an anonymous tip," she began, "a recording, and they believe it's reliable, but they don't want to sidetrack personnel on something that may go nowhere, especially with all this crap happening in the Middle East after the Middle East Plague. It's all hands on deck for that."

She didn't know of Jason's involvement in that and he saw no reason to tell her. His great friend Sali Bryant, and his former secretary, the beautiful Celine Venturi, had miraculously survived and nobody from the Agency or the Bureau was keen for the word to get out on that one. Codon Zero could remain a secret forever as far as they were all concerned.

Jason turned his head to her and waited for her to continue as the south Florida sun beat down upon them. He caught a waft of her "Mariel" perfume and felt a stab of regret for their separation back then. They had broken each other's hearts, but remained close after the salve of time.

"They want to subcontract you to follow up on a lead," she said, as they continued their slow walk, "See what's there. If you find something, then we'll follow up and take care of it."

"So, what's the tip?"

"We got a call from a man who says that a woman named Julene is supposed to be receiving a large number of stolen jewels from a man whom the informant described as a tall fat captain of a yacht with a face that looks like Bluto from the old Popeye comics—big white teeth surrounded by a jet-black mustache and beard. He wears a blue sailor's cap with no insignias or marks on it. The transfer is supposed to happen this coming Saturday at a restaurant in Fort Lauderdale called Aruba's Beachside Cafe. I checked it out online. It's on the beach at the end of Commercial Boulevard."

"Ah, yes, I know it well. I've been there a few times. Great place. Right on the beach. Live music every night."

"The source said the jewels are part of an international kidnapping and human trafficking scheme. That's what makes it HSI business, as well as the Bureau's business, and the Department of State's, if it's true."

They stopped. "I'm embarrassed to say I don't know much about human trafficking except from what I've read—I mean I've never witnessed it. I don't know how to recognize it because it's apparently so well hidden, and I don't see the connection between jewel smuggling and human trafficking anyway."

"We don't know what the connection is, except, thing is, you can't just grab the jewels, especially since we don't even know if there are any jewels, and we have no probable cause and don't know enough, but if you see a man who fits the description handing anything over to a woman, then follow the woman and see what you can find out about her. Maybe you can get Sali's help, too, and follow the captain and find out where he goes and what he does."

Jason nodded. "Let me check up on a few things and I'll give you a yes or no tomorrow."

"If you decide yes, we'll bankroll you as an outside contractor up to a point—just let me know what you want to do and how you want to do it, along with a budget, so I can report it up the chain."

Jason smiled and nodded. "Okay. Would you like to stay for dinner?"

Her eyes glistened and she smiled. "I'd love to."

* * *

Jason's internal clock woke him at four-thirty the next morning. He lit a candle next to his bed then turned gently so as not to awaken her. She was asleep with a small smile on her face, just as he had always remembered her. He never knew any other women who did that—smiled all night long. It was so nice to be with her again.

"Hey, sleepyhead," he murmured. "Time for your morning exercise program."

Her grin widened and she put her arm around him without opening her eyes. "Are you leading?"

They kissed and the exercises commenced.

* * *

"It's good to be with you again, Jason," she said as she dressed.

Jason smiled. "Indeed."

A short while after a delicious breakfast of island fruits and scrambled eggs with bell peppers, onions and cheddar cheese, Jason stood in front of his house and waved goodbye to her as she roared off to the Miami Airport in her compact rental car. He would miss her, but it was nice to know they were working together again, and nice to know neither sought to possess the other. He turned and walked back into the house and called his partner in Key West, Sali Bryant, recently retired from the FBI and now part of Jason's recently formed private intelligence gathering firm, Tiger's Eye.

"Hey, what's for breakfast," yawned Sali as he answered his cell phone.

"Can you make it to The Stuffed Pig any time soon?"

"Well I don't know, I'm pretty busy watching flies shit on the dishes right now. This life of retirement is exciting."

"We've got a job. Can you pack for a week or so and come on up?"

"Be there in sixty."

* * *

There are at least two great old breakfast spots in Marathon—Stout's across from the airport, and The Stuffed Pig, across from the jail. Jason had arrived early at the Pig and was reading the local paper, *The Keynoter,* when Sali pushed through the front door.

"How come I can never get a decent cup of coffee in this joint," barked Sali. Everybody in the restaurant looked around to see who this rude person was. He stood there in the doorway, a rather short and stocky man with a thick brown beard and wearing sunglasses.

"Good morning, Sali," said Sue the waitress. "You love our coffee and you know it. What'll you have?"

Jason stood and shook hands with Sali, like two pythons battling over a rat. "Chow's on me. I already ate. Good to see you again."

Sali settled in and ordered his usual meal, Sue hovering about, laying silverware and a napkin, then Jason turned the chat to Jamie's visit and what she wanted them to do.

"So, I was thinking," continued Jason, "this job sounds like we could maybe use your old friend, the famous ex-jewel thief Masen."

"Ah, yes," said Sali as he put down his coffee cup. "Masen Williams." He nodded and chewed on his remaining piece of bacon. "Not a bad idea. I'll give him a call. When do you want to leave?"

"Soon as you finish eating."

* * *

On the way to Jason's safe house on Grassy Key, one island north from Key Vaca on Overseas Highway, Sali pulled out his cell phone and called his old nemesis and now friend, Masen Williams.

"Hey, you being good?"

They exchanged a few pleasantries then Sali said, "You remember I told you about Jason Stouter? Yeah. We're heading up your way; you going to be around? We've got a little project you might be interested in."

Sali listened. "Beautiful! Can't wait to see it!"

Another pause. "Great. Okay, we'll be up there in about two or three hours. See you then."

He turned to Jason. "All set. We'll meet him at a place called Pelican's Landing at Pier 66 off 17th Street Causeway. And get this: he's bought a motor-sailor since the last time I saw him. A thirty-six-foot Cheoy Lee. Lots of bunk space. He said we could stay on his boat if we'd like."

"Can't wait to meet the guy."

The safe house on Grassy Key was a place few people knew about and fewer still its whereabouts. It was a fortress of sorts nestled back in the mangroves on the Florida Bay side of the island, surrounded by a gate and fortified with security cameras and alarms. Jason pulled up to the gate first, unlocked it, then swung it back for them both to enter and park inside the grounds. Jason relocked the gate then moved toward the stairway leading up to the main body of the house. He gestured with his chin toward a white surveillance van parked under the house. "We'll take the van after I double-check everything."

Jason punched in the number sequence on the digital lock on the front door and they entered. "Want some more coffee or anything?"

"Nah, I'm good."

Jason nodded then waved him to follow. "Help me pick out some toys, then let's book."

They moved down the hallway to the first bedroom on the left. Jason unlocked and opened up a large walk-in cabinet that folded out into three large sections. On the walls of the cabinet were an array of pistols and assault weapons and knives of different sizes and grenades, GPS trackers, binoculars, flares, C-4, various killing tools, a drawer holding ammunition, and a box of miscellaneous combat goodies. "Take your pick," said Jason as he grabbed his favorite all around gun, the Heckler & Koch Mark 23. "You never know what we might run into. I still like the Mark 23 for an all-around good gun. It uses a .45 ACP cartridge, even +P, it's waterproof, and it's rugged as hell."

Sali hesitated for a moment. "Nice! Can we take all of them?"

"Hmmm, I don't see why not—you never know…"

* * *

The surveillance van was decked out with all the necessary tools of the trade: periscope, a pan-tilt-zoom camera, microphones around the outside of the van, an antenna system for audio and visual data feeds, a bank of batteries to run all the gear, battery chargers, computer recording system, a remote access system for controlling cameras and microphones from afar, a refrigerator, an air conditioner and a heater, a carbon monoxide detector, two comfortable seats, and a fold-down cot.

In the front seat, Sali drove while Jason dialed Jamie's number.

"So, you made it back okay?"

Her field office was in Miami, off northwest twentieth street, so it hadn't taken her long.

"Yeah," she replied, "not too bad of a trip, actually."

"I met with Sali and we're in. In fact, he's here in the van with me and we're on our way up to Fort Lauderdale right now to meet an associate of Sali's then we'll come up with a plan."

"An associate? Jason, be careful. I'd rather he didn't know this is HSI business if you can help it."

"Don't worry, I'll be careful."

"Keep me posted," she said with a sigh, then hung up.

"She's a great lady, Jason," said Sali as Jason crawled back up front. "How come you two never stuck with each other?"

Jason reminisced for a moment. "Well, you remember the place she and I had up in Silver Spring after we met at The Farm. You took off to do your thing for the Bureau, and after that she and I had some good times then we didn't see each other for a while until we ended up on the same job. We hooked up, but then we got to traveling so much we spent more time apart from each other than we did together. We started getting into stupid arguments then realized we'd be better off as friends before we hated each other. I guess that happens to a lot of couples. She moved to the HSI field office in Miami and I stayed in DC until that flap with the Mossad, then I moved to the Keys."

He was quiet for some time, then changed the subject. "So, tell me about Masen Williams again. I don't think you ever told me the whole story. You just said he was one of the greatest jewel thieves of all time, but you finally caught him."

"Masen always worked alone after getting busted when he was a kid because of his knucklehead accomplice who did something stupid, I don't remember what. Over the course of his years of stealing, Masen made off with up to thirty-five million dollars in jewels."

"Thirty-five million?"

"A true master jewel thief, maybe the best ever in America. Or worst, depending upon how you look at it."

"So how did you catch him?"

"We never caught him in the act of stealing any jewels—we got him on circumstantial evidence, then we found his stash. We suspected him for a long time, but couldn't pin anything on him. Then we stopped him right after a robbery in the neighborhood and I found an address book on him. It was the same address book that was taken from one of his victims, and it had the names and addresses of hundreds of movie stars and other famous people in it, many of which ended up being his victims."

"But that was all you needed?"

"It was enough for a search warrant. We checked out his place and found a key to a safe deposit box at his bank. We got another search warrant for that, then we had him. We opened the box, which was the biggest type they offered, and the jewels in there were enough to melt your eyeballs. Emeralds, sapphires, diamonds, rubies, necklaces, bracelets, earrings…just absolutely astounding stuff. A true king's ransom in jewels, and that was only some of it. He'd already fenced most of it by the time we got him."

"So, he went to jail."

"Yes."

Jason looked over at him and waited a moment for him to continue, but he didn't. Sali slowed as they came upon a pickup overloaded with lobster traps.

"So how did the two of you end up friends?"

Sali snapped out of his reverie. "During that time I was bird-dogging him, I quite often talked with him, just to keep him looking over his shoulder. We even got to having lunch together a few times, but I never could get him to trip up and give me any clues. At any rate, we finally got to liking each other. Crazy. Here I was trying to send him up the river, and he just smiled and never gave me any clues."

"And after he was in the can, what then? Did you find out how he pulled off the jobs?"

"Yeah, he told me quite a bit, actually. He used to check out the society pages in the Sunday papers to see who might be good targets. His view was: 'They could afford it'."

A fast Harley passed them and drowned out any conversation, then Sali spoke again.

"He always worked alone. The more people that knew what he was doing, he figured, the more his chances of getting busted."

"Makes sense."

"Also, he never fenced the jewels locally. He'd drive long distances to do that."

Sali paused in thought.

Jason prodded. "Doesn't seem like you'd still be friends after busting him."

"Well, the guy had a sort of Robin Hood mentality. Sometimes when he'd fence the jewels, he'd give the money to charities, anonymously, of course. In fact, he gave most of it away. That's why it was so hard to find him at first—no outward signs of unexplained wealth. At any rate, after he was busted, he told me about that and I did some researching and found traces of evidence that proved he was telling the truth, so I spoke up for him at the trial and the judge reduced his sentence by half."

"Ah, no wonder you're friends."

A mile passed as Sali explained a bit more about Masen's personality and capabilities, then Jason spoke.

"So, here's the deal," he said as they passed Bud & Mary's Marina in Tavernier. "We have to see if we can spot this lady named Julene at a place called Aruba's at the end of Commercial Boulevard, downtown Lauderdale-By-The-Sea. I know the place well. I figure we can get a table at a place called The Village Pump right next to it, or Mulligan's across the street. We'll hopefully notice if we see her meeting a captain-looking guy." Jason gave him the same description Jamie had given him.

"Well," said Sali, flicking the ash of his cigarette toward the ashtray but missing, "if we're each going to follow the captain dude or this Julene, how are we going to do that if we're both in a surveillance van?"

The smell of Sali's cigarettes was unique but annoying and caused Jason to try and wave it away from his face. Sali always smoked Djarum Blacks, a black Indonesian brand of tobacco and cloves he always seemed able to find.

"I figure we can rent a car when we get up there."

"Wait, I've got a number for Enterprise—I used them a couple months ago. Hold on…" Sali reached for his cell phone and did a search on his cell phone while carelessly running oncoming traffic off the road.

"New experience for you, is it? Driving high speed while doing a Google search on your phone?"

"Hello, Enterprise? Yes, can I get an SUV for a week to ten days?" Pause. "Lexus LX? Is that the big one? Yeah, I'll take it. Name is Sali Bryant, and the credit card number is…wait a minute…"

Sali sneezed as he reached for his wallet out of his back pocket, fetched the card, then slipped quickly between an oncoming Peterbilt and passed a pickup truck full of crab pots.

Jason held up his company credit card and shrugged. "Why not use mine?"

"Don't worry, all tickets are covered for now." He switched back to the phone. "Okay, the number is…" He finished the transaction, lit another Djarum Black and coughed deeply for a few seconds.

Jason waved the smoke away again. "Do you mind if I drive for a while? I don't know what's going to kill me first, your driving or your cigarettes…"

Chapter Four
Fortress

The island from the sea appeared to be just another mangrove choked, coral reef-encircled, limestone-encrusted, mosquito-ridden, jungle hell with a single mountain on it, but behind the wall of green a carefully engineered and elegant fortress had been built to keep people out as well as to keep them in.

Zoran Marek, known to his condo-rent-for-sex mistress Julene and American authorities as Michael Fieldstone, stood in his robe as he ended his phone conversation with his half-brother Brevon Reznik. He surveyed the seascape from his balcony which was cut into the cliffside and helped hide the island fortress from prying eyes from the sea as well as from the skies. The ocean was rough this morning and whitecaps studded the angry deep blue expanse all the way to the horizon. Miles to the north he could see a lone container ship braving the seas and bringing food supplies to his hidden fortress. They would anchor about a mile off shore, and his crew would ferry the supplies using the Chris Craft.

He called for his right-hand man, Beldam Gorsh. He was a colossal specimen of a man—two inches over seven feet tall, three hundred and twenty-two pounds of muscle, tremendous arms and chest, and no fat. The guy was to a linebacker what a gorilla was to a chimpanzee, yet with a trim waist. For exercise, he swam around the island three times a week.

"Reznik got the jewels okay," said Marek, "but Amber Spring jumped overboard. They couldn't find her so they left her out there to drown." He removed his robe and reached for his pants and shirt. He was flabby and white, and covered with obscenely coarse, black hair.

"But I know she swam a lot for her morning exercise program," he continued, "so it's possible she was able to swim to shore. Highly doubtful, but possible. I want you to send some men to watch his house and follow her husband. If she makes it ashore, sooner or later she'll call him and he'll go to see her, or she will go to see him."

Gorsh started to leave.

"Wait. How are things with the new group?"

"The children are just finishing breakfast, the women after that."

Marek nodded. "I'll meet you down there in five minutes."

Gorsh turned and left.

Marek moved from his office past his private dining room to his bedroom. In the bed his companion for the previous evening, a young teenage girl with long black hair and olive skin, was still asleep. He had ravaged her all night long.

"Wake up," he barked. "Go down and get some breakfast then go back to your cell."

The girl grabbed her clothes off the chair, dressed quickly, then left without a sound.

Marek soon left and walked downstairs to the main dining area for the captives. It was a large room with fluorescent lighting and a series of folding dining tables and steel metal chairs. As he entered the middle door of the dining area a group of twenty-three children had finished their lunch and were filing out. The twenty-fourth, the girl from Marek's bed, was rapidly stuffing cornbread and bacon into her mouth. Marek motioned to Gorsh, who had just walked in through the opposite door, to let the girl eat.

Marek looked to his left and called out to a boy leaving the room at the end of the line. "*Oye, tú, ven aquí.*"

The boy turned to look at Marek, then turned his eyes downward and froze, terrified.

"*Ven aca,*" commanded Marek.

Slowly the boy walked over to within a few feet of him and stopped, his eyes still facing downward in fright.

Marek held up the boy's chin and said, "*Dime, cómo te llamas?*"

Very quietly, the boy said, "*Juan.*"

"*Juan, ¿cuántos años tienes?*"

"*Trece años.*"

"Thirteen" Marek said out loud for the benefit of Gorsh who didn't speak Spanish.

"*De dónde eres?*"

"*De La Habana.*"

Marek nodded and waved him away: "*Ya te puedes ir.*"

The boy ran away quickly.

Marek turned to Gorsh. "He's from Havana. He'll do fine. Keep him healthy."

"Okay, let's do the weekly inspection. I'm getting concerned about fuel for the generator."

As they left the cafeteria for the slave-children, they took a left and walked deeper into the mountain, within a minute they came to a door marked "Do Not Enter," and which was locked. A loud hum was emanating from behind the door. Marek took out his keys and unlocked the door. As soon as he entered, he reached for the two pairs of earmuffs to protect against the overbearing sound of the two diesel generators. He handed one to Gorsh and put one on himself. They walked over to the two large fuel tanks that had to be painstakingly filled, barrel by barrel, before they started operation. There were at least twenty spare barrels of diesel within this particular room. Marek stopped for a minute to remember the large project.

* * *

Marek inspected the two humming diesels and the fuel gauges of both and made a mental note to arrange for another transport of fuel in barrels at his earliest convenience.

"They sound pretty good," said Gorsh. "I think they'll last for a long time."

Marek nodded, then they hung up their earmuffs and left the room.

As they stepped outside, he said to Gorsh, "We're going to need more fuel soon, but you might as well make an order to bring the usual food and drink in on the same freighter, save us some money. Give the captain a bonus, too, for keeping his mouth shut, but with the usual threat about his family disappearing if he talks."

"You got it," said Gorsh.

"Let's go take a look at the lagoon berth to make sure it's ready for the submarine Kostya is loaning us. She'll be bringing us our main prize."

Chapter Five
The Master

Back in 1956, Phillips Petroleum, of Bartlesville, Oklahoma, bought a piece of land on the east side of the Intracoastal Waterway, near Port Everglades in Fort Lauderdale, Florida, with the intention of installing a gas station. Because of its prime location near the beaches and boaters, money was invested to build a pier and a marina for a hundred yachts. Its popularity grew as the marina was enlarged to accommodate one hundred twenty slips. A seventeen-story hotel called Pier 66 was built, complete with a revolving cocktail lounge at the top that attracted big shots from all over the world, although today it is open only for special occasions.

On the northwestern part of the property sits Pelican Landing, a small two-story restaurant that is visited mostly by yacht owners in the marina. In the wind was the smell of a fisherman's filleting of freshly caught fish, and in the background, you could hear a tourist ship blasting its horn as it began to dock next to the Seventeenth Street Causeway Bridge.

As Jason and Sali approached the restaurant, they looked up to the second floor and saw a man with long flowing thick gray hair and sunglasses parked on top of his head. He was wearing a black t-shirt billowing slightly in the breeze and smiled through a three-day old growth of gray stubble. "Sali, my long-lost friend!" Masen shouted. "Come on up you guys!"

As he shook hands with Masen, Jason was startled by the man's brilliant blue eyes which owed nothing to that oceanic northward-flowing warm and swift river of the sea, the Gulf Stream. His powerful grip, as Jason later found, was due to his occupational practice of hanging by his fingers from balcony ledges of the condos he had plundered over the years for gems and jewelry.

They sat at an outside wooden table. A slight breeze refreshed them as they basked in a radiant afternoon sun.

"Are you boys hungry?" Masen asked. He hailed a waiter to their table and turned to his two guests: "The conch chowder is to die for."

As they waited for chowder and smoked fish dip, Sali offered a toast with their newly arrived cold beers to their new alliance: "Chowder for three by the deep blue sea."

All three took healthy swigs then Jason spoke up.

"Masen, I know you're wondering why we came up here. Here's the deal. I have friends like Sali here in the FBI and also the CIA, where I used to work, but also in Homeland Security Investigations, or HSI. Those agencies use me now and then at arm's length as a contractor to do stuff they can deny but still need to get done, or just because they're overloaded with routine work. One of those times has come up. They got a tip there may be some kidnappers who ask for gemstones and jewelry as ransom for captives. I remembered Sali telling me that you'd gone straight and I thought maybe if we did find or acquire any of these jewels that maybe you could help us determine if they are genuine, or maybe even identify the source."

"Kidnapping? Sounds too dangerous for me. One thing I liked about being a cat burglar was I never had to confront or even see anybody. I don't really see me going up against kidnappers. Not my style." He held Jason's gaze from across the table.

"And I wouldn't ask you to," said Jason. "I just need your expertise on jewels, maybe about boats, too, since apparently a boat captain is involved."

Masen glanced at Sali who shrugged, then back to Jason. "Well, I suppose so," Masen said, "not really doing anything else I can't drop right now. What's the plan?"

Sali piped in. "It makes sense for us to get a room here at Pier 66, since this is where you are. It can be our base of operations for now, until we figure out if this story we've heard from Jason's contact is true."

Masen nodded and stared at Sali for a moment. Turning to Jason he said, "What's the story on the kidnapping?"

"A man who didn't give his name called my HSI contact. He said a woman named Julene is supposed to be receiving millions in stolen jewels from a man the contact describes as fat with a big black beard and a blue captain's hat. The transfer is supposed to take place at Aruba's Beachside Cafe on the Saturday before Memorial Day in the afternoon. We're supposed to follow this Julene and the boat captain and see what we can find out. That's about all we have to go on. I can pay you a good daily wage just for being on call until we find out something they can use; I mean if we do."

Masen looked into his beer mug, thought for a second, then took another swig. "Okay, I'm in. Just don't get me busted—I can't go down that road again."

They finished the meal and paid the check. Masen said, "Would you like to see my pride and joy, the Booty? She's a thirty-six-foot Cheoy Lee ketch and she is a beauty if I do say so myself."

"Lead the way!"

They took a short walk past two-multimillion-dollar superyachts and quite a number of beautiful lesser yachts and sailboats and finally to the *Booty*, tied at the very end of one of the finger-piers. Masen was right: she was a gorgeous motor-sailor meant to handle any seas, but in the greatest comfort. She had teak all around and was freshly varnished.

"Right this way," said Masen. They stepped off the dock onto the deck. "Check out this helm," he said. "New cushions all around and plenty of room for visitors." Pointing aft, he said, "I love that little Zodiac dinghy, and it's got a brand new five horsepower Lehr propane-powered outboard that starts right up, no mixing gas and oil. A real pleasure. Also," he continued, as he touched the mast and looked aloft, "I had an especially strong GMT Composites carbon mast stepped, just in case I get caught in a killer hurricane. Oh, and of course you noticed my wonderful solar panel for cabin lighting. Love it."

They followed him down the companionway to the galley and dining room, with its sparkling stainless steel gimbaled three burner stove, beautiful teak cabinets and shiny wooden table with comfortable seating all the way around. On the bulkhead amidships was a large LCD TV and near that a miniature propane space heater for cold nights, as well as an air conditioner that ran on propane for any blistering hot nights. There was plenty of bunk space for up to four people.

"She's got a Perkins diesel that I've learned to maintain myself," he glowed, "and I try to keep up with the best in navigation and telecommunications gear and software. We could take this baby anywhere in the world, under sail or power, and be comfortable doing it."

"Stowed up under the bow is my dive locker—it's got everything I need, plus extras. Four tanks, four buoyancy compensators, masks, snorkels, fins, even a miniature air compressor—you name it. I've done a lot of diving from here down to Key Largo. I love it, but it sure is sad about the die-off of corals from that stony coral tissue loss disease."

They settled down at the table for more beers. Finally, Masen said, "You guys can stay at the hotel if you want, but you're welcome to stay here."

"Hell yeah," said Sali. "I'd be honored."

"Sounds good to me, too, but I'm thinking we might need some of the amenities of the hotel, like their computer and printer and so forth. I should probably get a room. The place looks pretty swank."

"Oh, it is," said Masen, "you just wait. Nice pool, excellent rooms, and you can take nice long showers there, too—you can't really do that on a boat since you want to save the water."

"All right," said Jason. "I'll check in with Jamie Horgood, my contact, and make some calls and update you later."

"If we don't see you tonight, come by for breakfast," said Masen, "and I'll cook you up my special morning concoction—it's excellent."

Jason headed toward the van first. He'd have to make it comfortable for surveillance purposes, just in case. He walked past the gigantic superyachts, worth tens and hundreds of millions of dollars, rising stories above him, floating on the gently lapping wavelets just under the Seventeenth Street Causeway Bridge, hundreds of feet overhead. As he moved toward the hotel, berths on his left were filled with every description of fishing or pleasure or sailing or yachting or almost any type of non-commercial vessel you could imagine, but none shabby in any way—they were the sanctuary and playthings for the rich and famous of Fort Lauderdale and its visitors.

* * *

As Masen had said, the rooms were very nice. Two large twin beds overlooked the pool, and the south-facing tall windows allowed the brilliant south Florida sunshine into the room. He called for room service and settled for a six-pack of Sierra Nevada, then sat and watched the pool and thought about how tomorrow might work out. The woman named Julene may not show, in which case he'd ask Jamie "What next?" It might be that they just pack up and go home, probably after a bit of partying with Masen. Or maybe this Julene would show up and they could follow her somewhere. Or maybe they get caught following her by somebody unknown. What then? He decided to call Jamie and check-in.

"Hey, it's me," he said.

"Jason, what's up?"

He filled her in, then finished another beer and went for a swim.

* * *

The next morning Jason arrived at the *Booty* at sunrise. Masen had his nice stainless-steel propane-powered grill on the deck where he cooked up a hash of potatoes, bacon pieces, green peppers and onions sautéed in butter and served with ice cold guava juice.

"So, what's the plan," said Masen as he took the first bite.

"Sali and I will go to Aruba's and wait for the boat captain and the woman to show around noon. Hopefully we'll recognize them. Sali will follow the woman, and I'll follow the captain. We'll call each other when we can and compare notes. I'll call Jamie later and let her know what we've found, if anything. She calls the shots after that, unless we see something we know looks like a promising lead. I'll call you when I can so you're in the loop."

"What are your plans, skipper?" said Sali.

"Not much really. I need to do a little work on the radio, but I'll keep my cell handy in case you need me."

They finished and cleaned up the table and galley, then Sali and Jason went to the van and rental Lexus and split up the things out of the van they might need separately in surveilling the woman and the captain: cameras, three VHF secure radios, a satellite phone, GPS units, directional microphones, headphones, guns and ammo, and laptops.

"What are we forgetting," said Sali.

"Hopefully nothing. See you there."

Chapter Six
Julene

The end of her favorite TV show came an hour before noon, at which time Julene Northly began what she laughingly called her daily commute. She took her bicycle down the painfully slow elevator from the third floor in the condo where she lived down to the ground floor.

It was going to be a bright, hot, sunny, humid day, and that was just how she liked it. She stepped the bike down to the top of a small incline that led down to the street then gave a push and swung her leg around to the other pedal and was off on her daily commute—a five mile bicycle ride east down Las Olas Boulevard to A1A along Fort Lauderdale's famed beach, then north to Commercial Boulevard where she'd meet her friends at The Village Grill, Aruba's, and other establishments in the heart of Lauderdale-By-The-Sea.

But today was the Saturday before Memorial Day. There would be a glut of tourists as well as locals to enjoy the beach and listen to the jazz, rock and blues groups there for the yearly Reef Fest and to get wasted on beer and mixed drinks served by the bars. Her boyfriend Michael had been specific, though—the first thing she had to do was to meet the skipper of the *London Blue*, whom she remembered as a thoroughly unpleasant lecher who couldn't keep his eyes off her breasts every time he met her, which had only been twice before.

Ching-ching! Ching-ching!

The sound of her bicycle bell not only signaled the bathing-suit clad pedestrians along her beach route to be aware of her approach, it also served to alert her seemingly thousands of friends that she was on her daily run and would doubtless wave at them with her big smile and stop and say hello or yell to them long and loudly, "Loooove yoooou!"

Julene was a real head-turner in every sense of the word. She had a body she kept fit and trim by her daily commute, but her appearance was also complemented by her fake boobs which she didn't mind everybody noticing because that's why she had them. "Breasticles" she laughingly called them. And if that wasn't enough to make every heterosexual male swoon, her beautiful long blond hair and large sparkling blue eyes and her gleaming white teeth in an omnipresent smile certainly did. She was just plain drop dead gorgeous, as they say, but what was really amazing was that she was forty-eight and looked more like the healthiest thirty-four-year-old woman within twenty miles.

She coasted down El Mar street until she got to The Village Grill then dismounted her bicycle and ignored all the stares as she locked her bike and went inside to change into her "appropriate" beachwear for the bar.

Everybody who worked in the bar took their turn at saying hello or giving her a hug, and heads turned as she began the first of her many loud laughs that cheered everybody's day.

From the vantage point of her favorite seat at the end of the bar, she could glance out now and then as she spoke with her friends and keep an eye out for the scurrilous and scruffy and totally unpleasant skipper of the *London Blue*, although she did not know his name nor the name of his vessel or in fact that he was a skipper at all. All she knew was that Michael had instructed her to meet the man and retrieve what he had for her. He was emphatic, though: do not inspect the package.

* * *

The ocean end of Commercial Boulevard is the heart of Lauderdale-By-The-Sea, and the city's pride is the decorated open plaza bordered by restaurants and bars. Anglin's Fishing Pier attracted those who chose to try their luck at catching snook and cobia. The long stretch of Florida's Gold Coast stretched north and south, anointed with the golden sun over the sea in the morning and bathed in purples and saffron as the sun set. The unique smell of fresh seaweed filled the air as its windrows piled higher and broader, and the gentle waves continued to gently murmur their somnolent lullabies to the sandy beach.

The design of the plaza favored all aspects of the beach, from the inspiring vista for those who'd never seen the Atlantic Ocean, to the daily sun-worshippers who soaked in the rays all day, and to the fishermen who enjoyed the pier. And there were those who just came to drink themselves into a stupor and those who came for the music at Aruba Beachside Cafe every night and there were those who came to conduct illegal business as at any popular place. This was the Memorial Day weekend, though, and the special Reef Fest had been organized around the usual "Battle of the Bands" theme, but with proceeds to go toward the purchase of mooring buoys along their precious reef—better to moor your boat to the buoy than drag anchor and destroy the reef.

Jason and Sali had parked the van and the SUV a block away from the plaza and surveyed the throng of people.

"Oh, brother," said Sali, "talk about your needle and haystack…"

"Oh, I don't know," said Jason, "we know what the boat captain looks like—he's an ugly son-of-a-bitch."

"Big help—I see plenty of those around."

"Present company excluded, I hope? Let's get a table over there." Jason pointed to an outside table at Mulligan's bordering on the plaza, right across from the Village Grill. They sat and surveyed the menu.

"Howdy gentlemen, my name is Bambi and the special drink of the day is a watermelon margarita." The waitress handed them a couple of menus.

"I'll have the fish and chips," said Sali, "and the margarita sounds tasty, but I don't think the boss will let me. I'll have a Coke."

"He's right about that. I'll try your burger and the pink lemonade."

"Pansy," said Sali to Jason as the waitress departed.

Jason had the description of the skipper, and he knew the meeting was at noon, but he had no idea who this Julene person was or what she looked like. That fact alone would make identifying the pair during the meeting hard enough, but the building revelry for the gathering of Reef Fest to begin on a crowded Memorial Day weekend made the task seem ridiculously impossible.

He turned to Sali. "If he does have any gems with him, he'll probably be carrying them in a case or a bag or a backpack. It'll probably be small."

The wait for the food was unfortunately long due to the crowd, but when it arrived, they ate slowly to hold the table for as long as they could as they waited for the pair to show up.

Then from over the sound of the ocean waves not so far away, came the sound of a single chord from an electronic bass guitar, amplified enough to shake windows and put ripples on people's' drinks, and a slowly growing roar of the crowd like an awakening animal, and made itself known through happy cheers and hoots. A drummer rattled a quick cadence and a bass drum expostulated thunderous amplified booms like the sound of an approaching storm.

Then came the loud voice from the microphone and speaker system: "Good evening ladies and gentlemen, we are Mister Nice Guy!"

The rock and roll exploded in a deafening roar with the sounds of a globally favorite Santana song and the crowd screamed its collective throat out.

Suddenly the captain with the black beard and the huge chest and blue skipper's hat appeared walking quickly as he rounded on to Commercial Boulevard near the 101 Oceans restaurant making his way through the throng of people. He had a small backpack slung around his right shoulder that was a dusky purple and a windbreaker with a bulge under it which suggested to Jason a sidearm.

"Don't look at him just yet," said Jason, "but there he is."

Sali took another sip of his Coke then glanced inconspicuously. The man was making his way toward the small pagoda at the end of Commercial Boulevard and the plaza and looking around as he did so. Sali looked back at Jason and said, "Damn, the chest on that guy is huge."

The skipper sat down on one of the benches facing the sea and sat without motion facing east toward the ocean.

From just behind them the rear door of the Village Grille opened up and Julene stepped toward the blaring music and screamed "Yay!"

She walked straight toward the man. She sat down next to him, gave him a friendly smile and some kind of greeting. The man reached into his backpack and retrieved something they could not see from their vantage point.

"So that's Julene," said Jason. "How interesting."

"Amazing," replied Sali.

Julene said one or two words, smiled and laughed, then stood and started back toward the bar. She was carrying a small cloth bag which she held by the cords that held it closed. The man's eyes followed her—he couldn't stop staring at her beautiful behind as she walked in her high-platform silver sandals.

"Okay, we're on," said Jason. "You follow him and I'll follow her. Call me when you find out where he goes."

"Hey wait a second. Wasn't it supposed to be the other way around?"

"Yes, but I changed my mind."

"Gee, I wonder why…" Sali stood and began to move toward the corner where they'd first seen him enter the plaza. "You get to pay the check, then."

Jason signaled the waitress and stole a glance at Julene. She put the small bag she had just retrieved inside her knapsack, then waved and said hello to another one of her friends. She didn't appear to be at all concerned with leaving. She said a few words to a waitress, then sat down at a table outside. Soon the waitress brought her a split of champagne.

Jason signaled his waitress and asked for another lemonade.

He sat for another few minutes drinking lemonade and watching her laugh uproariously with her many friends who came by or apparently sent text messages to her phone. Finally, he saw her take a call from the cell phone and step away from the table, apparently for some privacy. She laughed loudly as she paced back and forth on the boardwalk outside the bar, then she hung up and walked back to her table. She motioned to the waitress for her check, then started getting ready to leave. Just as she paid her tab, Jason could hear her say rather loudly in a long-drawn-out voice to her friends around the outside tables, "Loooove yoooou!"

She stepped away from the table and started packing her things on to a blue Trek bicycle.

"Oh, shit," Jason mumbled to himself. He didn't know that she had come by bicycle. He signaled the waitress for the tab and left what he knew was more than enough. He knew he couldn't get to his car in time, so he waited to see which way she was going.

She headed south on El Mar.

Jason jogged to his parking spot two blocks away in the municipal parking lot in the opposite direction—north.

Quickly he retrieved the keys from his pocket, opened the door, and started the engine. He realized in a panic that he could not drive straight back the way he came because the road was blocked by the concert.

He decided to head south on A1A, the main thoroughfare that ran parallel to El Mar. The Memorial Day traffic did not help—it was jammed. "Damn," he said as he slammed the steering wheel with his palm. The light changed and he was moving again. He finally came to where El Mar intersected with A1A. He turned on to El Mar, then headed north back toward the festival. No sign of her. Of course! She was hauling ass when she left: She's probably a mile from here by now!

He turned back the way he had come, then came to the light at A1A and El Mar where he'd have to turn left to follow the direction she was hopefully going.

But the light must have been the longest on the planet for he waited what felt like ten minutes. Finally, he looked both ways, then ran the light and took off heading south on A1A.

He strained to look ahead as he raced between the cars, knowing that the cops would most surely stop him if they saw him. Finally, he saw her ahead, moving fast and easy with the traffic, her long blond hair flowing behind her like flames from an afterburner, her shapely tan, brown legs moving somewhat slowly and indicating she was in high gear. He slowed and held back, but not so far back that he'd miss the light coming up at Sunrise Boulevard.

But the light did change, and she stopped, first in line at the light. An old '57 Chevy convertible packed with fraternity guys pulled up next to her and started whistling and talking to her. She tried to ignore them, but finally she turned to them and laughed loudly, and so did they, slapping the side of the car with their open palms. The light changed, she waved bye-bye to them, then took off at warp speed continuing south on A1A amid the horrendous traffic, easily leaving the car full of testosterone and Jason, too, many cars behind her.

Jason pulled as far to the right side of the street as he could while the guys swerved over into the left lane and tried to pass the big panel truck in front of them. Then he saw her take a right at the first light onto Allamar Street just as the guys passed the truck—she had lost them.

Jason swung right onto Allamar and followed her from a distance. She turned left onto Beach Road then continued to make her way south moving at top speed.

He continued to follow her from a distance as she went the full length of Beach Road, never once looking back as Jason followed her. She took the curve near the Ritz-Carlton Hotel, then came to Las Olas Boulevard where she stopped and waited for traffic to clear and adjusted her top which had been making a valiant effort to retain her high full bosom. Jason pulled over into a parking slot. The traffic slowed and Jason waited a moment then took off after her again.

The Las Olas Bridge is steep and the view of Bahia Mar and its many luxurious yachts is spectacular, but Julene ignored it and kept her face forward, pumping her legs as she shifted to low gear and meeting the steep challenge with apparent ease.

Ching-ching! Ching-ching!

The happy sound of the bicycle bell alerted the parking attendants at the Chima Steakhouse and they waved at her and sang her name out loudly as she waved back with her big happy toothy smile.

"This woman is incredible," Jason muttered aloud. "What's a woman like you doing wrapped up in a jewel caper?"

He remained several cars back wondering briefly what had happened to the carload of fraternity guys she had lost earlier. *I bet this happens every day. I wonder how many car wrecks she's caused.*

He continued at the same speed, unobtrusively glancing in his rear-view mirror, but also keeping pace with Julene as she moved on rapidly. The two of them were pacing each other, then he noticed she stopped pedaling and began to coast. She turned right onto a street up ahead that went to one of the many islands in the Las Olas area—islands of extremely lavish homes and multimillion dollar yachts and occasional medium-rise condominiums.

He decided to go straight and did so without slowing down. He remembered that these streets were dead ends, though the dwellings were plentiful enough to give him a hard time finding her again. He glanced at the street name as he drove by and saw her pedaling easily down the street—it read "Hendricks Isle."

He drove down Las Olas a few blocks, then turned north on Southeast Fifteenth and kept on until he hit Broward Boulevard, checking his mirror to make sure he wasn't being followed. He pulled over next to a school and did a U-turn and drove back to Hendricks Isle driving slowly and looking for any sign of Julene's bicycle.

Finally, he saw it—the blue Trek bike chained to a bike-rack in the open garage that served as the first floor of a condominium building. He moved down the street and took a drive down to a small bridge then turned around and went back up Hendricks Isle.

He found a parking spot along the street, climbed in back of the surveillance van, trained the high-powered camera on the front of the condo and sat back and waited to hear from Sali.

Chapter Seven
Reznik

Sali glanced back over his shoulder at Julene as he left the table he had just occupied with Jason, then looked ahead to match the pace of the man he was following. Indeed, he did look like the Popeye character Bluto, and he didn't appear to be concerned that anybody might be following him.

It was just a few short blocks to the municipal parking lot. "Bluto" entered a Toyota Camry with an Uber sticker inside the windshield just as Sali was almost to his white rental Lexus SUV. The Toyota headed north on the A1A highway as Sali unlocked the Lexus. He let a Volkswagen get between them, then another car as he followed them at a slow beach-traffic pace.

They continued north until just before the Hillsboro Inlet bridge. The Toyota pulled into the marina parking lot of the Hillsboro Inlet Fishing Center. Sali turned around quickly in the drive to the Center and parked on the other side of A1A at the Hillsboro Inlet Plaza. He grabbed his small backpack and then ran across the street to move close to where Bluto was being dropped off.

Bluto exited the Toyota and walked down the dock to a yacht's dinghy tied up at the end of the pier. He eased himself down into it and started the outboard engine with one pull then went about untying the lines that held it to the dock.

Sali looked around frantically to see if he could rent a boat from somebody in a hurry.

At the other end of the dock, three college age young men were stowing snorkeling gear and an ice chest into their twenty-six-foot Contender, obviously getting ready to head to sea. Sali walked quickly to catch up to them.

The boys were just finishing up and about ready to go, but Sali called out to them.

"Hey, wait a second! How would you guys like to make a quick four hundred bucks? Two hundred now, two hundred when you bring me back."

The young men looked at each other for a moment then the captain said, "To do what?"

"I just want you to follow a boat for me. It shouldn't take long."

The young men consulted briefly, then motioned Sali aboard.

"That's him there," Sali said pointing, "but stay as far back as you can."

"Why are you following him?" asked the young skipper.

"Because he's a bad guy."

The young skipper nodded, "Fair enough," then headed toward Bluto's outboard which was just now turning to go under the Hillsboro Inlet Bridge and out to sea.

The current was swift as the tide was coming in and the day was brilliant and cloudless and the ocean was gently rolling, but there was no wind so the surface of the sea was smooth and reflected the glare of the hot midday sun.

As Bluto headed out of the inlet he looked around and no doubt saw the pursuing boat, but Sali had instructed the kids to act normal so they removed their shirts and passed around some beers. Sali had donned a cap and sunglasses from his backpack and quickly looked up the coast when he saw that Bluto was turning around for a look.

Bluto gave the outboard full throttle and headed southeast toward a large yacht about half a mile offshore, anchored and facing south.

"Easy on the throttle," Sali said to the young captain. "Aim a little south of him, don't follow directly behind him."

A moment later he said, "Do you have any field glasses?"

"Of course." The young skipper opened a small door beneath the wheel and retrieved a very well-made binocular case and handed it to Sali.

"Nice," said Sali as he pulled the Zeiss glasses from the case. He held them to his eyes and scanned the yacht and saw Bluto heading for it. He saw him casually look back, but the boys were heading in enough of a more southerly direction that he didn't appear concerned.

A few minutes later Bluto's skiff pulled alongside the yacht.

"Slow down a little," said Sali, "but keep heading this direction."

Sali moved to sit on a starboard cushion and tried to steady the binoculars so he could read the name of the ship. "London Blue," he said. He turned to the crew: "Any of you guys know that boat?"

"Nope," they said, shaking their heads.

Sali pulled out his cell phone and chose the navigation application that displayed latitude and longitude. He minimized the window on the phone and called Jason.

"Talk to me," said Jason.

"I'm out in a boat off Hillsboro Inlet. I'll send you the coordinates. The target just climbed into a yacht northeast of this spot, maybe two hundred yards away. The name of the boat is London Blue."

"Hmmmm. Ask Masen if he can bring his boat around and pick you up—just keep an eye on it for now. Offer him an additional five hundred a day for his boat. Let me know if he says no. I wouldn't blame him."

"Will do. How are you doing on your end?"

"Followed her to a condo off Las Olas. Now that I've heard from you, I'll call Jamie and see if she can give me some info on this address. I'll update you then. Later."

Sali hung up and called Masen. "Hey, Masen, do you mind if we commandeer your boat for the mission? Jason says he'll pay you an additional five hundred per day."

After a short pause, Masen said, "Depends. What's up?"

"I followed the captain we told you about out to a yacht named London Blue, anchored off Hillsboro Inlet. Jason and I were wondering if you wouldn't mind coming out here to pick me up and we keep an eye on the dude."

"And?"

"Well, until Jason finds out more about the woman he followed, we just keep an eye on the yacht to see what it does, or if the dude gets back off it."

Masen paused. "Okay, I'm in. I'll crank her up and be on my way in just a bit. Send me the coordinates just to make sure."

Sali hung up and looked back at the crew who were all ears, looking at him. He sent both Jason and Masen the coordinates.

"My ride will be here shortly," he said. "I'll pay you the rest of the money now. Just wait until he shows up and I'll be on my way. And you, sailor, pass me a beer, if you don't mind."

* * *

An hour later after the college kids had caught some fish and gone snorkeling and Sali had quaffed half their stash of cold beers, the *Booty* pulled up alongside their boat.

"Request permission to come aboard, Captain," hailed Sali.

Masen waved him aboard, Sali thanked his helpful crew and paid them the remaining $200, then waved them farewell as they struck out to return to the dock.

Sali pointed out the *London Blue* to Masen. "Nobody's been aboard or left since we anchored here," he said. "We've just been fishing and acting like we're not looking at them."

Masen surveyed the area, then said, "We can tie up to that mooring buoy over there and keep an eye out."

After they'd accomplished the task, Masen said, "Now what? What happens if they weigh anchor and decide to head for Panama or some place?"

"No idea. Jason's waiting to hear back from Jamie, then he'll call and give us an update."

* * *

Considering his enormity, Brevon Reznik, whom everyone just called Reznik, climbed easily from the skiff onto the deck of the *London Blue* with surprising agility.

His first mate, Vlasta, glanced briefly at him as he surveyed the horizon for any signs of trouble, then said, "Any problems?"

"No, I gave her the stones and told her to go straight back to the condo and stash them in the safe. Did he call?"

"Not yet, but you know how he is—he's punctual and it's not quite time."

Reznik finished tying off the skiff to the stern, then entered the main cabin where the two kidnapped women sat at the dining table. They cut off their discussion the moment he walked in. Standing by the starboard window was a guard, Nadav, who just watched and listened.

"You'd better eat as much as you can and get as much rest as you can before we leave tomorrow," Reznik said to the women. "You're going to need your strength and rest, especially if you get seasick. We're heading out to the open ocean and there's a good chance it'll be a bumpy ride."

The women were silent for a moment, then the woman with the long red hair, spoke up. "Why haven't you let us go? You got your ransom jewelry, now you're supposed to let us go home."

"Not until I say so. Now shut the fuck up."

His cell phone rang—he could see by the caller I.D. it was Marek calling. He stepped outside the cabin onto the open deck and answered it.

"Yes," he said.

"It's me. Did you give the stones to Julene?"

"Yes. I told her to put them in the safe, just like you said."

"Good. Be ready to sail tomorrow or the next day instead of tonight. I still haven't heard back about Amber Spring. If she made it to shore and is back with her husband that could change everything."

"Highly unlikely she could make it back—just too far—but we'll be ready, just give us the word."

Reznik hung up then spoke to Vlasta who was still surveying the surrounding seas. "We're leaving tomorrow or the next day instead of tonight, but keep your eyes open."

He moved back inside the cabin.

"Listen up. We're leaving tomorrow instead of tonight, but it's the same deal: eat and rest up as much as you can before tomorrow."

He looked at the guard, Nadav: "Stay focused."

Reznik moved from the cabin to the wheelhouse where the navigator, Vlad, was turning the dials of the VHF radio and listening intently. "We leave tomorrow or the next day instead of tonight," he said. "Let me know of any change in the weather. I'll spell you at sundown so you can get some chow. Get some rest. It will be a long run once we get going."

Chapter Eight
Michael's Condo

Julene coasted her bicycle to a stop in front of the condominium building on Hendricks Isle where she lived. She punched in the combination to the locked gate then parked her bike in a garage that was below all the condo units. With her little backpack still slung on her back she took an outside elevator up to a third-floor condo and unlocked the front door and stepped inside.

The place was immaculate, but not because Julene kept it that way, rather her sugar-daddy Michael had a maid come by once a week to tidy up the place while he was gone, which was often. The only reason she had to stay there was so that she would be available for him when he came to town. There was no love, just a business deal: sex and arm candy for him when he was in town, and an expensive beautiful place to stay rent free for her.

She walked into the bedroom and put the backpack containing the jewels up on a hook in the bedroom. She retrieved her cell phone from the front pouch of the backpack, then dialed her friend Charlie's number. She opened the front door and stepped out onto the balcony.

* * *

Down below, Jason was watching her through the telephoto lens of the surveillance van's camera. He turned up the sensitivity to the high-powered directional microphone to listen to her conversation.

* * *

"What up, girl!"
"Hey, Julie," said Charlie in her naturally loud voice. "How are you?"

"I'm good. Just got back from my daily commute!" She laughed.

"Hey, so how's it going with Michael ever since he slapped you around?"

"He apologized, just like he always does after he roughs me up."

"Julene, you've got to get away from that guy. It's only going to get worse—it never gets any better. You just ask around and you'll see. It almost never gets better."

Julene paused. "Yeah, I know. I wish I could get away from him, but he never gives me any money, and it's hard for me to get a job because I don't have a degree."

"Maybe you can work for that veterinarian again."

"I asked, no luck."

They chatted some more, then Julene said, "Are you singing at Blue Jean Blues tonight?"

"Yes, I am, and you'd better be there!"

"I'm there! See you tonight."

She hung up and closed the front door then walked to the opposite side of the condo and opened the glass doors to the verandah and sat down facing the sun and kicked her feet up on Michael's bamboo-framed stool and loosened her top as she looked out over the Intracoastal and the condos along the seawall across from her about fifty yards away. The sound of the cars close by on Las Olas Boulevard and the light wind lulled her to a light nap, and after a while she went back inside and closed the glass doors.

* * *

Jason settled back on the stuffed chair in the van and called Jamie.

"Hey, Jamie, it's me."

"Hey, big fella, what've you got?"

"Well, the meeting happened pretty much as you described it: the guy you described as "Bluto" was pretty accurate: he's a big guy with a captain's hat. He met an attractive blond and handed her a bag of something. Sali called me a while ago and told me he had followed our Bluto back out to a yacht anchored off Hillsboro Inlet. I followed the woman to this condo address where I'm in my van right now and I'm hoping you can give me some information on who owns it." He gave her the address and descriptive information of the condo.

"Also, the yacht where the guy went to is called London Blue. Can you see what you can find out about it?"

"Okay, give me a few minutes and I'll call you back."

Thirty-five minutes later she finally had something and called him back.

"So far, I don't have anything on the boat, but the owner of the condo is one Michael Fieldstone," she said. "He has a clean record, except a mention of his name in a human trafficking report at the FBI. It's unofficial—it was found in an interrogation report of a trafficking suspect in Chicago. Unfortunately, said suspect disappeared less than an hour after that interrogation. Nobody—not even his wife and kids—have heard from him since. It sounds as though he could have been disposed of."

"So now it gets interesting. Anything more on this guy?"

"Nothing bad that I can find, and maybe that informant was talking about a different guy, maybe some other person named Michael Fieldstone."

"On our end," said Jason, "we're just continuing to follow. At some point I may have to trust Sali's friend Masen and tell him what we're trying to do."

She was quiet, then said, "I'd rather you didn't, but I trust your judgement."

"Thank you. If we discover that she does have the gems, things could get dicey in a hurry."

"One other thing," she said. "Our informant who told us about Julene is apparently in your area and he wants to meet me tomorrow and tell me more about what's going on. I think he must be checking up on me to see if I took him seriously."

"And you said…"

"I told him I'm not in the area, and besides, you are the lead on this now and to talk to you. He wants to meet you tomorrow at the Boatyard Sunday Brunch. He'll be wearing a turquoise shirt. I described you to him, so you two shouldn't have any trouble connecting."

"That might be difficult, but I'll try. I'm still in the middle of verifying if this woman does indeed have a bag of jewels."

"Sounds to me like you really need to talk to him."

They broke off the call and the obvious solution that came to him was to ask Masen to break into Fieldstone's condo while Julene was out at Blue Jean Blues tonight—wherever that was. But when would that be, and would Masen agree to imperil his future by breaking and entering again? That could put him in jail again for a very long time. Such was Jason's quandary. Human trafficking was about as ugly an enterprise as there was on earth, and he wasn't even certain Fieldstone was involved in trafficking, but asking Masen to gamble his life behind bars for this was a tough call.

* * *

After much thought and some consulting Google Maps, Jason dialed Sali's cell. "How's it going out there?"

Sali checked the field glasses again and surveyed the *London Blue.* "I've seen two women come up briefly on deck and one guy pacing around with a very big pistola. Our guy Bluto hasn't come back on deck since he got there, except once for a phone call."

Jason was silent for a moment, then said, "So, now the game changes. We're definitely dealing with some serious dudes. Can you put your phone on speaker and ask Masen to listen in?"

In the background he could hear Sali call Masen over to the phone and their movement to the inside of the cabin.

"Okay," said Sali finally, "what've you got?"

"I talked to Jamie. She hasn't found anything out yet about the London Blue, but maybe they didn't register the name like they're supposed to, or maybe it's from out of the country. About Julene, the place where she's staying is owned by a guy named Michael Fieldstone. It appears, but not certain, that he might have a connection to human trafficking. Now you tell me the London Blue has a guy on deck with a gun and I'm definitely thinking we've got some bad guys here. So, I have a proposition for you Masen, and I won't blame you if you say no, and I've got a little recreation for you, Sali."

Jason waited for a response, but got none.

"Masen, how do you feel about breaking into the condo and seeing if you can find the jewels that Julene possibly received today from the London Blue captain? Unfortunately, Jamie will likely not approve of this, but I'm not going to ask her and put her on the spot."

"Oh, brother," said Sali. "Masen, it's your call. We would of course defend you in court as best we could, but if you get caught, it's going to be tough."

Masen was silent, then said, "Well, I have to admit, re-stealing stolen jewels does have a certain appeal to it, but I told you, I'm out of that racket. I wouldn't be here now, enjoying the yachting life, if it weren't for the deal I cut with Sali and the court."

"But I'm not asking you to steal them," said Jason. "I just want to know if they're there. The most you'd get caught for would be breaking and entering."

"Very good point, but if the jewels are there, I'm sure they're not just sitting out in a fruit basket on the dining room table. They're almost certainly in a high-security safe."

"Which you could probably break into. You've been called the most successful jewel thief of all time. Look at the end game. This might save kids from sex slavery."

Masen said nothing as he gazed through the porthole out over the gentle seas and the bright sunlight shining on the *London Blue*. Jason just let his silence be his argument.

Masen sighed deeply, then said, "What if I'm caught?"

"How's that going to happen? I'm going to be right outside watching for Julene to come back, or I'll be following her, one or the other. Besides, you've never been caught breaking in—Sali just caught you with a list that led to your eventual undoing. Your chances of success are good. And anyway, you'd be leaving with nothing but pictures."

"That could be bad, too: intent."

"Okay, take the pictures with your phone, send them to me, delete them, then leave."

"It'll take weeks for me to case out the joint."

"The longer you wait, the greater the chance we miss something or they leave. You've got to do it tonight."

"Tonight!" he shouted. "Jesus Christ I can't believe this. You're guilt-tripping me into breaking and entering."

"In and out. Nothing taken but some pictures. A walk in the park."

Silence. "You're going to owe me big time for this."

"I know, Masen, I'll make sure you're compensated."

"I mean seriously. My fee just went up."

"Don't worry about that. If you find the stones, I'll do my best to get more from HSI. Or other sources."

"Maybe I should keep one of the stones?"

"No! Pictures only! Just take pictures and everything will be fine."

"How do I get there?"

"Do you have Wi-Fi reception on your laptop out there?"

"No, but I've got a hotspot I can use through my phone to connect to the Internet."

"Good. Use Google Maps and look up Hendricks Isle and Las Olas. I'll text you the exact address and unit number, then delete the message. I can't get in back there because of a security fence, but it looks to me like there's a dock out back and the best way to approach it is by way of the Intracoastal—use your Zodiac to get there. You should be able to quietly take it right up to the dock and tie up, or maybe some other place close. There's a gate all around the garage on the first floor, so it doesn't look like it would be easy to get in that way. However, if you could, there's a stairwell going up." He continued to describe the building as much as he could, and where Fieldstone's condo was positioned in the building.

"All right, I'll get the Zodiac ready. I've got enough spare propane if I need it, too."

"So, what about me," said Sali to Jason. "What's your plan?"

"I need you to make a night dive. Remember those little GPS units we loaded in Marathon? I need you to somehow make one of them waterproof and stick to the outside of the London Blue."

Silence.

Jason said, "Hello? You got a problem with night diving? You used to do that all the time, and I know you did it with the SEALs."

"I don't have a problem with a night dive, I'm just thinking this through. I don't know the bottom or the current or the tides, and I won't have a dive buddy. I may end up surfacing in Bimini."

"I can help with the current and the tides," said Masen. "I just need a few minutes to look them up. And as far as waterproofing the GPS, I have a small Pelican case that I use for my phone in heavy seas—you could use that. I've got some Marine Tex that works like putty then hardens up—that should work."

"Hmmm," mused Sali. "I'll use Masen's Zodiac to go back to the dock and retrieve the GPS unit from the Lexus."

"Good. When you do that, why don't you also pick up some bugs for Masen to plant when he visits the condo."

"Oh, good," said Masen in a huff. "To breaking and entering we also add illegal surveillance."

"I'll get them when I go ashore," said Sali.

"Fine," said Masen with a sigh.

"So, elsewhere in the news," continued Jason, "I used the directional mic on Julene when she was out on the front porch and she said she was going to a place called Blue Jean Blues tonight. I looked it up and it's a nightclub over on Thirty-third Street. Her friend is singing there tonight. I'll let you know when she leaves the condo and follow her there. That's when you guys start."

Masen said, "I might go earlier than that so I can scout out the place. It would help if I had an idea of the layout, who's coming and going, stuff like that."

Sali said, "I'll get the dive gear squared away and Masen and I will figure out the tides and stuff before he takes off."

* * *

In a little under an hour Masen and Sali had prepared Masen's Zodiac skiff for his ride to break into Michael Fieldstone's condo. Sali checked Masen's stash of dive gear to make sure all was in good operating condition, and that the underwater light and other items were squared away and ready to go.

Masen stayed aboard the *Booty* and watched briefly as Sali took off in the Zodiac toward the harbor where Sali had left the Lexus, then turned his attention to the *London Blue* and studying Google Maps to figure out how he would navigate the Intracoastal to get to the waterway where Fieldstone's condo was. According to Jason, Julene was still there and it was daylight anyway, but he wanted to get close enough to see what sort of boat and people traffic were moving in and out of the area. He would bring his fishing pole so he could pretend he was fishing while conducting the surveillance.

He took another look at the *London Blue.* A woman with long flaming red hair, flowing easily in the breeze, was on deck with her arms crossed and looking toward shore. Masen trained his glasses on her and in a start thought he recognized her. She was a long way off, but she looked almost exactly like Colorado Jacquette, the woman whom the news said had disappeared several days ago. He grabbed his cell and called Jason.

"Hey, Jason, did they ever find that missing singer Colorado Jacquette, that gorgeous redhead? I could swear I just saw her on the deck of the London

Blue." As he spoke while he watched her, he saw a man appear and motion her back down below.

"No, I don't think so. Are you sure?"

"Not really—she's a long way off. Anyway, thought I'd call and tell you."

"Duly noted. Let me know when you take off."

A short while later Sali pulled alongside the *Booty* and climbed aboard.

"How'd it go," said Masen.

"No sweat—got all we need, I hope."

Chapter Nine
Night Dive

Masen met Sali at the stern of the *Booty* and helped him put on his weight belt and underwater buoyancy compensator. He handed him the marine epoxy and the GPS transmitter in the little Pelican box as Sali put them into his BC pockets and zipped them up. Finally, he turned the air on for his scuba tank, then handed him a little metal plate from his own compressor that said Yamaha which Sali would put on top of the Pelican box to confer legitimacy to the package.

Sali strapped his underwater compass on to his wrist, put his portable underwater light in the other BC pocket, donned his face mask and fins, then asked, "How do I look?"

"Like you know what you're doing."

Sali held his face mask tight to his face and with his other hand held the strap firmly on his head. He slipped backwards into the water quietly at the same moment the sun dropped from view along the Florida Gold Coast.

Masen looked briefly at Sali's bubbles and barely perceptible silhouette as he dove deeper and passed under the *Booty* and made his way toward the *London Blue*.

Masen sent a text message to Jason's cell phone: "Our man is on his way."

"Good," Jason replied. "Julene is still silent. Keep me posted."

Masen moved over to the cockpit. He retrieved his field glasses and set up a lookout position, eyeing the *London Blue* from stem to stern, looking for any signs of trouble. It was getting dark quicker than he had anticipated, due to gathering storm clouds in the west. He wondered how that might help or hurt Sali's dive when he got close to *London Blue*, and also about whether or not any rain would make visibility worse from the dappling on the surface, distorting whatever faint remaining sunlight there was, or moonlight that was expected to shine.

He also wondered how this rain might affect his own mission to begin when he got word from Jason.

His phone chirped with an incoming text from Jason: "She's on the move. Will follow. Go!"

Masen texted back a quick "OK. Leaving now."

* * *

Even though he'd done hundreds of night dives during his stint with the SEALS, each new night dive brought a rush of adrenaline with the chill of the sea and the foreboding darkness as Sali slipped beneath the waves. Looking down at the bottom of the sea, only twenty feet below, Sali could see the bioluminescence of the animals and plants. It was like being at an altitude of a thousand feet looking down onto the lights of a city. There were thoroughfares, but they were actually the grooves of a brain coral, there were the lights of the apartments and buildings, actually the individual lights of cnidarians or pteropods or crustaceans bearing little bioluminescent collections of the phytoplankton responsible for the amazing bluish-green light. Little powerhouses producing the miracle of light which influenced so many animals around it. The connection. Plant to animal, in a microscopic landscape, the electro-physical connection across the division between plant and animal. In that meeting a light that he perceived as he dove.

On the ocean floor Sali looked again at his compass and surveyed as best he could the spur-and-groove of the reef and tried to commit formations to memory. The light was fading rapidly, until finally a new host of crepuscular critters began to move about with some showing little bioluminescent lights, while others moved about a little more brazenly than others, their large eyes more adapted to this nocturnal hunting ground, seeking prey caught unaware, or perhaps just a little too slow.

But he had to ignore these colorful distractions and pay close attention to the speed of the current and his direction of travel. And he'd better be damn good at approximating the distance of travel, because he could go too far to either side, or even go under the *London Blue* and not realize it. And he had to be careful with his light, so he stuck close to the bottom, showing just a sliver of light peeking between his fingers onto the compass.

The time was approaching quickly when the sunlight would go completely with the moonlight not yet appearing. Total darkness. He decided he had to chance surfacing and taking a peek to make sure he was close. Very slowly he swam to the surface, restricting his bubbles as much as he could, straining his eyes for any sign of boat lighting above, but he saw none. With one last squirt of air into his buoyancy compensator he rose the last few feet to the surface, until finally his mask broke the surface and he could see the *London Blue* perhaps thirty yards in front of him, her lights brilliantly lighting the deck and the surrounding sea. *Shit*, he thought to himself, *I'm entering a three-ring circus with lights every-fucking-where.*

He looked to the stern and saw that despite what looked like stadium lighting all over, right at the stern, where the lower unit was, the light was dimmer, and better yet, there was nobody near that area. He let air out of his BC and slipped below quietly again, down to the bottom, and moved steadily toward the *London Blue*.

As he got closer, the lights above lit up the underwater reef like a majestic play, then all went black—they had shut the deck lights off. Sali waited a few moments to get accustomed to the darkness, then moved cautiously ahead.

There was enough illumination from the running lights for Sali to see that he was now directly under the *London Blue*. He positioned himself under the stern and once again used his BC to rise slowly to the surface. He exhaled quietly. He completely held his breath and pulled the mouthpiece from his bite, making sure when he did so that the first stage mouthpiece was facing downward so as not to release a loud barrage of bubbles. He looked up from his position at the stern to the gunwale above him and saw no one. He slowly and quietly removed the waterproofed GPS from his BC pocket, then the marine grade putty he had prepared. He slowly and quietly put a blob of the putty on the stern, just above one of the outdrives, then pushed the box with the GPS unit containing plenty of small NiCad batteries and an antenna into the putty. He trimmed the putty with his dive knife and squared up the box to make it look as though the unit belonged there, then embedded the embossed metallic plate which read Yamaha in some putty on top of the little box. It all looked very official.

Finally, he was done and released the air from his BC and dropped until he reached the bottom, a small patch of groove amid the lively lights of the coral reef. He once again placed his hand over the light and opened a few fingers to allow a sliver of light to illuminate his compass. He noted the direction back to the *Booty* and headed back slowly, retracing his path back over the reef.

Chapter Ten
Timbo's Tale

Jason had just texted Masen that Julene was on the move and to begin his part of the operation to break into Michael Fieldstone's condo.

He closed down the directional mic and camera and slipped up front into the driver's seat.

Julene took the elevator down to the first floor and stepped out front and waited.

Shortly, a late model Toyota with an Uber sticker pulled up front and she stepped in. Jason started the van and followed from a safe distance.

Fifteen minutes later he saw her step out of the cab and laugh through the open door at the driver. She turned around and stepped into the bar called Blue Jean Blues on Thirty-third Street, just a block east of the Intracoastal Waterway north of Oakland Park Boulevard.

Jason struggled to find a parking place, but found one where he could keep an eye on the front door of the bar. He checked his phone to see if Sali or Masen had contacted him, then approached the bar. A beautiful, well-endowed brunette with a big, friendly welcoming smile said, "Hi, there! My name is Tina. Welcome to Blue Jean Blues! We have music every single night of the week. The cover charge to pay the musicians is five dollars per person." Jason happily paid the cover charge, then went inside the bar.

Inside, a band was just starting up and the place was already filling up fast. He could see Julene talking and laughing with what must have been her friend the singer Charlie and members of her band. She was totally captivating by her beauty, no doubt, but also by her laugh, which was contagious, and ebullient with energy.

Jason found a seat near the end of the bar and ordered an India Pale Ale from one of the twin tall blond bartenders whose name was Diane.

"How do I tell you apart from your sister?" asked Jason.

"Denise is slightly taller. What'll you have, my friend?"

Julene continued to talk with Charlie and the band members until it was time for them to start the show. Julene stepped over to a spot next to the kitchen where she could watch the band while she stood. A guy walked over to her and tried hitting on her, but she said nothing and held up her hands to either side of her eyes, like they were blinders, and the guy got the hint: she just wanted to watch and listen to the music and was not interested in talking to some guy.

The band started and Julene gyrated modestly in place. When the band would stop playing a tune, she would be the first to hold her hands up to her mouth and yell, "Yay!" as loud as she could.

On his right he heard the guy sitting next to him utter softly in admiration, "Damn, Julene…"

Jason turned to the guy, then looked back over at Julene, then back at him as though he didn't know who Julene was, but could see who he was talking about.

"Do you know her?" Jason said. "Man, she's something."

"Yeah, she sure is." He sighed. "She's also a heartbreaker."

Jason assessed the guy who apparently had been a lover, or at least very close. Age had probably taken away some of his good looks and certainly had taken away some of his hair, but he still had a handsome face and was dressed well. He was rather short, maybe five-and-a-half feet, and slight of build.

"I take it you speak from experience," said Jason.

The man took a sip of his drink and said, "Yeah, I'm afraid so. I actually met her at another bar a couple of years ago, a place called Alligator Alley. She was doing just like she's doing now—just listening to the music and totally into it. I couldn't stop looking at her—she was just my size, shorter than me, and God, just look at her. Killer body. Beautiful face. Beautiful blue eyes. I was blown away. Somehow I got the guts to ask her to dance, but she blew me off and said she just wanted to listen to the music. I think I said 'Rats' or something, then I asked her if she wanted to smoke a joint. I couldn't believe it—she said yes. We went out to her car, a beat-up old piece of shit, and she took just one puff, then was happy to let me smoke it while we chatted. My parents had both passed away in an accident just before then, so it was really nice to have somebody to talk to. She was genuinely sorry to hear my story."

They both took a swallow of their drinks and continued looking at her.

"She gave me her phone number, one thing led to another, and we went out to dinner a couple of times then finally shacked up at my place. My almost-adult kids live with me, so that didn't work out with her living with me."

"So, I guess she has her own place?"

"You interested in her?"

"Well, yes and no. I mean I'm from out of town, and I'm married," Jason lied, "but she sounds intriguing. Just curious."

"Yeah, intriguing. Over time I find out she's living in an expensive condo over off of Las Olas, but it's not hers—it's her boyfriend's."

"Oh shit. A love triangle."

"Well, the guy doesn't live here. Much. He mainly lives in Chicago. Guy name of Michael. Turns out they have this arrangement: she gets to stay in the condo so long as he can fuck her when he's in town, and take her out as arm candy or whatever."

"Jesus, how could you live with that?"

"Good question. I just became so in love with her I fooled myself into thinking I could steal her away. I mean look at her—not only is she gorgeous, she's got a great laugh and sense of humor, and she never says a bad word about anybody. Ever. And my God you should see her naked. Perfection."

"So, why didn't she come around to you? Obviously there was something about you she liked."

"So, I guess it was because I kept her alive by giving her money and taking her out to dinner and helping her pay for stuff she needed. She doesn't have a job. She just rides to the beach on her bicycle every day and makes the rounds to the beach bars and drinks and meets all her friends. So, I was her temporary sugar daddy while Michael was out of town."

"So, what happened when Michael finally showed up?"

"He showed up a couple of times, and I saw him with her, but she wouldn't let me ruin her gig by introducing me or anything like that. I didn't really want to meet him anyway. I was sort of getting used to this arrangement, then he flew in unexpectedly one day. Shit, I hate thinking about that day. It was Veteran's Day and I had rented a hotel room for us to be in that night. I was getting ready to go pick her up when she called and said that Michael was at the airport and she had to go pick him up. She did and they just took off to Key West. Just plain dropped me like a hot rock and took off with him."

"Ouch."

"Yeah. Ouch. After that we never had sex again and I forced myself to keep away from her. She didn't seem to give a damn and never called or texted."

Neither said anything for a few moments, then Jason said, "By the way, my name's Jason," and he extended his hand for a shake.

"Timbo," he said as they shook hands.

"So, you never met the guy."

"Michael? No, I never did. I saw him sitting with her once. The guy never smiled. To me the guy looked like an ugly son-of-a-bitch, and he looked mean. But the guy was obviously rich. Nice clothes, gold chain around his neck, big diamond ring, very nice Lamborghini. What woman wouldn't like being with a rich guy like that?"

"Yeah, I've heard that song before. What does he do for a living?"

"I don't know, and apparently she doesn't either. I asked her and she said she didn't know."

"Damn, Timbo, sounds like you've had a rough time with her."

"Yeah, well hell," lamented Timbo, "she was straight with me, though. She never really lied to me about anything, so I can't really say she was deceiving me, and she really helped get me through that time after my parents passed away. I have to think about my own motivations, too. I mean, I was proud—too proud, I guess—to be seen with this woman, even though she didn't want anybody to think we were an item. It was always: 'This is my friend Timbo,' but my ego got the better of me and I had to have more. I couldn't just be happy with what I had, I had to have more. So, as much as she hurt me, she was just being herself, and she never hid what her life was and never made excuses for it."

The conversation slowed, and after a while the band stopped for a break and they heard her yell "Yay!" again, and the chatter in the bar picked up to fill the void of the stopped music.

"Well, nice meeting you, Jason. Maybe I'll see you around again."

"Yeah, it was a pleasure Timbo. Take care of yourself."

Jason decided if he sat around the bar too much longer he was going to get drunk, no matter how slowly he drank, so he paid his tab and went out to sit in the van and watch for when she came out.

* * *

An hour later Jason's cell phone rang—it was Sali.

"Done," he said. "I attached the package to the stern, right next to the outdrive where you can't really see it too easily from inside the boat. You'd have to be outside to see it, and then you'd pretty much have to be looking for it."

"So, you're getting a signal from it okay?"

"Yeah, strong signal, no problem. Have you heard from Masen yet?"

"Nope, not a word."

"What's up with the broad?"

"I met one of her former boyfriends, a guy named Timbo. Poor bastard, she broke his heart. He told me a little more about the guy Michael who owns the condo she's in. The guy lets her stay there so long as she makes herself available for him when he's in town."

"Available. How nice."

"Apparently the guy doesn't spend much time here—just breezes in from Chicago now and then. Neither Timbo nor Julene knows what he does for a living, though, and by the sounds of it, she's a straight shooter and isn't the type of person to lie."

"Would love to meet this guy Michael. So, it looks like the captain has maybe passed some jewels in a bag to Julene, who may or may not know there are jewels inside, yet she doesn't know what he does for living, or so she tells Timbo, and this guy Michael may have a connection to human trafficking, but we don't know that for sure yet either because there is no proof of it and no other evidence of it. And our Bluto character may or may not be up to something nefarious, and all this depends upon what some informant told Jamie is happening, which may be a part of the informant's agenda somehow, but it may also be true. In the meantime, I just risked my neck on a night dive, alone, and Masen is about to do a breaking-and-entering adventure into a condo that we don't know for sure is a hiding place for jewels. Have I got all that right so far?"

"Pretty much. Are you trying to make me feel bad or something?"

"Oh no, not at all, glee is shooting out of my eye sockets. I'm rock solid with the plan. Only challenge is, none of us has really done anything illegal yet, except Masen is about to, so I hope he doesn't get caught."

Jason said nothing, then, "I hope there's nobody else living in the condo."

"Fuck. Well, he went early so he could see if in fact there is anybody else there, and also about neighbors. Let's hope he picks up on that."

"Wait a second: I see Julene leaving the club. If she's going to another one of the bars I'll follow her in. If she gets a cab, I'll call you."

Jason hung up and slipped out of the van and began walking her direction. She was facing away from him and crossing the street, and it didn't look like she was hailing or waiting for a cab.

She headed straight for the club across the street, the Thirty-third Street Wine Bar. The club had several tables outside and as she approached it, several of the people recognized her.

"Julene! Sit with us!" One woman stood and held out her arms for a hug.

Julene sang out: "Love you!" She hugged the woman and they both smiled in warmth for a long moment. "Going inside to listen to the music!"

Jason walked idly up to the scene and followed Julene as she walked inside the club.

The band featured a singing band leader named Anthony who had a torn earlobe and also played saxophone, plus a beautiful blond pianist who also sang, and a drummer who looked like he was still locked in the sixties. The songs were old favorites, and Julene swayed along with the music, but again stood by herself. The band stopped and she turned to lean against the bar and chat with the proprietor.

"Hi Candace!"

"Well, hello, Julene, what are you having?"

Julene opened her wallet and picked through it long enough to find a few crumpled bills and tossed them on to the bar. "What can I get for seven dollars?"

"I'll let you have a half a glass of wine for that."

Julene started to protest, but Jason broke in as he leaned up against the bar next to her.

"I'll get it." He turned to Julene: "What are you drinking?"

Julene turned to him then straightened up and looked up at him. "Oh my God! It's Elvis!"

Jason laughed in spite of himself. "I've never been called that before, but thanks for the compliment."

Julene laughed heartily then turned to Candace with a slight slur of speech from the previous club's drinking. "Doesn't he look just like Elvis?"

Candace laughed. "Well, if you hold one of your eye's closed and blink with the other, yeah, I see the resemblance." She turned her attention to Jason: "Well, you certainly are tall and that hair does look a lot like Elvis', that's for sure. What are you drinking, Elvis? I know she prefers a split of champagne."

Jason chuckled. "It's Jason, and I'll have any good IPA you've got."

"You got it," said Candace as she turned to gather the drinks and glasses.

"Well if you ain't Elvis," said Julene, "who are you? And thanks for the drink."

"Jason," he said again. "I'm from out of town. I heard about Thirty-third Street and the music, so here I am."

Candace poured the drinks and they toasted: "Cheers."

"So, what do you do, Elvis?"

"I sing rock and roll and produce hit records and surround myself with beautiful women."

"Oh, so you are Elvis!"

Jason chuckled and Julene laughed heartily again.

* * *

Usually, Jason's self-imposed limit of three India Pale Ales ("cold glass, please"), meant it was time to call Uber, or get a cab, or walk, or whatever. Drinking four was asking for it. Drinking five meant borderline fun or insanity. Sometimes both.

Anthony was still playing soprano sax and everybody including Jason was digging it. Suddenly, in the middle of an instrumental, Julene said to Jason, "I gotta pee," and she started heading back to the Ladies Room.

After a minute or so, right at the end of one of Anthony's numbers, Jason heard a loud, "Psssst!" from the Ladies Room.

Embarrassed, Jason looked around one-eighty, casually, to see if anybody else heard that. Nobody was paying any attention to him or Julene.

Jason put his glass of IPA down and walked over to the Ladies' Room. Julene had the door partially opened, and Jason could only see her head and hand motioning him in. Jason walked up to the door and peeked in the slightly open door.

"Quick, come in," said Julene, emphasizing the command with a wave inward with her hand.

Jason stepped inside the Ladies Room. Julene looked up at him and said, "I need some help with my blouse." She was busting out of her blouse with all but one button at the bottom undone.

Jason stepped back and put his hands up and said, "Whoa, I can't do this." Professional ethics and all that.

Julene laughed. "Wanna bet!" She proceeded to unbutton and take off her blouse, and unbelievably quickly, her bra.

Julene's breasts were magnificent. When she pulled off the bra, her breasts did not sag an inch. Her breasts were sticking out like they had been slightly inflated, and her thimble-like nipples were big and rock hard. She sat down on the toilet seat lid and pulled Jason over to her. Quickly and expertly, she unbuckled and unzipped him.

He had no underwear and there was no doubt about his desire now.

"My God, Elvis! You got a license for that thang?" She started laughing again, then she took him in her mouth and hummed with admiration and appreciation. After moments of mutual bliss, she looked up at him with her Alaskan Husky blue eyes, and said, "I want you to come in my mouth." Then she smiled and went back at it.

No man could resist. She didn't want him to do it right away, she wanted him to have a little fun along the way, so she drew the process out as long as she could—bringing him to near orgasm, then backing way off. She put him between her breasts and moved them up and down, smiling and looking up into his eyes, then she put him in her mouth again.

Finally, she won her bet, and Jason let out a groan of undeniable pleasure. Fortunately, Anthony and the band had started up again, so probably nobody heard them. Maybe.

Jason cleaned himself off and she got dressed, laughing all the time like a naughty child. When she was finished dressing, she pulled his head down to her mouth and kissed him quickly.

"Thank you, Jason," she said. "That was as good for me as it was for you."

Jason didn't know what to say.

Julene said, "I'm sorry, honey, but I've got to go home. I don't suppose you have some cab money, do you?"

"Oh, yeah, sure." He fumbled into his wallet and gave her a hundred-dollar bill.

She looked up and smiled. "Thank you, honey. I'll take Uber and save some money. You be good now! I'll see you around!"

With that she opened the door to the Ladies Room, but instead of turning right to go back into the bar, she turned left and went out the back door.

Jason left the room and came face-to-face with a line of three women waiting their turn. Two were scowling, one was smiling broadly.

"Sorry, ladies," he said, then also took a left, waited a couple of seconds, then peeked out the back door to see which way she had gone. Outside was an alley where the owners of the shops on Thirty-third Street parked their cars and placed their garbage for pick up. Julene was scuttling down the alleyway, heading east. He saw that the alleyway turned back towards Thirty-third Street. He closed the door and went back through the Wine Bar to the street out front—Thirty-third Street.

Julene had come back towards Jason but stopped at another bar several establishments down the street called Fishtales, where she sat at the outside bar and made a phone call with her cell. He sat down at a table outside the Wine Bar and waited to see what she was going to do. Soon, a car with an Uber light in the window pulled up front of Fishtales, and Julene stepped in.

Jason walked quickly back to his van and was able to catch up to the Uber driver and followed discreetly several cars back.

Chapter Eleven
Condo Boogie

Masen knocked the throttle back to its slowest speed—a minor *chug-chug* that moved the boat forward inches at a time. Getting into Michael Fieldstone's condo was going to be difficult—he had to do it while Julene was out, but at least Jason would be following her and would alert him when she was coming back. Jason had just texted him that he was following her into a bar on Thirty-third Street, but for now he had other people in the neighborhood to worry about. He could see lights were still on in other condos in the building, so he was going to have to be extremely quiet—perfectly so. But that wasn't the big problem on the approach. The touchier problem was the lighting all over the side of the building and the three floors below Fieldstone's condo. He was going to have to get up there in hopes that nobody decided to walk out on their back patio, or that someone from across the Intracoastal wouldn't see him as he climbed up and entered from the back…if he could. With his binoculars he scanned the area around the condo, and on the other side of the Intracoastal. He saw nobody outside, and from what he could tell there was nobody simply gazing out of their windows.

He slowly pulled the skiff up to the free side of a beautiful old classic sixty's era forty-six-foot Chris Craft Constellation and just floated there for a few minutes, waiting and listening for any movement from within. The size of the boat prevented people from up the Intracoastal from viewing him and restricted the view of others who may see him from the condominium building.

He grabbed the yacht's gunwale with one hand while he placed a rubber bumper between the hulls then moved quickly to the bow of the skiff to fasten the bow line, then to the stern to fasten the stern line to the yacht. He stepped carefully and listened intently again then he pulled from his bag a stethoscope with batteries for amplification that he often used in cracking safes. He put it against the hull and listened as he looked at the traffic driving by on Las Olas and the condominiums and yachts across the Intracoastal. He heard nothing, save the creak of a five-decade old vessel moving oh-so-slightly with the oh-so-small fading wake of Masen's original approach.

After a few moments of intense listening and watching, he donned his tennis shoes, grabbed his bag, then pulled himself up to the gunwale of the yacht and on to its deck. He crouched and listened.

She was a wonderfully maintained vessel—polished fittings and lines smartly coiled. He stopped and listened again for any souls on board, but he heard none.

All was well, so he slipped silently on to the short pier, then ran crouched to the seawall. Much was hidden by palms and hedges along the seawall, but he used that to his advantage to hide as he approached the wall of the condominium building. As he did, he noted what Jason had told him, that a gate protected the garage, front and back, and served as the first floor of the building. Inside the garage was a stairwell, so he knew if he climbed over the gate he could get into the stairwell. Only problem was there would almost certainly be the need for an access key or card, or a punch-button code device to get onto the fourth floor. But that left too much chance for running into neighbors. It was much better to go up the outside wall if he could. In Florida they call such robbers "condo crawlers," and condo crawler he would become.

One of the keys to his success as one of the greatest cat burglars of all time was his preparation. He removed from his tool bag several black garbage bags. He quickly ran along the outside wall which was lit with upward facing lights and placed a bag over each one, completely eliminating the flooding light along the wall he decided he was going to climb. Moving more swiftly now, he went to the dark corner of the condo and removed his rappelling gear and began to scale the balconies of the four floors of the condominium until he reached Fieldstone's.

An amazing thing he had discovered was that these rich folks who spent so much money on high security systems rarely locked their big sliding glass doors on their balconies! They obviously didn't feel that a cat burglar would be on the prowl. But even if it was locked, he had the equipment to cut his way in and bypass most in-glass security systems. You just had to know what to look for.

He quietly crept onto the outside balcony. The kitchen light was on, and so was the one in the back hallway, probably leading to the bedroom. He crouched silently for a long minute, watching and listening intently. He tried the latch to the sliding door and sure enough, it was unlatched. He remained still for another long minute, then slid the door open very slowly and slipped inside and closed the door slowly behind him.

The only sound was the very low hum of the central air conditioning, yet he waited for another full minute waiting to hear other sounds. He stood and surveyed his immediate surroundings. He was next to the dinner table, which in turn was adjacent to the kitchen. On his right was a living room adorned with long low couches with a glass coffee table in between. The view perpendicular to the facing couches was a big plate glass window overlooking the Intracoastal he had just arrived from. Between the living room and the kitchen was a small foyer off the front door, and to his right was the hallway which must lead to the bathrooms and a bedroom or two. Along the walls were various stylistic paintings and one ivory figurine on a pedestal. A hidden safe could be anywhere, if there was one, but most likely it would be in the bedroom. However, he decided to make a quick look around the living room, and after finding nothing obvious, placed his first bug on top of a large painting in the living room.

The first bedroom was on the right and appeared to not be in use—the beds were made tight, and there were no clothes in the closet, except a long raincoat, and none elsewhere in the room. He looked for the safe anyway. There were three paintings on the wall and he carefully inspected each one with his penlight before lifting them and looking behind. Nothing but wall. He placed his second bug under the night stand next to the bed.

There weren't many other places to look in that bedroom, but he did inspect under the toilet tank lid in the bathroom, in the medicine chest for a secret compartment behind it, and each tile along the wall for an open joint between. Nothing.

He heard a faint click, like that of a key in the front door lock, but it was something in the hallway. He checked his cell phone to see if there had been any texts from Jason. Nothing. He moved on to the next bedroom.

This was obviously the master bedroom where all the living was done. The bed was made, but the pillows disarrayed. The closet was jammed with clothes—hers on one side, his on the other. There were four paintings on the wall—Cezanne and Ansel Adams prints, and two others he couldn't identify. He went straight for the Ansel Adams and scored. The painting swung back easily and there in plain view was a Tigerking Digital Security Safe—arguably the best on the market without spending a ton of money. This was not going to be easy.

He opened up his kit and pulled out his battery powered stethoscope. Just as he turned it on he noticed a text message from Jason flash onto his cell.

She's leaving 33rd Street. Probably going home.

Shit. He knew this job would take at least an hour or more to hopefully open the safe, and that was under the best of conditions.

Reluctantly, he packed the stethoscope in his bag, and turned to go. Looking right at him was a backpack hanging on a wooden peg with something in it. *No, it couldn't be.* Masen walked over to Julene's backpack and took it off the peg. He turned back over to the bed, opened the backpack, and spilled the contents onto the bed.

Jason's text flashed on Masen's cell: *Looks for sure like she's heading home.*

A little box with a keyhole to unlock the box was the sole contents of the backpack. It was old wood and badly maintained, but solid. He tried to open it—no luck. He opened his robbery bag, pulled out a long thin lock pick, stuck it into the wooden box lock, twirled it around a bit, and the little wooden door opened. Inside were little bundles wrapped in cloth. He opened each bundle and rolled the contents of each onto the bedspread.

Jason's text: *Hurry!*

Bingo! An emerald. A ruby. Another emerald. A blue diamond. Another emerald. A ring with pink diamonds. A solid gold treble clef studded with sapphires and meant for a necklace. And there were more.

Masen stifled a gasp: "Holy shit!"

Of course, he'd seen these gem types before, but these were all bigger. Much bigger.

He grabbed his cell phone and took a picture of all the gems pooled together on the bed. He sent it to Jason with a text, "Done," put all the gems back into the box and deleted the photo on his phone, just as Jason had told him, then put the backpack back on the peg. He planted the final bug under a similar nightstand as in the other bedroom, then left at a quiet run.

She's home!

He sprang quietly down the hallway and across the living room, then through the sliding glass door, closing it quietly and easing over the balcony just as Julene entered the condo.

* * *

He scrambled down the outside condo wall, quickly packed his rappelling gear and the bags covering the lights, sprinted soundlessly down the dock to the boat, then pounced into his skiff and started it. The engine was still warm and chugged quietly as Masen turned the craft into a slow one-eighty so as not to draw attention to his hasty retreat. He increased the throttle at the end of the turn and headed back up the sparsely lit Intracoastal, barely able to contain his excitement. He wanted to shout, "Oh my fucking God!" but he knew it might draw attention. He reached for the radio and called Jason. "I'm out and on the water," he said breathlessly.

"Did she see you?"

"No."

"There's a small bridge at the end of Hendrick's Isle—you're probably almost there. Pull up there and I'll meet you in a couple of minutes."

Masen maneuvered the Zodiac up next to the bridge, found a cleat and tied up. Jason pulled up seconds later and pulled into a little parking area next to the bridge. Masen crawled up out of the boat with his robbery bag and walked over to the van. Jason stepped out and motioned him to the back door. They crawled into the back of the van and Jason shut the door behind them.

"Jeezus, that was close," said Masen. "What a rush!" He sat down on the cot, pulled the folding table down, and turned on the table light.

"So, what happened? How did it go?"

Masen opened his backpack and pulled the little box out and emptied the contents onto the table. The jewels were no longer wrapped, but loose. He pointed the table lamp right at the pile of jewels.

With stunning refulgence, the assemblage of jewels and jewelry sparkled regally: crystalline diamonds clear as mountain air; twinkling oceanic deep blue sapphires; Burmese "pigeon blood" deep red rubies; emeralds green as the dense and dark Amazon forest; one deep green Tanzanian tourmaline at least twelve carats; and one oval blue topaz the size of a marble and the color of Bombay gin.

Jason gasped and held his breath for long seconds as he got his first close look at the extravagant collection of sparkling stones.

"Masen, you idiot!" screamed Jason. "You weren't supposed to steal them!"

"Jason, my man, that's retirement! Big boats, big houses, and beautiful women with big tits! Come to Masen my little darlings…" He reached over and started to scoop them up.

Jason stopped him. "Masen, you knucklehead, you can't keep those! This is part of a criminal or maybe even a human trafficking investigation! You want the Bureau and HSI both coming after you, not to mention the bad guys you took them from?"

"So how are we going to find said Bad Dudes or Dudettes?"

"You put the bugs in his apartment, right?"

"That I did—all three of them."

"Crap. You've put me in a world of hurt." He paused for a moment to think. "Okay, sooner or later he's going to call her and say, 'Hi, Honey, where are my jewels?' So, with any luck, we'll be able to hear their plans and follow them and find where they hide out and nab them."

He stopped and sighed. "Jeezus, Masen, I'm going to have to think this over. Might as well head back to your boat—you sure as hell can't go put them back."

He reached for his phone. Time to call Sali.

Chapter Twelve
Gulf Stream Challenge

As the sun rose, Julene's phone rang and she rolled over to answer it.

"Michael!" she scolded. "Why are you calling me so early?"

"Good morning, Julene," he said in an unconvincing tone. "Did you put the box in the safe yesterday like I told you to?"

"Good morning," she said grumpily as she struggled to sit up. "Yes. Well, no, not yet. It's still in my backpack."

His voice rising, he said, "I told you to put it in the safe as soon as you got home! Go do it now!"

"Sheesh, what a grouch. Okay, okay."

She arose wearing nothing and tossed the cell phone back onto the bed and walked over to her backpack hanging from the peg next to the doorway leading into the bedroom. She lifted it and feeling that it was now light hurriedly opened the zipper on the backpack and felt and looked inside.

"Oh shit," she said quietly. "Oh fuck no." She stopped and stared at the bedroom wall, trying to remember where she might have put it that she hadn't thought of, or maybe some place she might have stopped on the way home and left it; but no, she had gone straight home and she remembered the weight of the backpack as she had hung it up on the peg.

Now she was scared. When Michael lost his temper, he didn't just lose it, he went apeshit. If he were here now, he'd be smacking her around. Shit! She drew a breath and went over to her cell phone on the bed.

"Michael! Somebody stole it from the bag!"

Total silence for long seconds from Michael; then, quietly: "Did you stop anywhere or talk to anyone on the way home?"

"No!" she said panicking.

Calmly, he said, "Could you have put it somewhere else in the house?"

"No. I walked straight into the bedroom and put the backpack up on the peg just like I always do. I was going to put it away as soon as I got in, but I had to pee and while I was doing that my friend Charlie the singer called me and I totally forgot about it."

More long silence, which scared Julene even more. She knew his rage was building.

"Look around the house and see if anything else is missing, or if anything has been moved around—any sign that somebody else was in the condo."

She walked all around the condo, inspecting every detail that she could think of. Finally, she said, "I don't see anything gone or anything out of place, but I swear to you, Michael, that box was in the backpack when I went out last night."

As soon as she said it, she realized it was a mistake.

"You went out last night. You went out without locking the box in the safe." They were statements. Condemnations.

Julene replied meekly, "Yes."

Michael exploded: "You dumb fucking cunt! How could you be so fucking stupid! Why do you think I asked you to put it into the safe in the first place! It's worth more than that whole damn condo, more than five condos!"

"I'm sorry, Michael!" She started to cry. "What the hell was in the damn box anyway?"

He ignored her question and said, "Go to the safe and open it and tell me if the other boxes are in there."

She went to the safe and opened it using the combination Michael had made her memorize and swear never to tell anybody or even write it down. "They're both still in the safe. Both boxes he gave me before are still in their little bags and they're sitting there just like I left them."

Michael's silence returned as Julene started crying again.

Finally, he said, in a more measured tone: "Don't go anywhere. You stay right there. Pack your bags and get ready for a trip."

"What? I don't want to go anywhere," she said defiantly.

Calmly, Michael replied, "You stay there or I will find you and kill you, do you understand me?"

"Michael! Don't talk to me like that!"

"Shut up, you fucking bitch! You start packing and don't you dare leave or I will have you killed. Do you understand? Now do it!"

* * *

Michael had hung up abruptly. Julene looked down at her phone and realized that now was her chance, if she were ever going to do it, to leave Michael and disappear. Just as her friend Charlie had told her, things would only get worse if she stayed with him, and there was nothing that he was doing for her other than giving her a place to stay. It was take, take, take sex from her, and he never really did anything for her or gave anything to her, except this place to stay. Oh sure, now and then he would buy her a ring or a necklace, or take her out to fancy places to eat, but what was that doing to make her a better person, to improve her life? In fact, she was basically there just to be on hand for sex and to exhibit a presence in the condo to help keep burglars away. And he played rough. She hated having sex with him. He treated her like he was about to kill her at the same time he got off. The man was mental. She had to get away from him, but how?

She began to wonder about the boxes, and if they were so damn valuable, maybe she could steal them and sell the contents and escape from him. She went back to the safe and opened it. She pulled out one of the little bags that held a box and retrieved the box from inside. The box had an inlaid lock in it, and it was made of heavy metal of some kind. It looked indestructible and would be impossible for her to open or crush. If she took it, she would have to get somebody else to open it, and if it was worth as much as Michael said, that person just might kill her and take it, or at the very least just take it from her. Maybe not, but if it was something that valuable, there was definitely that chance, or maybe they would tell the cops and she would go to jail. Or maybe she could give it to the cops, but if she did that, Michael would most definitely find a way to get to her. She didn't know if it was anything illegal, but the whole scene surrounding it certainly sounded like it. She put the box back inside the bag, and put the bag back into the safe, then sat on the edge of the bed, put her head in her hands and began to cry. She was trapped. There was nothing to do but pack and wait for Michael's next move, then hope that another chance came up to escape.

* * *

In Marek's rage he screamed at the top of his lungs and threw a chair across the bedroom. Gorsh came running in, his pistol drawn and ready to fire.

"That fucking cunt!" he roared. "Simple job," he bellowed to no one in particular as he paced around the room. "All she had to do was take the jewels from Reznik and put them in the safe for me. Be a simple go-between so Reznik and I aren't connected, our cutout, a simple dumb blond whom nobody would suspect and who doesn't even know what's in the boxes. But no! She fucks it up."

He turned to Gorsh and continued. "Somebody must have known Reznik was passing her the jewels and broke in when she was gone and took the jewels. She's not smart enough to do this on her own. Somebody knew."

"Could it have been Reznik?"

"No way. He's my half-brother, he would die for me, but he also knows that if he ever betrayed me like that I would rip his skin off while he was still alive. He'd never do something like this, and I know you wouldn't either."

Gorsh's face blanched. "Boss! Never! I would never do something like that!"

Just then Gorsh's cell phone rang. "Yes," he answered. "Are you sure?...Okay, wait one."

Gorsh looked to Marek: "They followed Joseph Spring and just saw him meet up with his wife, Amber. She's alive."

Marek held up his hand in thought, looking down at the floor. "There's a connection. Amber Spring must have made it back alive, and she must have told somebody about the jewels. The question is who. It couldn't be the authorities or they would have busted Julene. Somehow, somebody knew Julene was collecting the jewels from Reznik."

He paced back and forth for a few seconds, then said, "I know Amber Spring's and her husband's routines. They always go to a place called the Boatyard in Fort Lauderdale for brunch on Sundays—let's hope they do it again. If your men hit them there, they'll never get through the traffic and cops will be blocking the roads. Tell them to rent a boat under a false name and pull into the Boatyard's docks and kill them there. Send your men their pictures if they don't know them already. They should be able to get back out on the Intracoastal and out of there in a hurry. They can ditch the boat back over at Pier 66 and have their man pick them up there."

Gorsh repeated the instructions and left the room.

Marek dialed Reznik.

"Yes," said Reznik after one ring, "it's me."

"Tell me again that you gave those stones to Julene."

"I did. I told you that. What happened?"

"They're gone. The fucking jewels are gone. She forgot to put them in the safe and somebody broke into the condo while she was out and took them. They didn't take anything else, just the stones, so they knew the stones were there."

"Jesus fucking Christ! But who? How? Did they get the other ones, too?"

"No, so whoever did it didn't know the combination to the safe. Nobody knows that combination except Julene and me. I want you to go get her and the stones, and after you get them get ready to sail. As soon as she's onboard, take off and head for the mountain."

"Will do, but remember, I haven't been there by sea before—just seaplane. I suggest we get a captain who knows those channels, since I don't."

Marek paused. "Okay, but tell him you're taking the girls to a party and you don't know the waters, and don't let him talk to them. Choose carefully. Make sure he's not a blabbermouth. We can off him later when we're sure we don't need him anymore."

"On my way."

* * *

Down below the condo in the surveillance van, Jason sat up sharply as he heard loudly over the van's speakers the transmission from the microphone that Masen had hidden in the bedroom. All he could hear was Julene's responses to Michael Fieldstone, and from those conversations he pieced together what might be happening. First of all, Fieldstone now knew the jewels that were in her backpack were missing, but that the ones in the safe were not; therefore, Fieldstone would guess that somebody on the inside knew about the transfer of the jewels—namely, either Julene or Bluto, at the least—and that someone had been hired to steal them. He could also hear her crying and cursing and opening drawers and closets, so he inferred she was packing. Apparently, Fieldstone threatened her and was telling her to get ready to leave. Maybe he or somebody else was coming to get her, maybe he told her to leave on her own, or maybe Bluto was coming to get her. He had to let Sali and Masen know the latest.

He called Sali who was already up on his shift to keep an eye on the *London Blue*.

"How's it looking over there?" asked Jason.

"All quiet. What about you?"

"Well, it seems Fieldstone called Julene, found out about the jewels being taken by our friend, and now I think he's asked her to pack her things. I don't know if she's leaving in a cab or with a friend, or maybe Fieldstone's coming to get her, or maybe Bluto's coming to get her, or what, I don't know. But I'm supposed to meet Jamie's informant later this morning at the Boatyard for brunch, and I don't know how I'm going to cover all the bases. I can't do that meeting and watch her, too."

"You want me to go watch her while you go meet the informant?"

Silence, then, "I guess so. I don't know what else to do at the moment."

"Wait," said Sali. "I see movement over there."

Jason waited impatiently for Sali's observations: "Well?"

"They're taking the Zodiac down, so probably somebody's going back to shore. I'll bet it's Bluto and he's going in to get her."

"Follow him to make sure, but try not to alert the crew on the London Blue."

"Okay, I'll have Masen take over the watch, then I'll be on my way."

Seconds later Sali answered Masen's phone when he saw it was Jason calling and handed it to Masen. "Hey, wake up you bum."

"Jeezus," Masen grumbled, "don't I get any sleep on this job?" He grabbed the phone and shouted irritably, "What!"

"Get your boat ready to roll, Captain. I've got a feeling the London Blue might be sailing today."

"Wait a second, sailing where? I didn't know we'd be leaving the area. Are you increasing my pay?"

"Are you going back to jail for grand larceny?"

"Shit. I should have seen that coming…"

"Glad you see the light. Don't worry, you'll get your reward. Check to make sure that GPS tracker is working and call back if you see the boat taking off."

Jason hung up and sat back and continued listening to Julene's movements around the condo. It would take Sali a while to crank up the skiff, drive it over to the dock, tie it up, then hop in his car and catch up to Bluto. It was still about three hours before the time when he had to meet the informant at the Boatyard. This could be tight.

* * *

Thirty minutes later Julene heard Bluto banging on the condo door, while Jason listened from the van and Sali watched from the Lexus a short way from Jason's van.

"Okay, okay! I'm coming! Stop banging!" said Julene.

As she turned the knob Reznik shoved the door open and screamed at her: "Get the stuff out of the safe and grab your shit—we're leaving immediately."

"Why do I have to go with you?" she yelled back at him. "Just take the damn bags and go!"

"You're coming with me. Now do what I said and let's get out of here. You don't want me to ask again, because I won't ask."

"Shit. Bastard!"

She turned and walked into the bedroom with Reznik following. She turned the dials on the safe and handed the three boxes over to him. He saw her two bags packed on the bed and grabbed one of them. "Grab the other one and let's go."

* * *

From the van, Jason talked to Sali: "Here they come. Make sure they're heading back to the London Blue. If they are, drive to the Boatyard off Seventeenth Street Causeway and take a seat at the brunch tables and I'll get a separate one. Our informant will be meeting me there. Keep your eyes open while I'm talking to him. Masen will tell us about any movements on the boat."

"And if he's not going back to London Blue?"

"Just keep following. I'll stay here for a while then take off and arrive at the Boatyard at eleven."

Just as Jason hung up, his phone rang and he saw it was Masen.

"Masen," he said. "What's up? Are they moving?"

"No, but get this—they're repainting the name on the back of the boat and putting new numbers on the hull, so obviously they're getting ready to move and they don't want anybody being able to identify them."

"Damn. Is the GPS Sali planted on them still working?"

"Yes."

"Can you tell the new name of the boat yet?"

"No."

"Call Sali and update him and let me know if anything changes."

Jason watched Bluto throw Julene's bag into the back seat of his car. Julene was obviously barking at him about something, but he couldn't make out what she was saying. Bluto yelled at her and started to come around the front of the car to apparently force her into the car, but she relented and got in and they finally took off.

Sali called Jason.

"Masen just called me. Them changing the name of the boat tells me they're probably getting ready to take off all right, but I'll follow them anyway. Hey, do they serve mimosas at the brunch?"

"Hell if I know, but I guess we'll find out."

Sali continued following Bluto and Julene until he saw them pull into the parking lot at the Hillsboro bridge, then crawl into the Zodiac. He turned around the Lexus and started heading back toward the Boatyard.

He called Masen as he drove. "Keep your eyes open—Bluto and Julene should be on their way to the yacht in just a few minutes. If you don't see them, call me immediately."

He hung up and called Jason. "They're heading to the yacht all right. I'm on my way to the Boatyard."

"See you there shortly."

Chapter Thirteen
Singing at the Boatyard

The Boatyard is an upscale restaurant that has the distinction of having a branch of the Intracoastal go right along the back of the property. Large expensive yachts tie up there, as well as the many pleasure craft of various sizes that traverse the so-called Venice of America, as Fort Lauderdale is frequently called.

The restaurant had free valet parking for the Sunday brunch, so Sali let a young man park the Lexus for him. He made his way to the inside of the restaurant, registered for the buffet, then sat outside at the far end of the patio where there was a nice little Tiki bar in the open air.

Two minutes before eleven o'clock, Jason arrived and parked under some shade at the near end of the parking lot out front of the restaurant. He started to walk into the front entrance, but heard singing and noticed there was a walkway at the east side of the restaurant and a sign that indicated the patio was at the end of the path.

As he arrived at the back patio he saw Sali sitting at the Tiki bar, and he noticed a blond woman, apparently in her early forties, singing on the makeshift stage. A sign on the stage said, "Liz Sharp Sings!"

Jason removed his shades and looked around the patio. He saw his contact in the turquoise shirt, but also noticed he was sitting with a very attractive woman with jet black hair wearing sunglasses. The man lifted his chin slightly in recognition, but immediately held up a walkie-talkie and spoke into it.

He noticed three other men, apparently the man's security detail, scattered among the crowd, put their fingers to their ears and immediately looked over at Jason.

Jason approached the couple and sat in the only available chair, facing the singer.

"I'm Jason," he said to the man, glancing briefly at the woman.

"I'm Joseph Spring," the man said. "And this is my lovely wife, Amber Spring."

The woman had hair the color and luster of ebony. Her small nose was hard and angular, her cheeks had just a hint of rouge, and her complexion was flawless; yet through all that beauty, she wasn't smiling. She did not remove her sunglasses. She shook Jason's hand as he sat down. A waitress brought him coffee and asked if he'd also like a mimosa—a Boatyard special of sparkling wine and freshly squeezed orange juice. He declined.

"I agreed to meet you," said Joseph, "but actually it's my wife who has the story to tell you."

Jason nodded at her slightly and said, "I'm all ears."

"I'll start at the beginning, and it's a long story, so if you want to serve yourself some of their delicious buffet, now's the time."

"It does smell good. Hold that thought." He got up and nodded discreetly at Sali, who joined him in the line at the buffet.

"Apparently it's the woman who has the story to tell," Jason said quietly to Sali. "Just keep your eyes open. I saw at least three men from his security detail." He described them as he served himself from the buffet.

Jason returned to the table and started to eat, while the couple sat over cups of coffee, no food.

"I was kidnapped," she continued. "I was coming back from my usual weekly workout at the gym and pool, walking out to the car, when two men threw me into a van with its side door open."

Jason stopped eating and placed his fork down. "Could you recognize them if you saw them again?"

"Doesn't matter—they're dead."

Jason glanced briefly at Joseph, then said, "What happened?"

"There's so much to tell. My husband is a very wealthy man," she continued, "and he's a fabulous husband at that." She put her hand on Joseph's and squeezed it gently.

At the stage, singer Liz began singing Patsy Cline's classic, "Crazy."

She continued. "The kidnappers had a peculiar demand—they wanted Joseph to give them one million in gemstones. Not jewelry, but loose stones. They told him which types of stones to get, so he did."

Jason took a sip of coffee.

"But they cheated him. He met them, but they kept me, and took the stones, too. They said they needed to keep me for safe passage, but they'd give me back later."

"How did you get away?"

"I'm coming to that. I wasn't the only one kidnapped. There were two others."

"Taken by the same kidnappers?"

"I guess so, but I don't know that for sure. They were the only ones we saw."

"'We', you say. You and the other ladies?"

"Yes. Beautiful women, but you haven't heard about them missing yet. Hopefully you won't, and you won't hear it from me, either. They'll be killed and their families will be killed if the word gets out."

"But you say the kidnappers didn't release you back to your husband. Obviously, you got away, but what were they going to do with you and the other ladies?"

"I don't know."

Jason stared into his coffee cup for a moment. "Please, go on."

"They put all of us on a big fancy yacht and we were in there for a couple of days. They fed us well, we had showers, change of clothes, and we could go up on deck. I didn't know where we were, and we never saw land until the day I escaped. That night, we met another yacht at sea, and that's when all the killing happened."

Jasen stopped eating or drinking and leaned back in his chair and listened. She continued her tale for some minutes as she described her escape.

"Then, from just under the bow, I heard him yell out to the crew that he'd meet a woman named Julene this Saturday at Aruba's, and that he'd call somebody named Marek. That's what I told Joseph, and that's what he told your colleague, Jamie."

"Marek?" said Jason. "Jamie didn't mention that name."

"Yes, that's what it sounded like. I don't think I remembered that before when I told Joseph, but I remember it now."

"Please, go on," said Jason.

"Well, then the boat sank." She stopped and just stared ahead as the singer began to sing that famous old favorite, "At Last" by Mack Gordon and Harry Warren.

Joseph's head bowed and shook a little bit as he recognized the song. The morning breeze was cool and had picked up the pungent aroma of the frangipanis surrounding the patio and the palm tree fronds swayed slightly. The sun was bright. It was a gorgeous morning for a Sunday brunch.

"Yes, the boat sank," she began again, "and the sound of the flames died and then there was no light and I could see the boat that I might have been on, maybe should have been on, sail away. The lights of the boat faded and I noticed it was only a quarter-moon. Then it was dark. I was so scared I just can't begin to tell you, but I was clearheaded enough to know the only thing I could do was swim to shore and hope to see a boat. I used to be a mile swimmer in college, so I had some confidence that I could do it."

The waitress came and took away Jason's plate but left the coffee.

Amber continued. "So, I started swimming toward the lights on the shore, a long way off—maybe it was a mile, maybe three, I don't know."

"Then I saw what I thought were sharks next to me," she continued, "or they looked like sharks at first, but then I saw they were porpoises. They rolled up next to me and made squeaking sounds, so I knew they were porpoises. They came close and at first I was afraid, but they didn't do anything except come right up next to me and actually rub up against me. It was like they were trying to help me stay afloat or something. I swear, there must have been a hundred of them—they were all around me. I couldn't hold on to them or anything, but they stuck with me and helped keep me going. I don't really remember much more about it. It was truly amazing. Finally, I got close to shore and they left and I was able to swim in. There were people there with flashlights looking for something and they heard my screams for help and saw my approach and began pointing and shouting until I was close enough to walk in. They asked if I was okay and while they took care of me they explained they were looking for freshly hatched sea turtles, wrapping towels around me and getting me dry clothing. I asked them to please not call 911, but I did ask to borrow a phone."

Jason glanced over at Sali who sat up stiffly and was looking fixedly at something happening over at the Intracoastal.

"Then I called my husband and told him I was safe and that after I found out where I was, I would call him back. Long story short, he got me, and I am just so thankful to be alive."

Jason asked, "Do you know what happened to the other women?"

"No—how could I? But since they had the jewels and the women, I would say it doesn't look too good for them. Those poor ladies," she said, then started crying.

The waitress came and asked if everything was okay and could she get them anything, but Joseph waved her off and said to Jason, "Now you know why I didn't tell you much more: if the boat had been caught, the women and their families may have been hurt or killed by the kidnappers; and you can see that I couldn't let anybody know Amber was still alive or the kidnappers might try to kill her so she wouldn't talk. We didn't know where they were going anyway, but we did know this Julene woman was supposed to meet the captain at Aruba's, so at least you'd be able to do something. So now it's your turn. Tell us what you've found out, and what happens next."

Jason put down his coffee and cleared his throat. "We saw the guy I figured must be the captain by your description to Jamie, and he met with the woman who we did ultimately verify was named Julene. She took the bag he gave her and went to the place where she lives. I can't tell you how, but we verified the bag did in fact contain jewels. A lot of them."

"Who is she and what did she do with the stones? Who else is involved?"

Just then two men stepped on to the dock out of a Gulfstream 26 boat that Sali had been staring at; two other men stayed aboard as the boat idled. The two men walking up the dock were carrying short canvas bags and hastened toward the restaurant.

Joseph Amber's security detail also noticed the men and reached for the pistols in their shoulder holsters that were covered by their windbreakers.

Sali stood up and started walking toward the men as they in turn started walking faster up the dock. They opened the canvas bags and tossed them aside as they each pulled out an Uzi.

Jason stood and reached for the gun in his fanny pack and screamed to Joseph and Amber: "Run!"

Joseph and Amber froze for a moment then stood quickly to begin their escape. All three men from the security detail pulled their pistols at the same time and began to take aim at the closest man with the Uzi.

The two attackers had planned ahead, though: one was to take out any shooters, and the other was to take out Joseph and Amber.

Sali pulled his gun from the holster also hidden under his windbreaker and fired at the same time the security detail fired at the attacker. The man with the

Uzi fired at both the security detail and Sali. The attacker had a Kevlar vest and took several shots to the torso, but a shot from Sali blew the man's head apart.

The other attacker began shooting at the same time at Joseph and Amber just as they began to run. Amber tripped and fell and missed getting shot, but Joseph took several shots to his back as he tried to run away and he fell lifeless to the sidewalk.

Jason dove to the ground to his right as he pulled his pistol and also blasted the shooter in the head.

The people inside the restaurant began screaming and yelling and knocking over tables and chairs as they headed for the exits. Several people were dead at the outside dining area, as well as several inside the restaurant. Blood was everywhere; people were moaning and screaming for help.

The men in the boat started backing out of the slip. Jason and Sali rose and ran after them. The security detail ran to take care of Joseph and Amber.

The remaining attackers quickly turned the boat and gunned their engine. Jason and Sali continued firing and one of the assailants turned and continued firing as the boat straightened out and began racing down the Intracoastal. Jason and Sali stood at the end of the pier and continued firing. Jason told the cowering skipper of a boat in the next slip to get out, that he was going after them, and the skipper quickly obeyed.

Jason screamed over to Sali as he reloaded his Mark 23: "Call 911 and tell them to alert the Coast Guard!" Jason quickly untied the lines as the boat's owner ran for the restaurant. Jason started the boat and backed it out and gunned it to chase the assailants.

* * *

The killers had a good start and a fast boat, but Jason's ride was just a bit faster. They sped down the access canal past the "Watch Your Wake" sign and the Fort Lauderdale Police boat dockage, generating high waves with foam and spray and completely drenching a couple getting married in a beautiful Donzi 38ZR and nearly swamping a woman in a kayak heading for the Intracoastal. The killer ahead of them in the stern of the lead boat braced himself so as not to fall out of the boat with the next burst of gunfire. He opened fire at Jason who was slowly catching up as he bobbed and weaved haphazardly past the many boats tied up along the sea wall. The bullets shattered the windscreen, but Jason ducked and slowed, then peeked out the corner of the windshield and returned fire. The bullets missed as the attackers reached the Intracoastal and took a quick turn to starboard on a track to leave Port Everglades and head for the open sea.

Jason flew past the locally popular yellow Water Taxi, spraying the drunken tourists who laughed and cheered him on, obviously clueless of the danger. The attackers ahead flew past the Broward County Marine Patrol as they continued shooting at Jason.

The men in the Patrol boat shouted at the boat through a bullhorn just as Jason sped past them, returning fire at the assassin's boat.

The men in the Patrol boat scrambled to give chase, their siren wailing, lights flashing, and guns drawn and ready to fire as the two boats ahead of them flew toward the mouth of Port Everglades.

The wave chop began to build as they all approached the sea. The lead boat of attackers fell to a disadvantage in their lack of sea legs as they tried to brace themselves instead of bending their knees to the bouncing hull, and they began to steer erratically as Jason began to draw closer. The man in the stern with the Uzi had finally run out of ammo, then both men looked ahead as they maneuvered around an incoming gigantic tanker and a handful of pleasure boats and continued speeding toward the open ocean.

The pursuing Patrol boat was faster than the other two and was quickly approaching Jason's boat, which was now coming abeam of the lead attackers' boat just as they passed through the Port Everglades entrance and past the outlying large rock jetties. The attacker in the back of the boat threw his empty gun at Jason as they pulled up next to him, then the attacker in the back of the boat lunged up over the beam of their boat toward Jason's. Jason quickly pulled to port and the man fell into the water just as the pursuing Patrol boat pulled up close to both of their sterns. The man in the water raised his head just as the Patrol boat approached; the hull smacked him on the head then the prop of the outboard chewed him up into a red cloud as the engine groaned, stalled and died.

The remaining attacker screamed at Jason and pulled a pistol from his pocket and started firing at him. Jason swerved out to port again and slowed a bit, then raced up even and yanked hard to starboard as they both veered closely toward the jetties. The attacker's boat began to sway and the attacker overcompensated and the boat began a rhythmic rocking back and forth that he couldn't control. Jason smacked the boat again just as they drew close to the huge oceanic exit buoy of the Port. The attacker's boat crashed headfirst into the buoy and came to a dead stop, splintering the boat into a thunderous cloud of shards. The attacker flew through the air but his head smacked against the buoy light, just as Jason swung to port to avoid hitting the buoy himself.

The stricken man now in the water, his head split open and bleeding, began to sink. Jason swerved the boat around just as the patrol boat again reached him and the officers held their guns out, screaming at him to stop his boat and raise his hands. Jason nodded and pulled the throttle back to neutral and an idle and raised his hands. The man in the water began to sink in a red cloud with fish swirling in and around him, then the rising waves and outgoing tide carried him quickly below into the deep.

Chapter Fourteen
Charise

Florida State University's Strozier Library, a member of the Center for Research Libraries, is one of eight libraries on the Tallahassee campus plus four libraries from their overseas campuses. In 1967 the main library was enhanced to include a five-story annex at the rear of the original library, and in 1971 added its one millionth volume. On the fourth floor of the annex the U.S. President's polite and cheerful daughter, Charise Pearl, was seated at a long table under fluorescent lights, along with other students, studying for an exam on Friday.

But she found it hard to study that day, as the Secret Service was hovering close to her, as they usually did, and it made it difficult to meet and talk with the handsome young men who were always trying to talk to her. The agents scared away the exciting boyfriends who were always marginal with the law, the boys she was always most attracted to. However, her Secret Service protector sitting two tables in front of her alternately looking at her and perusing a book was a handsome hunk and she decided to mess with his head and try to tempt him. She smiled widely at him and stood to go talk to him.

Just then an older-looking student with a garnet-and-gold colored Seminole Football jacket checked his watch, then opened a hollowed-out book and extracted an ice pick and a Belarusian Makarov pistol. He stepped up quickly behind the agent and shoved the ice pick haft-deep into the back of the agent's skull. The agent died instantly, his head dropping with a big thud to the table. The killer screwed on a silencer to the Makarov and looked over at his accomplice.

Students at the table gasped and were frozen in shock.

The accomplice, with an identical jacket, opened a similar hollowed-out book and came up behind the other agent who had been looking out the window and also dispatched him with an ice pick, the agent dropping immediately to the floor twitching involuntarily. Both killers turned to the stunned and momentarily silent students who had witnessed the executions and held up their guns.

The first killer spoke calmly: "Nobody screams or says a word. Put your cell phones on the tables and put your hands in the air and nobody will be hurt. Now stay quiet or we will happily shoot you in the head."

The students, gasping, crying and dumbfounded, clamored to unload their phones onto the tables.

A third and final man in the same style jacket stepped up behind Charise and grabbed her by the arm and said, "Right this way Ms. Pearl, and don't do anything stupid or you'll be dead too." She couldn't see a weapon, but it didn't matter—she knew she had no choice because the man's grip was strong and unrelenting. Her mouth was wide open with fright and tears welling in her eyes as her captor motioned her to move toward the staircase. "Please don't hurt me," she whimpered.

The three kidnappers moved with the President's daughter to the northeast emergency exit stairwell and ran down the steps to the bottom floor.

Just outside the black double door exit from the library was a custom black Ford E350 Diesel Van with a converted trap door on the floor, bullet-proof windows and a six-liter diesel engine for get-away speed. The van had been pulled up onto the curb and was idling over the top of a Tallahassee Stormwater Management manhole cover for access to the network of stormwater drains throughout the city. The driver of the van was calm with a cigarette dangling from his mouth. The man in the passenger seat was huge and muscular and leapt out of the van and opened the side door for the three captors and Charise who ran the few steps from the exit to the van and jumped inside. The kidnapping had occurred in less than four minutes and there were no Secret Service agents in sight.

The muscular captor opened the trap door in the bottom of the van, then removed the manhole cover over the storm drain, while the other two placed miner's lights on straps on their heads, then gave the other kidnapper his light.

Charise started to scream but she was slapped hard. "Shut the fuck up if you want to live." She suddenly found the cold steel of a gun pushed against her temple, and she began to cry.

The kidnappers pulled a telescoping portable ladder from the sidewall of the van, then stuck it down through the manhole down into the storm drain. One of the kidnappers went down the ladder quickly then Charise was pushed to do the same. The others followed and pulled the ladder down into the storm drain. "Okay, close it!" the last man yelled up into the van.

With only a little difficulty the muscular man inside the van replaced the very heavy manhole cover, closed the trap door of the van, then hopped up front. "Okay, let's go," he said.

They drove on to Honors Way then east on to West Call Street a short way, then north on Dewey Street until they came to a parking lot. The driver got out and changed the license plate, while the other stepped out and peeled the company name off the side of the van, revealing yet another fake company name. They got back into the van, pulled out normally onto Tennessee Street, then drove east at the legal speed limit.

Back at the library, the unreturned calls to the dead Secret Service agents sent the other agents scurrying up past screaming and hysterical students into the library. They found no trace of Charise and nobody knew where they had gone once they had run down the stairwell and through the library exit at the side street. Some students said they had seen them go into a van and take off, and they described it. The agents contacted all local law enforcement agents and told them to be on the lookout for a van fitting the description, but by then the van had driven up into the back of an even larger box truck, which had then driven away undetected.

* * *

Just as Charise and the two kidnappers dropped down the storm drain, the man above closed the storm drain cover and they were all in total darkness for a moment. Then both of the kidnappers turned on miner's lights and one of them said to Charise, "Here, put on this miner light and this breathing gear." She put on a vest with a small air tank on the back, and a regulator with a tube coming around the front and a mouthpiece for breathing, just like a regular scuba tank.

The one man crawled back up the ladder and fastened a long piece of metal with a lock on it so that nobody from up top could open up the hatch again.

Then the other man said, "Come this way."

They all had to bend down, but only had to go a few feet, then they came to three seven-foot-long sleds with four wheels that were motorized with small electric engines and batteries at one end.

"Lie down facing forward," the one man said to Charise. "Put your head at this end."

She did as she was told. The one man doing all the talking showed her how to work the levers to control speed and forward and reverse.

"I'm going to be in the lead," he said, "and you'll be in the middle, with my partner following up the rear. Don't try anything funny, just follow us and you won't get hurt. I promise."

The two men donned their breathing gear, then the three of them started moving forward and they traveled for what seemed about twenty minutes, making sharp and gradual turns along the way, then they stopped. The man in the lead got off his sled and stood up. They were in a higher and wider area of the sewer system. He took off his breathing gear.

"Okay," he said. "Here's where we get out. You can remove your breathing gear."

He pointed his flashlight at a ladder leading upward. "Follow me."

He started moving up the ladder, then as he reached the top, he used the butt of his gun to bang on the sewer cover immediately overhead. Somebody opened it up and light poured into the sewer, temporarily blinding all the occupants below.

Charise climbed onto a ladder and out of the darkness of the sewer into a clearing near a forested area where she recognized the Tau Kappa Epsilon fraternity house. The man who had lifted the storm drain lid motioned them to another waiting van and they all climbed in. He gathered the breathing gear, threw it into the back of the van, closed the door, then jumped into the driver's seat. They left the area within the speed limit and headed west on West Tennessee Street and away from the university. Only a short few miles later, though, they turned right onto a dirt road called Lazy Creek Run, where another large truck with a ramp was waiting at the dead end about a mile down the trail. The van drove right up into the box truck and then the doors to the truck were closed. This time, however, the truck went nowhere and just stayed parked.

As midnight came, Charise was met by another panel van that had come to meet them. Her captors had stayed behind to disperse the van and truck. Now gagged and bound and lying down on a mattress, Charise and her new captor drove for about fifteen minutes down the backroads of north Florida to a wide-open clearing where a helicopter was waiting.

The chopper took off and flew extremely low over treetops across the Florida/Georgia line and soon landed in a small field where Charise was transferred again to yet another waiting car. The car sped off—they had gotten away clean.

Chapter Fifteen
Jail Time

A megaphone blared at Jason over the choppy inlet just outside of Port Everglades: "Keep your hands where we can see them!"

Jason stuck his hands higher as a swarm of U.S. Coast Guard and Harbor Patrol boats arrived on the scene for his capture.

"I'm unarmed!" yelled Jason above the sound of all the engines of the surrounding boats. "Don't shoot!"

Jason wondered how in the hell he was going to get himself out of this one without alerting the authorities that he was one of the good guys and that he was a contractor for the Agency. They weren't going to buy that one, and even if they did it would be a bureaucratic mess.

One of each pursuing Coast Guard and Harbor Patrol boats jumped onto Jason's boat, but a Coastie said to one of the Harbor Patrol guys, "Stand aside sailor, this is our jurisdiction." The Patrol guy was pissed and looked to his captain for assurance, got none, and finally deferred and climbed back onto his boat.

Two Coasties patted Jason down then turned him around and put handcuffs on him. The other Coastie threw the bowline of Jason's stolen boat to a man on the Coast Guard cutter, then all three of them climbed aboard the cutter and pulled away from the scene. Jason was thankful for this: going directly through the government to get him off should hopefully be easier than going through the local city government.

The two Coasties marched Jason to the fantail where they met the captain. "What's your name and what's going on here?" the captain said.

"My name is Jason Stouter and I really need to make a phone call before I explain to you fully what's going on here, but I can tell you the reason I chased and killed these men is because they shot up the Boatyard and I think killed two of my colleagues."

"You're on a US Coast Guard cutter Mr. Stouter, and I may not let you make that phone call." He turned to the two men: "Take him below. I'm going to check out his story with the local authorities. No phone call. Not yet."

* * *

An hour later Jason got his one free phone call.

"Jamie, it's me. Wait, don't ask any questions yet. Turns out your informant and his wife Amber got themselves shot up at the Boatyard—somebody must have been following them. Anyway, I followed the shooters after the fire fight and I killed them both; then the Coast Guard arrested me. I'm in a locked office guarded by four Coasties at the U.S. Coast Guard station at Port Everglades right now. It's right next to Nova Southeastern University's marine lab. Can you pull some strings and get me out of here?"

"Jason, you dumb shit!" She railed at him for another few minutes, asking questions and not getting answers Jason couldn't give over the phone. Finally, she said, "I'll try, but no promises. Jeezus, Jason." She slammed the phone down.

* * *

"All right, Stouter, you're free to go."

A Coastie opened the office door at the Coast Guard station and led Jason out of the facility. Outside, Sali was waiting with the Lexus, leaning against it smiling and smoking one of his smelly Djarum Black cigarettes that Jason could smell the minute he opened the Coast Guard front door.

Sali grinned. "Did you get cornholed?"

"Very funny. So, what happened after I left the Boatyard?"

"The man you were talking to is dead. His wife is in critical condition at Broward General Hospital."

"Joseph and Amber Spring. Damn it. What's going on with Masen?"

"I just talked to him. He said the crew on the London Blue pasted a new name over the current one. The new name is Garnet Lady, and they're heading east."

"Is the GPS working?"

"Yes, for now, but it will be out of range before too long unless we go after them."

"I need to call Jamie."

Jason opened the passenger side door and climbed in as he pulled his cell out of his pocket. He dialed Jamie's number.

"Hey, it's me," he said to her.

"So, give me a sitrep," she said coldly.

"They changed the name of the boat to Garnet Lady, pulled anchor, and they're heading east."

"Shit. What about our contact? What happened to him?"

Jason recounted what Joseph and Amber Spring had told him and what had happened to them.

"Oh, brother. Thank goodness at least she is alive."

"Jamie, we have to leave right now if we're going to follow these guys. The GPS is still working, but if we wait too long, it'll be out of range."

"They're leaving the country, I'm sure of it."

"I would if I were them."

"What about Masen? Can we use him and his boat to follow them?"

"Haven't asked him yet. He's still on the boat, but I can tell you he'll be worried about getting caught up in something and going back to jail."

"Okay, if he'll play along and do exactly as you say, go for it, follow them, and we'll triple his fee and defend him in court if it gets that far. In the meantime, I'll see who I can get to help us."

They said their goodbyes, then Jason said to Sali, "Let's go talk to Masen. Have you got the skiff?"

"I do. It's at the Hillsboro Inlet." Sali accelerated and ran an oncoming Mercedes off the road as he swerved back to the right-hand lane. "Love this car…"

* * *

"Are you out of your fucking mind? I'm a cat burglar," said Masen, "not some action hero. These guys just shot up the Boatyard and killed people!"

"Masen, we just want you to help us follow them. Sali and I will do all the hands-on stuff."

Masen said nothing, but paced furiously around the small cabin.

"This would send me back to prison, for sure."

"No, Jamie said she'd take full responsibility, so long as you do as I say."

"My fee would be increased?"

"Tripled."

Masen stopped pacing and gazed out the starboard porthole for long seconds. Finally, he sighed, then said, "You guys kill me. Okay, I'm in."

"Good. Take us back to the marina. We'll settle things at the hotel, pack up what we need, park at Pier 66, and be ready to go. Keep an eye on the GPS to see where they're heading."

* * *

It was a bit of a hassle getting hotel management to allow them to park the van indefinitely on the Pier 66 property, but Jason suggested paying a larger daily rate and that settled it. The rental car company bitched a bit about picking up the rental Lexus, but of course they'd do it for the extra fee. Jason and Sali were ready for Masen before sundown.

With all three onboard, Masen powered the *Booty* out of the Pier 66 marina and under the Seventeenth Street Causeway Bridge.

"You really know how to pick a great time to learn sailing," said Masen as they passed the bridge and turned toward the sea channel. "That tropical storm took a turn to the north and we'll be heading right into its path."

Jason and Sali looked at each other and said in unison: "Shit." Jason knew that Sali was an old hand at riding the waves, but Jason was a landlubber who rarely went to sea, although he obviously knew how to handle small boats.

They passed the last buoy out of the Port Everglades inlet, then Masen showed Jason and Sali how to set sail as they headed east toward the Bahamas and the Caribbean Sea.

Chapter Sixteen
Berry Islands Encounter

It wasn't long before they hit the Florida Current—the southern extension of the Gulf Stream—as the light from the sundown diminished. To Jason the gentle up and down of the boat was rather a nice adventure, and paying attention to Masen instructing them how to sail kept his mind off the building seas. But the seas they hit in the Florida Current were nothing like those near shore. These were big and rising seas, and it wasn't long before they were in ten-to-twelve-foot seas in the sudden and terrifying blackness of a moon covered by black clouds.

"Hold on!" shouted Masen over the sound of the wind and waves. "It's going to get worse!"

Jason and Sali went below to check on the GPS reading from the renamed *Garnet Lady* and could see that they were still within range. Suddenly, Jason said, "Oh, God..." and ran to the head where he unloaded whatever he had left in his stomach.

He came back, blanched white and sweaty. "I gotta lie down," he said.

"Good idea," said Sali.

Jason groaned and crawled back to his bunk.

Sali scrambled up top next to Masen who was constantly being pelted by waves crashing over the deck and the stinging rain in the rising winds.

"Jason's sick," he yelled over the roar of the wind and waves, "but he'll come around after he gets some rest."

"Well it's not going to get calm any time soon, so I wouldn't count on it. Are we still tracking the Garnet Lady okay?"

"Yes, but she's moving faster than us. We'll lose her at this rate."

"Well this wind is going to pick up and I'm pretty sure every boat with a sail is going to pull into port soon, so let's hope we end up close to where she hauls in. We're going to have to find a port or lee side of an island very soon. Like now."

Within the next hour the wind picked up to near gale force winds, and by dawn the *Booty* was struggling against twenty-foot seas, and nobody was talking—they were just hanging on for dear life and doing what they had to do to stay afloat and keep on following the track of the *Garnet Lady*.

As the sun rose, Jason was feeling better—trying to see the horizon, which was difficult between the mountainous seas and getting sprayed by sea and drenched by rain, which at any rate, helped to keep him awake. He had to admit to himself that he was scared shitless. He'd been in all kinds of harrowing situations including the worst of firefights and attacks by armies of dangerous men, but being at the mercy of a stormy ocean with confused mountainous seas was something no sane human being could confront with anything but stone-cold fear. He went below to check on the *Garnet Lady* while Sali and Masen stuck by the helm, ready for whatever might change for the worse.

Jason viewed the track of the *Garnet Lady* on their tracking scope, versus their own, and he could see they were outpacing the *Booty*. However, both were heading in the same general direction: the Berry Islands, in the Bahamas.

* * *

The Berry Islands, sometimes called "The Fishbowl of the Bahamas" only has a population of a little over eight hundred, most of which live on Great Harbor Cay. The islands remain relatively undeveloped, with only two small airports, no hotels, and, according to the locals, the highest population of millionaires per square mile of any other place in the world. If you had the money, this is one place in the world where you could still buy your own private, beautiful uninhabited island. It has an annual fishing tournament and is often visited for its fishing, snorkeling and scuba diving attractions.

Jason shouted up to Masen, "They've stopped ahead. I can see they're pulling into a protected cove at Alder's Cay."

He thought for a moment, then pointed at the map and said, "They must be getting ready to anchor for the night inside that lagoon."

Masen came down to look at the map. "Look, there are two ways into the lagoon. They're going south and likely will anchor just outside the bridge because they're too big to go under it. We can go around to the other side, which is also protected, right outside another channel that exits the lagoon. It says Berry Islands anchorage, so we should be safe. We're too big to get into that lagoon, though. We can anchor outside and it's protected there, and if you guys want, you can go ashore and walk across the island and spy on them from the shore. But it's a private island and you might get spotted by somebody. Just play dumb. Sali, go up to the bow and guide me through the coral heads. Jason, you make ready with the stern anchor."

There was enough moonlight so Sali could see the black silhouettes of the big coral heads and smaller boulders against the brilliant bright sand bottom.

"Steady as she goes," said Sali. "Straight ahead, dead slow."

The quiet *chug chug* of the diesel broke the otherwise dead silence as they headed toward the island.

"Stop!" said Sali. "I don't think we can go in much further."

"Okay," said Masen, "Drop the hook, and make sure you've tied off the bitter end to the bow cleat, with the line going under the railing, please. Jason, as soon as he's set, drop yours, make sure it catches, then tie it off."

Sali finished setting the hook and tying off the line on the bow cleat, then headed aft toward Masen. Jason finished tying off the stern anchor, then they mustered below at the dining table.

Jason asked Masen, "Have you been here before?"

"No, just saw it on the map a few times."

Masen said, "So are you guys going to go ashore, or are we just going to wait out the storm overnight?"

"Do we know they've anchored?" They looked at the GPS locator for a minute, then Jason said, "Looks like they did. Okay, we'll go ashore and bring the VHF radio and some binoculars."

"Use the fifty-megahertz band," said Masen.

"Okay, then, we'll make ready the Zodiac," said Jason. "I'll scan the radio channels and see if I can pick them up talking to anybody."

Sali joined Jason on deck and they unfastened the Zodiac and readied the small outboard.

Masen came on deck and the three men stood quietly for a moment, then Jason said, "I hope they don't hear the outboard."

"I highly doubt it," said Masen. "The outboard is whisper quiet and those trees on shore with all this wind will help block the sound. Besides, like I said, it's a private island and they'd just think the owners were driving around."

Minutes later, as they were preparing to launch the Zodiac, they heard an outboard skiff off to their left as it went under the low bridge that enclosed the lagoon. They sat in the cockpit and trained their binoculars on the skiff as it headed under the far bridge toward the *Garnet Lady*. Aboard and handling the outboard engine was a thin old man with a gray beard, and one other man who wore a captain's cap, but was perhaps in his early fifties, a little heavyset of stature but taller than the old man. Both were looking toward the *Garnet Lady* and not speaking with each other. They slowed as they approached and pulled abeam the big yacht and finally stopped as the deck hands held her steady. Then the tall man with the captain's cap went aboard the *Garnet Lady*, and the old man immediately turned the skiff around and headed back to the lagoon. Through their binoculars Jason and Sali could see that the new arrival met Bluto, shook hands, then went inside the cabin of the boat. It was apparent that he was going to stay aboard the *Garnet Lady* for a while, most likely overnight at the very least.

Jason and Sali waited perhaps ten minutes to see if there were any further movements from the shore or the *Garnet Lady*, then the winds abruptly ceased and an eerie calmness settled about the island and the dark sea. Jason and Sali carefully put the Zodiac into the water and were soon on their way to the dark island between them and the *Garnet Lady*.

* * *

Sali killed the outboard as the Zodiac hit the beach. Jason jumped out, holding the bowline and pulled the boat further onto the shore. Sali grabbed their backpacks out of the boat and helped Jason pull the boat further up the beach. Sali handed Jason's backpack to him and they ran up to the edge of the palm trees surrounding the island. The sky was magnificently clear, for a change, and the stars looked close enough to touch. You could also see lights on the horizon. To the south they could see Chub Cay, and to the southeast, Nassau, and amazingly, far away to the west, they could still just barely see the glitter and brilliance of Miami and Fort Lauderdale as a bright haze on the horizon.

Twenty minutes later they were on the opposite shoreline of the island with the *Garnet Lady* in full view. They stopped and both pulled their binoculars out of their backpacks.

Sali said quietly, "It's a hell of a lot better view than I had at Hillsboro Inlet—we're a lot closer."

As they continued looking, they could see the men and women through the wheelhouse windows and on deck.

Finally, Jason said, "I count four men and three women, including Julene. Bluto appears to be in charge. Too bad we can't hear what they're saying."

"You want me to swim over and listen?"

"Nah, you always have all the fun. My turn."

Sali turned and looked at Jason. "Oh, so now you're Mr. Navy SEAL?"

"Give me the Mark 23, just in case."

As Jason entered the water's edge, the smell of the fresh *Sargassum* seaweed on the shore, the wading into the cool water, and the feel of the sand under his feet made him feel at home. A couple of minutes later Jason was slowly breast-stroking toward the *Garnet Lady*, his chest just inches over the elkhorn corals that could easily abrade his chest with a thousand scratches from their spiny skeleton. The waterproof H&K Mark 23 was tucked under his belt in the back of his pants.

As he slowly and silently approached, he could see the afterdeck was lit up brightly, but no one was there. Just as he arrived next to the hull, though, he could hear the cabin door open and a man bark at them, "Close the door! You trying to cool the whole fucking outdoors? And don't try swimming ashore—the place is loaded with sharks and barracudas."

The door closed and at first all he could hear was the low hum of the battery-powered air conditioner.

Jason waited under the bow, peeking aft, waiting to hear any conversation. He saw a lit cigarette go flying out into the water. He wondered about the sharks and barracudas the man had mentioned.

"So, what's your name?" It was a woman's voice.

"Julene. What's yours?"

"Colorado Jacquette. Some people call me Jackie, some call me Colorado, some call me Collie."

"Love it! Jacket? Like in what you wear?"

"No." She spelled it out for her.

"I like Collie," said Julene. "Reminds me of when I was a veterinarian assistant, working with dogs. Collies were always great to work with."

"Oh really? What sort of work do you do now?"

Jason couldn't wait to hear this himself.

"I fuck." She laughed.

"Oh."

There was a strained silence between them, then Colorado responded, "Don't we all."

"Well, I think you probably make love. I fuck to live."

Quiet again. "You mean you're a prostitute?"

"No! Well…It's different." There was a pause. "You know I wasn't really trained to be a veterinarian's assistant," she said, changing the subject. "I only finished high school. I've also been an extra on movie sets, too. What do you do?"

"I'm a country western singer."

"Yeah, really?" Julene said excitedly. "I love all kinds of music, but I don't listen to country music much. Sorry. Are you, like, famous or something?"

"Oh, I'm pretty well known, yeah."

"Wow, that is very cool. Guess I'll start listening to more country western music now. If we ever get out of here."

They didn't say anything for a while, just looking out at the stars.

"Well," said Julene, "I don't like the way I live, but I do have a lot of fun, usually. I live in a beautiful condo, but I don't pay for it. I pretty much have to be available when the guy—his name is Michael—returns from traveling to go do fun things around town. He and the captain of this boat, what's his fucking name, Reznik, know each other, and for some reason, they're taking me along to go see him, wherever the hell he is. I have no fucking idea where he is or where the fuck we're going or why, so don't bother to even ask."

"Okay," said Colorado softly. A minute later she said, "Do you love this guy Michael?"

"Hell no! He treats me like shit. He's not even good looking, and he's horrible in bed. I'm basically a kept woman, and he doesn't give me much money, just enough to get by. I'm his show piece, and I give him sex whenever he wants it. But no, I don't love him—not in the least."

"Why don't you leave him?"

"Leave him? And do what? I don't know how to do anything except survive however I have to, and I'm good at that. You pros have book smarts and talent, but I have street smarts," she said proudly.

"But you're so beautiful! You're gorgeous, in fact. You could be a model. A blue-eyed blond with a killer figure like yours shouldn't have any trouble becoming a model. I mean, really, Julene, you are one of the most beautiful women I've ever met."

"Thank you," she said demurely. "Yeah, I tried a modeling gig, but the agent wanted me to fuck him to get the right connections. Big surprise, huh? Anyway, I don't know why, but I quit trying that."

"Damn, that's a shame. You deserve a break. You're one in a million. If we ever get out of this mess I'll try to help you."

Jason felt the boat shift slightly and he could see Julene put her hands on the gunwale and look straight out into the blackness of the night while a full night of stars twinkled all about her forward-leaning body. The very slight wind brought the smell of her perfume to Jason and reminded him of the night he had met her, amazingly just a few days ago.

"I'm just surviving, that's all. I'm not really doing anything important. I'm not making any changes to society or even entertaining them, like you. I'm not helping people in any meaningful way. I'm not helping fix the environment. I'm not helping people like doctors or nurses or veterinarians, any more. I don't help make people well again. All I do is try to eat every day to survive, so I'm nice and friendly to people so they'll buy me breakfast and dinner and drinks. So even though I have a lot of friends who help me out, I end up spending most of my days making guys think I'm interested in them so they'll buy me food and drink, and that they have a chance of fucking me when Michael's not in town, which I do if they're half-decent looking and buy me nice things. I just string them along so I can live. I haven't ever loved any of them, and that last guy I was with even told me he didn't think I was capable of love anymore because of the life I lead. I was married once, and I loved him, but that's been over for a long time now. They called us Ken and Barbie."

She stopped and looked far into the distance, into a future she wished she had. As she leaned over, a chain and locket around her neck swung as a pendulum over the calm and inky black sea.

"I just wish I could do something good with my life. I want to make a difference. I don't want to leave this world and nobody remembers me."

As Jason looked at her, he could see that tears were welling in her eyes and reflected in the moonlight. At that moment her necklace chain with the locket broke from her neck and fell into the sea.

"Oh no!" she cried. "Oh no!" She put her hands on her chest. "My locket!" She groaned and in a shaky voice said, "That was from my Mommy!"

Colorado stepped over to her, put her hand on Julene's shoulder and looked over the side and into the blackness of the ocean. "Oh, dear," she said. "Maybe they'll let us dive for it in the morning."

Julene was crying gently. "It was just sentimental—it wasn't worth anything, but I've had it since I was little."

After a long and deep sigh, Colorado said, "We may never find it, Julene. Make a wish and let's hope it comes true."

Julene sniffed and wiped away her tears and said very quietly, almost to herself, "I just did a minute ago."

Just then Jason heard the cabin door open and close again.

"Hi, ladies." It was a third female voice, a young one. "We finally get to meet each other. My name is Naieema."

"Hi," said Julene, "Nice of them to let us out of our cages."

"At least the berths are nice," said Naieema.

"I'm Julene, nice to meet you."

"I'm Colorado, very nice to meet you."

"I recognize you from somewhere," said Naieema.

"I'm a recording artist for country western music. Maybe you've seen me playing somewhere."

"Wow, how exciting!"

"So why do you think we've all been kidnapped, Naieema?" asked Colorado.

"No clue. I was just walking to class and they grabbed me and threw me into a van, and now here I am. I hope that woman who jumped overboard made it okay. That was a horrible scene. I can't stop thinking about that."

"What happened?" said Julene.

Colorado summarized, with Naieema filling in.

Jason listened below, and now had an even more complete picture of what had happened that night when Amber swam to shore.

Reznik bellowed hoarsely from inside the cabin: "Hey you broads! Come back in here and get some sleep. It's going to be a long day tomorrow and I don't want a bunch of cranky bitches complaining the whole way."

The ladies went inside and closed the door.

Jason continued treading water for a moment, then silently dove down to where Julene had dropped the locket. Though he didn't have a face mask on, and the salt water stung his eyes, in the moonlight he could see the chain and locket adorning a tall upright darkly colored sponge like a string of lights on a Christmas tree. He snatched it hurriedly, then turned quickly and swam back underwater toward the shoreline and Sali. At a safe distance he surfaced and exhaled, then turned and looked back at the *Garnet Lady* to see if they had noticed him. He turned again and breast-stroked quietly back to the shore and Sali.

Back aboard the *Booty*, Jason explained about the necklace and the three new names they had besides Julene's: "Colorado Jacquette, the country western singer, the guy we call Bluto—his name is Reznik—and Michael, the guy they are going to meet soon, apparently the same Michael from Fort Lauderdale."

They still did not know the name of the man who had come aboard, nor what his plans or intentions were.

"I'd better call this in to Jamie," said Jason as he reached for the satellite phone.

Chapter Seventeen
Presidential Heat

United States President Jonathan Pearl was not by nature a violent man; nonetheless, he threw his beautiful blue fluorite paperweight across the room where it knocked over one of the two table lamps in the Oval Office and shattered into a handful of pieces. He shouted at Nathan Kale, the Director of the Secret Service, "How on earth could this have happened! How can you have agents right next to her and downstairs, yet still she is captured and we now also have two dead agents?"

The President's wife, Helen, was beside herself, sobbing while she sat on one of the newly upholstered beige couches. She stood and held Jonathan's arm gently, but firmly he pulled it away.

"I want to know where our daughter is," he said loudly.

Nathan Kale started to say something, but was interrupted again by the President.

"How could they possibly hope to get away with this? What do they want and who are they?"

"We have had no word at all from the kidnappers, sir."

"Tell me how they got away."

"Well, sir, they had it planned pretty well, and we didn't even know how they had escaped, at first, but we took some first witness accounts from students and pieced something together. They exited the university library at the northeast corner stairs, then they moved to a van and the van took off. However, our agents later found that the sewer system opening manhole cover was ajar below where the van had parked, so we looked down inside it. They must have gone down through the bottom of the van somehow and used their own lighting system. The air in the sewer system is almost unbreathable, so they must have used breathing gear. They also had a vehicle made specifically for traveling in the sewer tunnel so that they could get away fast, it was a modified 'pig'—or so the professionals call it: a common device used to clean and inspect pipelines. We found it several miles away near the frat houses. From there they didn't go far—all they had to do was get to I90, then they could go east or west quickly, and from there the roads they could take are innumerable, and they could transfer vehicles multiple times. We set up roadblocks and deployed helicopters and called other law enforcement agencies as fast as we could, but we've come up with no other clues yet. We're looking at where they might have acquired the tunnel gear, checking with the van rental companies, and reviewing the tapes that were in the library."

"But still no clues? No clues from press coverage?"

"I'm afraid not yet, sir."

The President continued pacing. "Damn it all to hell!" he screamed. "Well what do we do now?"

"I'm afraid all we can do: wait until they contact you. From there we will hopefully get some more leads to follow up on."

"What could they possibly hope to gain by kidnapping my daughter? Surely they must know the heat on them will never cease until they are caught."

"Well, sir, it pains me to say this, but it's possible they don't want money."

The President turned, incredulous, and looked at the Director. "What do you mean by that? What!"

"Well, sir, I think we have to consider the fact that they might want to exchange her for a criminal or a spy we are holding. Or..." The Director paused, unsure he wanted to plant this in the President's mind. Too late now, though.

"Or what?"

"Or they don't intend to release her at all."

The President just stared with growing malice at the Director. "That is totally unacceptable. You use whatever reserves you can gather and move as fast as you possibly can to follow the slimmest lead you can possibly find. Now go! Make it happen!"

Chapter Eighteen
Stormy Crossing

It was late when Jason called Jamie at home, but she had instructed him to do so as the need arose.

"I'm sorry to be calling so late," said Jason, "but Sali and I just got back from a close up visit with our boy Bluto and company, and I thought I'd better update you with what we found out, because I think tomorrow we're going to be following them in some pretty rough weather, and it may be awhile before I can update you again. I mean if I don't drown."

"Yeah, sure," she said, groggily, "What's up?"

"First off, Bluto's real name is Reznik, and his boss, the guy they're going to meet, is named Michael. I don't know if Reznik is his first name or his last, but Michael must be the same one who owns the condo Julene was staying in. Besides Julene, there are two other women on board, a young lady, whose name I only got as Naieema, and Colorado Jacquette."

"What! Holy shit! Colorado Jacquette? She's a famous country western singer!"

"Yeah, that's what I found out by her discussion with Julene. Never heard of her—I'm a jazz fan, I'm sure you remember."

"What did you find out about the young lady, Naieema?"

"Nothing really, except they nabbed her when she was on her way to class, so I assume she's a college student. Maybe you can find out if anybody has heard of a kidnapping near a college."

"I'll check. How did you find all this out?"

Jason went on to explain how he had gotten close to the boat and overheard the conversation.

"I guess the reason we haven't heard about them in the news," said Jamie, "is just as Joe and Amber Spring mentioned at the Boatyard right before Joe was killed—that if the news media finds out, this Michael and his men will kill them, or the husbands, so that's why Joe had been in hiding until Amber was returned. As far as Colorado and her husband are concerned, there was an article in the paper saying they haven't heard from the couple in a while, and that her concerts were mysteriously cancelled for the foreseeable future. Nobody knows why."

"Any idea at all who the young lady might be?" asked Jason.

"None. I have heard nothing of any high-profile people being kidnapped, but you've got to remember that there are thousands of people per year who are reported kidnapped, missing, runaways, or trafficked, so that part of the FBI is constantly overwhelmed. A famous person disappearing, though, would be hard to hide."

"All right, Jamie, hope you can get back to sleep. Like I said, I thought I'd call while I still had the chance."

"Stay safe, Jason, and call me when you get safely to wherever it is you're going."

"Wish I knew. Good night."

* * *

When the old man with the long grey beard had dropped off his passenger at the *Garnet Lady*, he saluted the new passenger for the yacht and said, "Have a safe trip. See you next time." He turned the skiff around and headed back into shore full speed.

The men on board the *Garnet Lady* gave the new man a hand as he climbed on board the yacht. There were just Reznik, Nadav and Vlad to greet him on the afterdeck, with the captured women below locked in their quarters.

As the new man stepped on board, he greeted Reznik first. "Mr. Reznik, I presume?"

"You are correct. I trust Marek has finalized your payment concerns?"

"He has indeed. Half already sent; the rest given upon arrival."

"Good," said Reznik, then turned to his crew. "Men, this is our captain now. He knows these waters a hell of a lot better than me, and he's going to take over the ship now until we get there. His name is Chester..."

The new captain interrupted him, "Please, just call me Captain Chet. I'd rather the IRS and the few people I do business with not know my last name. I'm sure you understand."

Captain Chet knew every passage and every coral head between Miami and Trinidad, and had piloted everything from a surfboard to an oil tanker. His knowledge was legendary among charter boat captains of the Caribbean, and you could hire no better captain to take your yacht through the Bahamas during a gale on the verge of becoming a hurricane. He was in his early sixties but he retained the youthful resilience of a hard man in his forties. People could easily recognize him from a distance by his big, thick grey mustache, as well as his characteristic bearing, gait and laughing demeanor. His forearms and hands were large and extremely strong from reeling in so many fish and pulling on so many lines attached to anchors. His gut showed only a passing attraction to dark beers. His life on the sea had made him a strong and capable survivor, and he had the wisdom of a life on the ocean. He had mostly worked legitimate jobs, but he was rumored to have smuggled tons of marijuana and cocaine into the United States, yet he had never been caught, nor had the shipments apparently ever been witnessed.

He turned to Reznik. "If you can show me around, we can get started as soon as your men are ready."

Reznik introduced his crew, then said, "There are also three women on board, but they are belowdecks in their private quarters. I ask that you not speak with them, and don't ask any questions either. They are part of a surprise at our destination."

"Fair enough," said Captain Chet, then paused for a moment. "May I ask if there is anything illegal about their passage?"

"No," said Reznik, who stared back at him with a piercing stare and said nothing more.

The new captain thought to himself: Well does he mean, "No, you may not ask," or, "No there's nothing illegal about their passage," but he decided to keep his mouth shut and instead just said, "Good enough. Shall we continue with the tour?"

* * *

Masen volunteered to take the first watch while Jason and Sali turned in. He sat on the foredeck, remembering his life of crime and the wife who left him because of it, and the wife who stayed with him because she embraced it. Unfortunately, the second wife perished in the ravaging Corona virus pandemic a couple years back, while he remained unaffected. It just didn't seem right that he, who had led a life of crime for so long, would be the one who escaped that devastating disease, while she, so fun-loving and daring and beautiful, had not. His melancholy felt unbearable, and as he watched the night sky, he saw a falling star and wished that she would be with him in soul at some time in the future. Tears formed in his eyes, then the loud whump of a nearby fish—probably a snook catching some prey—brought him back around to the present.

Sali came on deck and said, "Ahoy, mate, you still awake?"

"Yep," he said as he started to stand. "Time to turn in for a bit?"

"Yes indeed, sleep tight, my friend, see you in the morning."

The rest of the night was uneventful, until shortly before sunrise, when Sali woke Jason and Masen with a loud: "They're on the move."

* * *

Aboard the *Garnet Lady*, which had just pulled anchor, the sound of the anchor winch awoke Julene who moved up the companionway and pleaded again with Reznik to wait until dawn so she could try to retrieve her chain and locket.

"No," said Reznik. "Now get out of the way and shut up. Go back down to your cabin."

"If Michael heard you talk to me that way he'd kick your ass," she complained.

Reznik scoffed at her. "I don't think so. And his name isn't Michael."

"What do you mean? What is it?"

"Go below."

As Julene grumbled and moved back down to her cabin, Captain Chet arrived from the afterdeck and said "We can make it there before noon and beat the storm if we get moving at full throttle."

Reznik nodded and Captain Chet took over the controls and pushed the throttle all the way as they pulled out of the cove and made their heading southeast.

* * *

Just after leaving the Berry Islands Captain Chet and Reznik were standing at the bridge while the building seas rolled under them. They looked out the front windscreen while everybody else was below trying to settle down and get their rest while they still could.

After they reached the open sea, Captain Chet said, "What's the story with the women? They don't exactly look like they're out here on a pleasure cruise, and they don't appear to be your girlfriends." He gave Reznik an uneasy smile.

Reznik looked over at the Captain. "Why couldn't they be?"

"You mean your girlfriends? Well, I guess because you keep them down in their quarters and don't really talk to them, you just order them around. I mean I'm not complaining, I'm just curious."

"You shouldn't be so curious. Just drive the boat, and don't ask so many questions. I already told you this."

"That one is a dead-ringer for the country western singer, Colorado Jacquette. Man, she's beautiful."

"Isn't she, though." Reznik said nothing further.

The captain looked over at him, waiting to hear more, but upon hearing nothing, stopped talking and just continued to look at the rolling seas, and did as he was told: Don't ask such questions. But he thought to himself that these guys are uglier than sin on a toilet, so of course they're not their girlfriends. And that one woman looked too much like Colorado Jacquette not to be her. So, what is the deal here? Maybe we're just going to one of those eight-figure private Bahamian Islands for some kind of party, or even a movie or something, and they just don't want the press snooping or anybody else around. He'd been captain for enough movie stars to know that could be the case. But the guns? What was with the guns?

* * *

Though the eye of the tropical cyclone was far away and heading away from them, one of the feeder bands was beginning to form and reached their location. The rain began to come down in torrents, the winds building to forty knots, and the seas in response would soon grow to twenty feet or more.

"Tie everything down!" screamed the captain. "Everybody put on their life vests, and tell the women to just stay in their bunks. If they get sick, tell them to throw up in a bucket. We're in for a hell of a ride."

* * *

Within the first thirty minutes of the sudden storm, Masen made the decision.

"We can't do this. We can't follow them. She's a much bigger boat than us and has more power. If we try to follow, and the winds increase, we're goners. There's just no way. We're going to have to turn around and head back to that same cove. It's our only hope."

Jason and Sali made no argument. "What do you want us to do?"

"Hold on really tight, because I'm going to turn her round. We'll have a following sea, which is dangerous as hell, so I'll have to take it in quarters and try to keep the stern from taking direct hits. The ride is going to be really, really rocky, so before I make the turnaround, make sure everything is tied down as tight as you can make it, make sure all the windows and hatches are closed, and close yourself in the cabin and hold tight on to something. Don't worry about me—I'll tie myself to the helm and bang on the door if I need you. And be close to the radio to call out a May Day if we need to. Keep an eye on the radar and make sure I'm heading in the right direction. Use the megaphone to yell out if you need to."

Jason and Sali scurried down the companionway and into the cabin, closing the door behind them. Masen kept steaming ahead with full throttle and no sail.

The seas were rising rapidly, with their tops turning to foam and filling the air with their white mist. The rain went from moderately light to torrential downpour. Masen struggled to keep his eyes open as the wind and rain went from strong and steady to gale force in short bursts.

"Okay!" screamed Masen at the top of his lungs. "Here we go!"

He waited until a trough between waves, then swung the tiller hard to port. The *Booty* responded at once, but not fast enough and the next wave caught her broadside. The *Booty* rolled a full three hundred sixty-five degrees as the wave crashed over them leaving them completely engulfed for long seconds.

Masen hugged the wheel tightly and held his breath as the water washed over him and the *Booty* began to righten.

Below, in the cabin, the crash of things that were not tied down or had come loose could scarcely be heard over the roar of the wave as it had washed over them.

The *Booty* had righted herself and Masen turned the helm back to starboard so that the craft was now catching the waves along the starboard aft.

The seaworthy ketch beat like a metronome as it bobbed its mast flat to the ocean in a near catastrophic pronounced roll again, then righted herself proudly.

Masen's senses were entirely trained on the precise maneuvering against each wave as it approached and passed underneath.

Belowdecks, Jason and Sali had tried to catch and reposition all that had gone flying about the cabin, but the vertigo from not being able to see the horizon and being able to anticipate each roll had made them both nauseous until Jason finally tried throwing up in the ship's head.

Masen finally got into a rhythm with the waves so that he could still retreat back toward their previous night's cove as the waves rolled under their starboard quarter. Waves were no longer washing over the craft, and the diesel engine was still chugging along, making its way forward steadily.

Sali cautiously opened the companionway door to check on Masen. Above the sounds of the roaring waves and howling wind, he screamed, "Are you okay?"

Masen took his eyes just briefly from the sea in front of him and down at Sali. "Yeah, just wonderful, how about you guys?"

"Jason's a little sick, but he'll be fine. It's kind of a mess and a little wet, but nothing we can't fix up. I wish you'd learn to drive this thing a little smoother, though."

Masen smiled, "Hey, practice makes perfect!"

Sali closed the door and latched it tightly. He and Jason continued trying to put things up as they could, considering they were still rolling mightily against the heavy seas outside the boat.

* * *

Aboard the *Garnet Lady*, Captain Chet handled the yacht, which was much bigger than the *Booty*, with careful attention and wariness, but the seas were no less frightening to the others on the ship. He looked over at the ship's radar several times as they left the Berry Islands and noticed that a smaller vessel had been following them. He turned to Vlad, who was in the pilot house with him, and said, "Those poor bastards will never make it if the storm keeps up like this."

Vlad had been watching the radar steadily. "They're turning around."

"Well, that's pretty smart of them," said Captain Chet, as he made a hard turn into the seas, "I'd do the same damn thing if I were in their boat."

Vlad hurried down the companionway to the next deck where Reznik was trying to play solitaire, with the cards held down by chewing gum.

"They turned around," said Vlad. "Do you think they were following us?"

Reznik grunted. "I doubt it. Not in a boat that small. But it doesn't matter—they won't be able to catch up, even if the storm stops soon. If they were chasing us and turned back, they'd call ahead, so keep your wits about you."

The *Garnet Lady* was making good speed, even in such wind and seas. The seas had steadied to twenty to thirty feet, which meant the air was full of white ocean mist, and the yacht itself was continually being smashed and drenched by threatening seas.

"I don't want to die like this!" screamed Julene.

"Calm down," scolded Vlad. "Just vomit and go lie down. We're not going to die. This boat and this captain have seen worse than this."

* * *

At last, the *Booty* had reached calmer seas as it rounded the cove at their previous Berry Islands retreat. Masen reached down and opened up the companionway door. "Okay, you can come out now and get some fresh air. One of you guys take the helm. I feel like I just got run over by a truck."

Sali stepped behind the wheel and gave it a slight turn toward their previous anchorage. The sun was beginning to peak out of the clouds as a rain band passed them by. A rainbow appeared on the horizon. There was a faint smell of the island in the breeze.

Jason stepped up on to the deck, inhaled deeply and positioned his face up to the sun. "Oh, man, that feels good." He paused a bit as he soaked up the rejuvenating rays, then turned toward Sali. "I wasn't sure we were going to make it back there."

Sali just nodded his head in the affirmative, and he, too, took a deep breath of fresh air.

Jason stepped down the companionway into the main cabin and retrieved the satellite phone. He returned to the upper deck and called Jamie.

"We couldn't catch up with them—we had to turn back. We got hit with a feeder band of the hurricane and some very heavy weather."

"I'm glad you're safe, Jason. What's the range on your GPS locator? Can you still see them?"

"Yes, but they're about to go off scope. Our range under the best of circumstances is fifty miles."

Silence. "We can ask our legal attaches to be on the lookout."

"Well good luck with that. That's going to be near impossible—they could change the name of the boat again, and there are way too many boats that look just like her. And are the FBI legal attaches doing nothing else? I rather doubt it."

"There have been no ransom demands yet. What could they be doing with the women; I mean besides obviously kidnapping them? Are they raping them? They can get better looking hookers, if that's their goal, so what's the point?"

"I don't know," said Jason, "and where are they taking them? I can't put it together."

* * *

By noon the next day the storm had cleared and the hurricane had taken an unexpected and sudden turn to the southwest, so the *Booty* set sail in the direction of the *Garnet Lady*, which had been heading southeast. Their only hope at this point was to pick up the GPS signal again, but it seemed hopeless when considering the enormity of the Caribbean islands that lay in front of them, as well as the extra capability of speed for the *Garnet Lady*.

"We'll stop at Nassau and re-provision and ask around," said Masen. "Maybe somebody saw them, or spoke with them. What I don't get, though, is they seemed to be heading more south-southeast than southeast, which would put them more to the west side of New Providence Island. There's a marina on that side of the island called Lyford Cay Club Marina. I'll bet that's where they're heading. Less people there than the east side of the island, where all the tourists and people are. I don't think they'd want an audience. Let's take a chance and head for Lyford's instead because that's the direction they were heading."

"Who am I to argue?" said Jason.

"If that's where they're going, then I'm pretty certain they're going straight down the Tongue of the Ocean and heading for the Great Bahama Bank. From there, it's anybody's guess, maybe even Cuba."

Chapter Nineteen
Lyford Cay Club Marina

It was only a little over thirty miles down to Lyford Cay Club Marina, so the plan was that if they found no sign of them there, they'd sail around the west end of New Providence island to Albany Marina. However, just before they reached Lyford's, Sali shouted up from below, "Hey, I'm picking up their GPS again!"

"Hot damn!" said Masen. "Where the hell are they?"

"Just as you guessed—Lyford's."

"Nice work, Masen!" shouted Jason.

"All right then," said Masen. "I'm sure they didn't see our boat when we were back in the Berries, so let's head on in and take a peek."

Lyford Cay Club Marina is a very exclusive yacht club with seventy-four slips for yachts, a magnificent eighteen-hole golf course, white sand beaches, and a modern and well-maintained tennis court.

"Let's cruise around the yacht basin while we wait for them to get situated," said Masen. They saw some of the most elegant homes they'd ever seen, and quite a few had their own docks for their yachts. This was where the rich stopped to mingle among themselves, away from the noise and tourism of downtown Nassau.

Finally, they returned to the marina to find a slip and fuel up.

* * *

The *Garnet Lady* was of course much bigger than the *Booty*, so she was docked at the eastern side of the marina, where all the big slips were. Masen picked one of the small slips on the southern side of the marina.

Jason called Jamie.

"Hey, Jamie, we're west of Nassau on Providence Island in the Bahamas."

"You shithead. I send you on a job and you end up in the damn Bahamas. Where did I go wrong in life?"

"Well why don't you come down for an official visit, then?"

"Never mind," she replied, exasperated. "What've you got?"

"Okay, here's the scene. We're just now stopping at Lyford Cay Club Marina which the Garnet Lady is also doing. We're going to try to be inconspicuous and find out where they're going. If we don't find out, we were still fortunate enough to pick them up on the GPS again, so we can still follow them."

"Well, if you can pick them up already on the GPS, why try to screw up the operation?"

"Because I'm curious, and I like one of the girls they've got."

There was a long pause. "Now you're a double shithead."

"I'll call you back when we find out more." He disconnected quickly.

* * *

Masen had decided they'd dock in the middle area.

"Jason," he commanded. "Jump up on the dock and take the lines as soon we're close enough."

Jason jumped on the dock and quickly tied up to the bow and stern cleats on the dock as Masen held her perfectly parallel and inches from the dock.

"Sali!" Masen shouted, "Go find the harbormaster and tell him we're here, then find out the fuel charges and have their dockhand fill us up."

"Roger that, captain," saluted Sali then scurried off.

After they'd locked up the *Booty*, they split three ways and headed for the *Garnet Lady*.

There was nobody on board that they could see when they walked by the *Garnet Lady*.

The man filling up the yacht was big but not fat, and wore bamboo-nylon white pants and short sleeve cotton blue shirt. He was an older and handsome Bahamian who looked as though he already had lots of money and was doing this deckhand thing just for something to do. He looked happy.

But he eyed the three of them suspiciously when he saw them all meet up a hundred yards away. Reznik had told the old man as he walked away for lunch, "Keep your eye out…"

The old man made a mental note and continued filling the yacht.

* * *

Jason, Sali and Masen met up past the *Garnet Lady*.

"I didn't see anybody aboard," said Jason.

"Me either, and that guy filling it up looked like he was making sure nobody would come aboard that didn't belong."

"Same here, but that doesn't mean there's nobody belowdecks or locked in their cabin."

"Maybe they went to get a drink or some lunch," said Jason.

"Not a bad idea. And if they aren't drinking, I am."

"Masen," said Jason, "I think it's better if you go back to the boat. Better they don't see at least one of us, and we may be in a hurry to get out of here. Make sure you're fueled up as quickly as you can."

"Shit. Okay. Watch yourself, damn it."

A short walk past their split with Masen they came to a sign that pointed the way straight ahead down Scepter Road to The Captain's Table, a bar and restaurant a short walk from where they were tied up. Jason stopped and turned to Sali. "I know Masen's your friend, but he's also the world's greatest jewel thief, and that box of jewels is in his boat."

Sali looked up at Jason. "And…?"

"Well it might be tempting to take off with enough jewels to live for the rest of your life anywhere in the world you wanted to, and leave your friends high and dry on New Providence."

Sali flicked the ash from his ever-present Djarum Blacks cigarette into the Surinam cherry hedge along the walkway and looked up at Jason through his dark sunglasses. "So, you set him up to see what he'd do," he stated.

Jason paused a beat. "Yes, I did. Do you want to go check on him, or do you want me to, and what are either one of us going to do if we catch him trying to do that?"

"How about we leave him here and take off with his boat and the jewels, just like he was going to do to us—if he was going to do that to us."

"That's one plan, a little less extreme than the one I was thinking of. You know him better than me, but why don't I go check on him, discreetly, and you go check into the bar up the road at The Captain's Table. Wait for us there, unless of course he skipped out on us. If you don't hear from us before too long, come back to the boat. And try to stay out of trouble."

Sali saluted and headed for the bar, while Jason turned back the way he came.

* * *

Jason walked back toward the *Booty* and found a big hibiscus shrub trained into a tree to hide behind. He saw Masen dutifully coiling lines and calmly cleaning the deck and the Zodiac, while the marina employee filled the fuel tank with diesel. Jason watched for a while and was finally convinced that Masen wasn't going anywhere. He came out from hiding and walked up to the boat.

The dock hand finished fueling and told Jason the total owed. Jason gave him a credit card and the man rang it up on his cell phone attachment and asked if he wanted his receipt emailed to him?

"No, just write me one and that'll be fine."

The man did so with an old receipt book.

"How's it going," Jason said to Masen as the dock hand walked away.

"Doing all right. We're ready to go when you are."

"Let's go join Sali for a drink."

* * *

As Sali entered the bar he saw the man they had called Bluto, aka Reznik, sitting at the bar with the same man they'd seen meet the *Garnet Lady* that night in the Berry Islands—the new captain—on his right, and one other man to the right of the captain. They were all at the end of the bar. There was a bar stool on Reznik's left. Sali decided that was his seat, and that he'd try to get Reznik to talk. He was pretty sure Reznik had not seen him back at Aruba's on the beach in Lauderdale-By-The-Sea, or when he and the college kids had spied on him from their boat.

He walked up to the bar and sat next to Reznik and asked the bartender for a Kalik beer with a cold glass and an order of French fries. There was nobody sitting on Sali's left.

"Coming right up, mon" was the reply in his distinct Bahamian dialect.

Reznik looked to his left at Sali, grunted, did a double take as though he had recognized him after all, then scooted his chair a bit to the right to give Sali a little more room. He continued his conversation with the other two men.

Sali noticed Reznik had a pack of Camel cigarettes next to him and was smoking one.

The waiter returned with Sali's beer and fries. Sali lit up one of his Djarum cigarettes, and blew the smoke sideways out of his mouth toward Reznik.

"Man, hot one out there today," said Sali, trying to start up a conversation, but Reznik kept up his quiet conversation with Captain Chet.

"I thought it would cool off a bit after that squall," said Sali, but Reznik turned his back to Sali and said nothing.

Sali grabbed the salt shaker to salt his fries, but instead of salting them like ninety-nine per cent of humanity does, Sali salted them with a back-swing, twisting his wrist in a full one-hundred-eighty degree circle and a little added arm motion as he salted his fries, spraying not only the fries, but Reznik's beer, Reznik's hair, and the whole bar in front of both of them.

Captain Chet started laughing loudly at Sali's maneuver.

Reznik turned around and glared at Sali, who took a deep draught of his beer and took a dainty bite, showing his teeth, on a French fry and stared straight ahead with a straight face.

"What the fuck?" said Reznik, pushing his chair back from the bar about a foot. "Do I know you?" he asked gruffly.

"I don't believe so," said Sali, turning in his chair, and extending his hand. "Name is Fudd. Elmer Fudd."

Captain Chet started laughing even more. "Elmer Fudd? Elmer Fudd?"

Nadav, who was on Captain Chet's right, wasn't laughing—he was looking directly at Sali with a stone-cold hard face, and his right hand went down to his lap. He had a filleting knife in a sheath on his belt.

"Keep away from me," said Reznik with disgust, and he turned back to the captain who was trying to contain his laughter and get back into the serious conversation he was having with Reznik.

"With this fuckin' hurricane coming," said Sali in a loud enough voice to be heard by all three of them, "I figure I ought to just find me a nice warm butthole I can crawl into and wait until it's all over."

"Fuckin' pervert," said Reznik over his shoulder in an audible low growl. "Leave us alone."

"You got something against faggots?" barked Sali loudly, as he turned again to face Reznik. "Who knows, you might like it. Care to tongue my asshole, cutie? I'll even let you do it for free."

"Get the fuck away from me!" screamed Reznik as he stood up pushing the chair back onto the floor. Nadav stood, too, ready for a fight. The captain remained seated and stared at Sali as the two men's confrontation came to a boil.

"Tell you what," said Sali, then burped loudly and put down his beer, still sitting calmly, "if you don't like it, I'll give you a hundred dollars; if you do like it, I'll give you a thousand dollars and a blow job. Only thing is, you have to lick the shit off my dick."

Reznik reached over and grabbed the shirt over Sali's chest with his left hand and swung his right hand back ready to slug Sali full on in the face.

A hand came seemingly out of nowhere and grabbed Reznik's right wrist and held it like a vice, freezing it in mid-swing.

"I wouldn't do that if I were you," said Jason calmly, who stood a good five inches taller than Reznik with forearms as big as his neck.

Sali took both of his hands and grabbed Reznik's left hand holding Sali's shirt and twisted the hand downward, forcing Reznik to his knees while Jason continued to hold Reznik's right wrist.

Nadav jumped away from the bar and pulled out his knife, but Masen appeared and stepped up between Jason and Nadav and pointed a seventeen-shot Smith & Wesson nine-millimeter pistol at his forehead.

As the tableau froze, the bartender pulled out his own persuader, a Mossberg 590 Nightstick shorty shotgun with a mahogany handle, and pumped it loudly, thus loading a shotgun shell into the breach and making the weapon ready to fire. He pointed the gun at Masen. "Drop the gun, all of you hold up your hands, and get the fuck out of here. Now."

The other people in the bar and restaurant took this chance to run out of the establishment, with tables and chairs making a loud screech and crash to the floor.

Masen held up his hands, then said, "I hear you, but let me just drop the bullets right here and keep the gun and we'll be gone."

The bartender waited for a few seconds, then said, "Do it nice and slow, or you'll be the first to get blown away."

Masen, with the gun held high with his right hand, reached up with his left hand slowly and unloaded the gun, allowing all fifteen rounds, plus the one in the chamber, to drop to the floor. He then very slowly put the gun in his back pocket and put both his hands back up in the air.

"Now, you three, pointing at Sali, Jason and Masen, you go first. Go. Now. And wait outside. You three," he said, "stay right where you are while I call the cops." He knew he couldn't cover all six of them with one shotgun against possibly more than one pistol he couldn't see.

Jason, Sali and Masen backed out of the bar, but when they were outside, ran like hell to the *Booty*. Masen started the engine as Sali and Jason untied the lines and spun around to leave the Marina at full speed, disregarding the "Watch Your Wake" signs, and raising the ire of a dozen voices yelling at them from their boats as they headed out of the marina.

Inside the bar, while the bartender looked down at the phone to begin calling the police, Nadav quickly got to him and poked the knife into the man's throat just enough to make him stop his dialing.

"Drop it," said Nadav, and the bartender did. "We're going to leave here nice and peaceful like, and you're going with us out to the boat to make sure you keep your mouth shut."

The four of them walked outside while the few patrons of the bar standing outside stared at them in stunned silence.

"Let's get out of here," said Reznik, and they ran at a trot to the *Garnet Lady*. As they got there, the man who had been fueling up the *Garnet Lady* told Reznik about the suspicious looking three guys. Reznik said, "Yeah, I had the pleasure of their acquaintance. You didn't let them come aboard, did you?"

"No, sir."

"Did you see which boat they went to?"

"No, sir, I did not."

Nadav told the bartender to get onboard the boat. The man hesitated, but did as he was asked.

In short order they were underway. About a half a mile out, Nadav told the bartender, "You're lucky I don't blow your fucking brains out, but that would attract too much attention. Jump in and swim back, and don't call the cops, or we'll come back and I *will* blow your brains out."

Without another word, the man jumped and swam as far as he could under water then surfaced, looked back at them, then began swimming to shore.

Captain Chet looked at the radar and asked, "Do you want to go after those guys? I think I see them on the radar."

"No," said Reznik. "It's bad enough that we might have the Bahamian Coast Guard coming after us; we don't need to be in the middle of a gun battle, not with these women on board. Just haul ass and make for Saba." He gazed out at the sea for a moment and said, "That little shit looked familiar, but I'll be damned if I can remember where from. Why in the fuck was he trying to provoke me?"

Captain Chet said, "Probably just some drunk locals looking for a fight," but he wondered again about the women, and wished he hadn't taken the job. These men were trouble, dangerous even, and this could not end well, but he couldn't see any way out of it, at least not yet.

* * *

Aboard the *Booty*, Jason screamed at Sali. "What the hell was that all about?"

"Well, I couldn't get the fucker to talk, so I thought maybe I could start a fight and get them arrested. We've got nothing to hide, but they sure do."

Jason just shook his head. "That was a hell of a gamble—we could have been arrested, too, and then who knows what would have happened."

Sali just looked at him and shrugged, took another drag on his Djarum, then threw it overboard and went to help Masen at the cockpit.

Just to make sure the *Garnet Lady* crew wouldn't think they were following them, they turned the *Booty* toward Nassau, thinking the *Garnet Lady* would go the other way, since that's the way they were heading before they stopped at Lyford Cay, and sure enough, that's what they did, according to the GPS onboard the *Garnet Lady* that was still transmitting.

"Okay," said Jason, as they all three looked at the GPS tracker, "let's turn around and follow them, but stay just far enough back so they can't see us."

"They might still see us on their radar," said Masen.

"Well, let's hope they don't, because if they do and come back after us, it's not going to be a pretty sight. But I kind of doubt they're going to waste time on us. They're probably still just wondering why in the hell Sali was trying to pick a fight."

Chapter Twenty
Odesa, Ukraine

Kostya Chugunkin had just walked down the plank from his superyacht the *Turquoise Lament* at the Yacht Club Odesa in Ukraine and entered the black Mercedes waiting for him in the parking lot. He stepped into the back seat and greeted his driver, Bodashka Debroshtan, with a quick handshake over the front seat.

"So where are we going this time, my old friend," said Kostya to his driver.

"This time we're going to a place called Gentlemen's Club Flirt."

"Have you targeted any of the girls?"

"Of course. I've got at least five girls who are showing real interest."

"I don't want any dogs. Only the most beautiful women."

"Would I do that to you?" Bodashka asked earnestly as he leaned back over the seat. "How long would I be in the business of finding girls for you if I found you women who couldn't come up with the money. Besides," he said, returning to his driving, "I don't think there are any dogs in Ukraine—they're all beautiful."

Kostya grunted. "We'll see."

Twenty minutes later they pulled up in front of Gentlemen's Club Flirt. Kostya stepped out and Bodashka went to park the car and join him inside.

Twenty minutes later they were at a table and had just ordered their drinks.

"That's one of them, there," said Bodashka. "The one with the very long blond hair and blazing blue eyes. Her name is Nyura. Nyura Kravchenko."

Nyura was just finishing up her dance as guys stuffed bills into her shoes, as that was all she was wearing. Bodashka caught her eye and motioned her over to their table.

After she had gone back stage and changed back into her skimpy floor outfit, she came over to their table.

"Bodashka, my darling, where have you been?" She leaned over and kissed him on the cheek.

"I told you I would bring you a miracle, and here he is. This is my very close friend Kostya, and he is going to take you to America in an elegant, unbelievably beautiful superyacht, the Turquoise Lament."

Nyura said, "Pleased to meet you, Mr. Chugunkin, may I join you?" Her scintillating blue eyes twinkled like wet Swiss blue topaz, and her lips were slightly puffy, but naturally so.

"Please do," said Kostya, "but please just call me 'Kostya'."

Nyura settled into the seat next to Kostya. Her elegant, flawless body was skimpily clad in black silk lace and Kostya's face grew red with excitement. "My goodness, Bodashka was right, you are extremely beautiful."

"Thank you," she said quietly and looked down, affecting bashfulness. Kostya stole a look at her magnificent, taut breasts. "It's nice to be appreciated by such a real gentleman such as yourself."

"How old are you, Nyura?"

"Twenty-three."

"Nyura," said Bodashka, "you mentioned that you wanted to find a way to get to America, and this is the man who can help you."

"It is true," said Kostya, "but I'm afraid I would have to charge you a fee, or else everybody and her girlfriend would want to be going. It costs money for me to make these arrangements, too, I hope you understand. People at the borders we cross need to be bribed, and there are fees as we cross borders."

"Bodashka said it would cost me three thousand U.S. dollars. That's an awful lot of money in Ukraine."

Kostya smiled and nodded. "I know it's a lot of money, but the good thing is, not only do you get to travel there in the elegance of my yacht, which I will be happy to show you, and with free meals by the best chef you can imagine, but I own modeling agencies in New York, Miami, Los Angeles, and Hollywood." He pulled out his wallet and gave her his business card, which was beautifully designed, but also fake.

"For a woman as beautiful as you," said Kostya, "I feel certain I can get you an audition in Hollywood for a minor part in a movie. No promises on the movie business, though. That is very tough to get into."

Nyura's smile broadened and she leaned over and kissed Kostya on the cheek. "Three thousand dollars, even for me?" she said. "I would dance to make you gloriously happy the whole way there."

"Oh, I'm sure you would, but I'm afraid I must insist. As lovely as you are, there are many others waiting for this opportunity, and there are only so many berths on my yacht. Besides, a woman of your beauty could I'm sure earn money from dancing for these American and European tourists in no time."

Nyura took his glass and took a sip of his vodka. "Okay," she said, "you show me your little boat and I will decide after that."

"Fair enough," said Kostya. "How about if we pick you up in front of this place at two o'clock tomorrow afternoon? We'll go straight there and show you around my 'little boat'. There will be other girls going on the trip, but I don't know yet when they will arrive."

She leaned over and kissed him on the cheek again and said, "Okay, see you tomorrow then!"

When she had left the table, Kostya said, "My God, what a goddess. She'll bring in ten grand a night." He wiped the vodka from his lips, then threw down his napkin. "Okay, where to next?"

"Oscar's. It's not a bad drive from here."

* * *

After the same sales pitch at Oscar's and three other strip clubs, Kostya and Bodashka headed back to the *Turquoise Lament*.

"Very good, Bodashka. Indeed, they are all extremely beautiful, and we have them scheduled just right so that we can set sail in just a couple of days and I can be on my way."

"Why don't you take me with you one of these times, boss?"

"Are you kidding me? Your dick would be so hard the whole time you'd have a heart attack in two days."

"Perhaps so, but what a way to go."

* * *

The next afternoon at two o'clock Nyura was out front of Flirt dressed in jeans, a sweatshirt and a floppy hat, but that did nothing to hide her beauty. As the Mercedes pulled up, Kostya stepped out of the car and opened up the back passenger door so she could ride in the back seat.

"Good afternoon," he said. "You look absolutely marvelous."

"Thank you, Kostya."

He walked around the back of the car and got in beside her.

"Okay, let's go," he said to Bodashka who was in the front seat driving.

The car sped off and within minutes they pulled up to the dock where the *Turquoise Lament* was docked.

"Oh, my," said Nyura. "That is quite a boat!"

"It's called a superyacht," said Kostya as he exited the Mercedes. "It's a little over one hundred and one meters. Follow me."

She stepped out of the Mercedes and walked up the gangway onto the yacht.

"She is my pride and joy," said Kostya, as he took her hand and helped her aboard. "It includes a large Jacuzzi at the afterdeck, a sauna, a fully-equipped gym, a full bar, and a hairdressing salon. It can host up to twenty-six guests in twelve cabins, as well as thirty-one crew members, but I'm only taking five of you so that you each have your own room. You deserve the best."

"Now I'm seeing why three thousand dollars is not such a bad price, if you can get me all the way to America in this!"

"I knew you would agree," he smiled.

They toured all the amenities of the yacht for another half hour, then had a delicious mid-afternoon dinner.

As the waiter cleared the table, Kostya said, "So, what do you think? Would you like to take the trip?"

"Yes!" she said emphatically. "How do you want to make the arrangements?"

"We will leave in three days' time, on Saturday morning at eight. Bring the three thousand dollars and your passport and whatever clothes you'd like to take with you, but best if you travel light, and be sure to put your name on your bags to keep them straight amongst the others. Also, in case something bad happens, which it won't, please tell me now what your address and phone numbers are." He handed her a notepad and a pen.

"Please don't lie or you won't be able to go on the trip—my associate will check it out discreetly. And don't worry: I won't call anybody unless it is absolutely necessary, so if you are leaving without anybody knowing, that's your business. I'll settle you into one of my agencies and will give you some clothes up front to wear, but if you want more, you will of course have to pay for them out of your earnings. I will leave you there in the good hands of my associate in Miami, and he will work out the details for whichever city you would like to go to. My agent will arrange to have a percentage of the modeling payments sent to me, and he will give you your fee for the work. The agent will receive fifteen percent for your work. I will return to Odesa and arrange to bring more girls back over, but please don't tell your friends or I will be inundated with requests by women who may not be as beautiful as you. I want only the best of models, of which you obviously are one."

"Oh my God, this is just too good to be true!" said Nyura. "I will have to get my passport tomorrow morning. I already know where to go and how much it will cost. I've been waiting for this moment, but just not believing it could possibly be true."

She arose from the dinner table and went over to Kostya and hugged him. "Oh, I am so happy! Thank you so much Kostya!"

"My pleasure," he said. "Now don't be late! We'll see you Saturday morning and the ship will sail on time. Now please return to the car and Bodashka will give you a ride back to the club, or wherever you wish to go."

This time she gave him a quick kiss on the lips and said, "Thank you again. I can't wait for this trip!"

She squealed with delight and walked briskly back to the gangway down to the dock where Bodashka was waiting.

* * *

At seven-thirty Saturday morning Nyura arrived at the *Turquoise Lament*. Four other girls were already onboard, sitting in the sun in their bikinis at the after deck having Bloody Mary drinks with stalks of celery with breakfast crackers and cheese, and if one thought Nyura was beautiful, the others were no less stunning. All of them were Russian and in their twenties and had thin waists; they introduced themselves to Nyura with a kiss on each cheek and a quick hug.

Dasha, who was also tall with brown hair down to her bottom, had eyes the color of mahogany and a high-pitched laugh that always seemed to wind down to a long giggle. She wasn't much of a conversation starter.

Elena had dark red hair, a taut large bosom, and open ocean deep blue eyes. She seemed to be the deep thinker and wasn't as quick to laugh as the others, but when she did, it was a full-throated loud roar. If she were the first to laugh, everyone within ear shot was likely to start laughing, too, whether they caught the funny line or not.

Natasha had raven-colored hair, and her sparkling eyes were the color of morning dew on fresh grass. She was the curious one—always asking probing questions that often didn't seem to pertain to the topic of discussion. Of the four girls, she was the envy of the others for her magnificently formed derriere.

Oskana was also blond, like Nyura, and had a physique to match, only with the blue-grey eyes of an Arctic wolf. She was the quiet one. She seemed to have a secret that she would never tell, and she didn't laugh as often as the others when they were together.

After drinking and chatting for a bit, Kostya boarded the ship with a big smile on his face and greeted the young ladies.

"Good morning, my lovelies! Are you ready for your big adventure across the Atlantic to America?"

They all shouted their delight in unison: "Yes!"

"Excellent. Let me give you a tour again of the ship and introduce you to our crew and show you to your private stateroom. You may leave your glasses where they are—the steward will clean up after you. He will also put your bags in the proper stateroom, so long as you remembered to put your name on your bags. All okay? Are you ready, then?"

Standing gleefully and smiling broadly, the girls put their glasses down, put on their throwovers or tops, if they had one, and followed Kostya, while the steward began cleaning up behind them.

After the tour, Kostya invited the girls to sit at tables served by the bartender down near the water line next to the tender garage at the aft of the yacht. The bartender arrived and the girls each ordered their own special choice of alcoholic beverage, while Kostya ordered Beluga vodka, neat.

"This is going to be a long, but very pleasant voyage. The trip of a lifetime," he said. "But first of all, let us get the business out of the way, the money and the passport. My associate has already checked on your parent's homes and phone numbers and advised me that they are all correct. I'm sorry for being so cautious, but it is necessary, as I described, and I assure you my associate was completely discrete."

Each of the girls reached into their pocketbooks and retrieved the fee, as well as their passports, and handed them over to Kostya just as the bartender was delivering the drinks.

Kostya took a big swallow of the vodka. The girls watched him as he counted the money and put it in an envelope he retrieved from his coat pocket, and put the passports in a separate envelope.

"Okay, very good—I'm glad we have that out of the way so we can go onto the more pleasant aspects of this adventure."

He now drank the whole glass of vodka in one long swallow. He put the glass down, then continued his monologue.

"First of all, we will travel west across the Black Sea to the rather small port city of Poyrazköy where we will stop and refuel, and get more provisions. It is best not to go ashore here—you will have a chance later on. From there we go down the Bosporus Strait toward Istanbul, passing under three very beautiful suspension bridges, the awesome Yavuz Sultan Selim Bridge, the Fatih Sultan Mehmet Bridge, and finally, the magnificent 15 July Martyrs Bridge at Istanbul, which we will hopefully pass under at night while it is lit up. It is extremely beautiful. The trip up the Bosporus Strait is something you will never forget."

The girls were beside themselves with joy and excitement, toasting each other and laughing and urging him to continue.

"You may go ashore in Istanbul for a few hours, but you must leave your passports with me because I will check all of you through customs at the same time. Don't be late coming back to the ship, because we will leave without you if we have to."

This made the conversation more serious and the titter of the girls had turned to serious looks of attention to details.

"The crossing of the Sea of Marma does not take long, and soon we will be at Gallipoli and enter the Dardanelles Strait. There are so many beautiful sites to see along the Strait, but we don't have forever, so we will just keep on steaming until finally we make it to the Aegean Sea. After a couple of days, we will finally reach the Mediterranean Sea, where hopefully we will have good weather and make it across the Alboran Sea to the Strait of Gibraltar. We will stop in Tangier, Morocco, where we will dock at Tanja Marina Bay; and again, you can go ashore and do some shopping and sightseeing while we refuel and gather more provisions, and clear your passports with customs. We will be there about twenty-four hours to double-check the integrity of the boat for the crossing of the Atlantic, and for resting, but Tangier is such a beautiful and interesting city, that you could easily spend a day there just sightseeing. I suggest you travel as a group and do not separate, and spend the night on the boat and nowhere else."

"But what if we meet some handsome guy whom we just can't resist?" said Elena, and all the girls started laughing and teasing her.

"This is exciting!" broke in Nyura. "I can't believe this is really happening. Finally, I am going to America!"

"Me, too!" they all chimed in. Kostya just grinned broadly.

All the girls cheered and toasted again and called for a second round.

"Okay," said Kostya, "I'm almost finished for today. From Tangier we take a day to go to the Canary Islands, and then we overnight there. Then, so long as the weather looks good and there are no hurricanes brewing off the coast of Africa, we make the long trip to a Caribbean island south of Saba. Once we get there, you will go ashore to meet my associate who will give you more information on the best modeling agency to place you in America. As we cross the Atlantic, I'll find out more information about the different agencies and can inform you further then. That's all I have for now ladies, make yourselves comfortable in your cabins and get ready to sail in about twenty minutes, and bon voyage!"

They all had a loud and cheery final toast, then excitedly headed to their new home cabin for the trip across the Atlantic.

Chapter Twenty-One
No Choice

All the women were back aboard the *Turquoise Lament* after a two day stop at the Port of Las Palmas on the Gran Canaria island of the Canary Islands. Kostya called the captain to the bridge and said, "Time to go."

The captain left the port and turned the superyacht to a two-hundred-sixty-four-degree course toward the northern part of the Eastern Caribbean Islands. He turned up the radio to hear the marine weather and began looking at the radar more often.

"I don't like it," said the captain. "It looks like winds from the African Easterly Jet are starting to pick up off Cape Verde, but nothing strong yet. You never know."

As they reached the open sea, Kostya announced on the public address system, "All passengers meet at the tender garage bar for a briefing in thirty minutes." He hung up the microphone, and turned briefly to the captain. "For now, it looks like smooth sailing. Do you concur?"

"Yes sir, I do. I think chances are good for a smooth trip. Let's hope so."

Down in the tender garage Kostya found the women waiting at the tables near the bar, all laughing and telling stories of their fabulous adventures so far.

Kostya sat at one of the tables. "Well, ladies, I hope you all had a good time, because now comes the long stretch, and it may not be so pleasant. Right now, the weather looks to be good, but it's entirely possible that a tropical storm could start to form off Cape Verde and it could get very rough. By rough I mean up to 10-meter seas—extremely difficult sailing with the highest of probabilities that you will want to puke your guts out. If it gets that bad, don't worry, we'll go to the closest port.

"But as I say," continued Kostya, "the weather looks good for now, so the trip, which will be about twenty-six hundred nautical miles, should last between two to three weeks, depending on the weather. We won't be pushing it, but I would like for you all to go to your staterooms and make sure everything—and I do mean everything—is fastened down as tight as possible so things don't go flying and crashing around in your rooms in case we do have a storm. Finish your drinks, then go to your rooms and make them ready. Dinner will be served at the usual hour. Then we'll be on our way."

* * *

After the girls had tidied up their rooms and had a delicious swordfish dinner, they joined each other at the afterdeck round table, the same place Marek and Kostya had originally made their plans for abduction of the famous women, but not these newly acquired assets.

As the yacht picked up speed and headed out to the deep blue eastern Atlantic Ocean, they began to feel the ocean swells, but the ship took them easily, and the ride was smoother than might be expected.

The bartender came to their table and politely asked what the ladies would like to have.

"What do you have?" asked Natasha.

The bartender smiled broadly. "Everything," he said. "Truly, there is probably not a drink you can name that I don't know and can make. Please call me Emile."

"Well, Emile," she said, "I think I'll just have a Campari and soda with a twist of lime."

"Johnnie Walker Red, straight up!"

"Vodka Gimlet!"

"Screwdriver!"

"What do you suggest, Emile?" asked Oskana.

"If you haven't tried it before, I'd suggest a pisco sour, Peruvian style."

"I'll take it!"

Emile left the women to themselves to chat about their adventure since leaving Ukraine, yet finally turned to other subjects.

"So, were all of you dancers, like me?" asked Nyura.

They all nodded agreement.

"I just couldn't find any work," said Natasha. "I haven't even had a steady place to live. My parents sold me to traffickers when I was only fourteen because she couldn't afford to feed all of us. I had two brothers and two sisters, no father, and my Mom had just lost her job. She was offered two thousand dollars and the man said he'd return me to my family in one year. My mom believed him. That was a long time ago."

Silence fell on the group as Emile delivered their drinks.

Oskana spoke up. "I was forced to marry some ugly slug for payment to my parents when I was only sixteen. I hated the guy, and I was so depressed my parents did that to me I tried to commit suicide. But I chickened out and just went down to Ukraine and started doing odd jobs, hooking, stripping, you name it. I got heavy into drugs and almost died, but some stripper took me in and helped me get back on my feet, if you can call stripping getting back on your feet."

"And on your back!" laughed Elena.

They all laughed and nodded their heads in agreement, except Nyura.

"I don't mean to dull the party," Elena said, "but because of my big boobs, I was a hot looking number at thirteen and my parents pimped me out for about a year until I got syphilis and almost died. The hospital took me in for free, and while I was lying there in that bed wondering how I could have gotten in such bad shape and be so young, I decided to leave as soon as I could. My parents never even came to visit me. As soon as I got better, I ran. I travelled all over Moldavia and then came to Ukraine and started dancing, and have been doing it ever since."

They all took a big drink from their glasses and stared out at the sea rolling behind them.

"You're not going to believe this," said Dasha, and she pulled up her shirt to show a scar on her back, on the right side. "My parents sold my right kidney to an organ trafficking recruiter. They knocked me out when I wasn't looking and just fucking did it while I was knocked out. I woke up in some nasty hospital, and they took care of me until I got better, but I wouldn't say they gave a shit one way or the other whether I lived or died, but anyway, I finally sneaked out when I could and never went back to my parents. That was just a short drive from Odesa, so I didn't go very far. The scar doesn't help for the tips, either, but at least it's covered with a nice tattoo."

They all had another swallow, then Natasha asked Nyura, "What about you?"

"I'm happy to say I don't have any horror stories like those," she said, "I just had to start stripping because I couldn't find any work. My parents think I'm a bartender."

"Well," said Elena, "it doesn't sound like their threat of calling home is going to mean shit for any of us except you."

"Ohhhh, damn it! Now you've got me scared!" Nyura put her drink down and her eyes began to tear.

There was a long moment of silence as the girls looked at each other and began to think and worry.

"Don't worry," said Oskana, without much conviction. "Please."

"Yeah!" the girls screamed in unison and toasted the last of their drinks.

Emile arrived. "Does this mean another round?"

"Yes!"

* * *

It wasn't but a day later, about ten at night as the seas were rolling gently, when Kostya called Nyura to his cabin. She arrived within minutes, dressed in her tight jeans and a V-neck leopard tunic long sleeve button down blouse, with her long blond hair loose and flowing behind her. Kostya opened the door for her and she stepped in to find Kostya wearing only his night robe.

"Hello, Kostya, you wanted to see me?"

"Yes, I did, beautiful Nyura," he said, as he closed and locked the door. "I would like for you to take off all your clothes for me."

She blushed slightly, then said, "You mean you want me to do my night club strip act?"

"You can, if you'd like, but then I'd like you to lie down on my bed, with your knees up and your pussy warm and ready for me."

He took off his robe and she saw his partial erection.

"Kostya, no, this wasn't part of the deal. I don't want to do that."

"I'm afraid you have no choice, my lovely. It's that, or you can swim home."

She turned to the cabin door but found it locked. She tried banging on the door and screaming, but nobody could hear her through the soundproof cabin and the sound of the ship's engines, and because of his location near the bow, away from all the other cabins. But even if anybody had heard her, it would not have mattered.

He grabbed her and with one tug threw her to his bed. She tried to get up, but he was on top of her immediately and gave her one hard smack across the face with his left hand, then another with his right.

"Now," he said, "are you going to fight me, or are you going to strip and do as I say?"

She started to cry as she removed her clothes, and it wasn't long before Kostya availed himself of every position and act he could think of until he was sated.

"You may go for now," he said, "and it doesn't really matter if you tell the other girls, because this is how I pay my crew. I give them a few dollars, but they get as much pussy as they want, so long as they get their jobs done. And don't try plotting with the girls to escape once we get to our destination, because I have all your passports locked in the safe, and if you try anything stupid, I have your parent's addresses and phone numbers, and my associates will find them and kill every last one of them. Don't underestimate me—I *will* do it."

Nyura moved to the side of the bed, crying and putting her clothes on.

"Just think of what a great vacation you just had sailing across the Mediterranean and the Canary Islands. An unforgettable trip, don't you think?"

Chapter Twenty-Two
Saba

The *Booty* had the advantage of the near constant trade winds to keep her traveling for long distances without having to refuel, while the *Garnet Lady* had to stop three times for fuel as she made her way to the Eastern Caribbean islands. As before, the *Booty* stayed just far enough behind the *Garnet Lady* so as not to be seen, but still within range of the GPS on the *Garnet Lady*. They followed them for three long days, then suddenly, as they approached the small island of Saba, the smallest island in the Netherland Antilles and a favorite of pirates from centuries ago, they lost the signal.

"Shit," said Sali. "Either the batteries finally gave out, or they found it and got rid of it."

Jason shook his head and thought for a moment. "Let's stop at Saba and ask around and see if anybody's seen them and which way they might have gone."

Masen turned the tiller and made a course to Fort Bay Harbor on the southwest side of the island. "They have a wahoo tournament there that I've been dying to see someday. Maybe we'll get lucky. Always wanted to see this place."

There's no commercial marina on Saba, but there is a secluded strip of moorings on the more sheltered western side of the island, away from the near-constant trade winds from the northeast and east. Everybody who visits has to check in with the harbormaster between six in the morning and six in the evening and fill out the proper forms, then register with the Marine Park. So, if the *Garnet Lady* had stopped in Saba, they figured the harbormaster would know.

* * *

As they entered Fort Bay Harbor they saw the two-story white harbormaster's office on the right, with a tender pier out front where they could tie up. The whole harbor was medium sized, with not much room for a lot of boats, especially large ones. A local kid helped them tie up, then Jason and Mason went ashore to check in with the harbormaster.

As they entered the office there was only one person there, so they figured he was the harbormaster. He was an old but well-built black man about six feet tall with a broad chest, large arms and hands and a big smile.

"Greetings, Gentlemen," he said. "You fixin' to stay awhile, or just passing through?"

"Actually, we're not sure. We've been hoping to catch up with some friends we met in Nassau. We heard they were heading this way, but we can't reach them on the radio. They're aboard a yacht called the Garnet Lady. I don't suppose they came by here, did they?"

"Well, as a matter of fact they did, just yesterday," the man replied.

"Well, I'll be damned," said Jason, smiling, "Our lucky day. Can you tell us where they were heading?"

"Well, now that's the funny part, now that I think of it. Most people head north toward the Anguilla group of islands, or southeast toward Saint Eustatius, or maybe even a little more southeast toward Antigua and Barbuda, but these guys headed straight south."

"South?" said Masen. "I don't recall seeing any islands south of here, but then again," he said dismissively, "I've never been here before—just been studying the maps."

"Well, there isn't much of anything, until you hit South America. But even if they were going to Venezuela or Colombia, hardly anybody goes straight down there, they go along the eastern chain of islands, like through Guadeloupe, Martinique, St. Lucia, and so on. I don't know why they went that way."

"You mean there's nothing south of here at all except South America?" asked Jason.

"Well, there is this one little island. It's called Dark Island on the map because it has so many trees, but people call it *L'ile des ames perdues*, which means 'Island of Lost Souls.' I went by it once a long time ago."

Jason waited for him to continue.

"They say anybody who goes inside the island never returns."

Jason and Masen looked at each other skeptically.

"How do we get there?" asked Jason.

The harbormaster looked at him warily, then pulled out an old map. "Well, it's on this old survey map I've got right here, but it's not on every map, because it's uninhabited and small, and few shallow places to anchor. I don't know why they don't put it on the map. Anyway, if you really want to visit it, there's a river on the south side that supposedly takes you into the interior."

"Supposedly?"

"Like I said: Nobody ever seems to come back, or at least so far as I've heard from the old sailors drinking over at the Deep End Bar and Grill. I guess they've just seen it or went up the river a ways—I don't really know. But anyway, when you get close, you'll see the only mountain on the island, called Rubicon Mountain. When you get close to the island you can see there's a line of mangroves around the island, then the interior is all jungle."

"What's the name of the river?"

"*La riviere sans nom.* The river with no name. Nobody really has a name for it, except that, I guess."

"Thank you," said Jason as he started to roll up the map. "What do I owe you for the map?"

The man stopped him. "Sorry, son, that's the only map I've got that has that island on it. But you can set a course for it from here and you'll see it when you get close enough." He looked at the map and jotted a heading down on a slip of paper and gave it to Jason. "Dark Island is approximately southwest of Saba on the western side of Saba Bank."

"Good luck," said the old man as he shook his head slightly, "but I wouldn't go onto the island, if I were you."

"Thank you," said Jason and they left.

* * *

Jason and Masen returned to the *Booty* and spread their own map out on the table, and Masen took his compass and protractor and the slip of paper the old man had given them and plotted a course.

"According to the old harbormaster, they should be somewhere along this line," he said to Sali. "They headed off in a direction where there's nothing but the island the harbormaster told us about, or further down, South America. He said the island isn't on every map because it's small and uninhabited, and there's not many shallow places to anchor."

"No wonder, I guess," said Masen, "It would be right inside Saba Bank, actually a sunken atoll—the top of an extinct volcano. That island must be where part of the atoll is still above water. The rest of the atoll sank a very long time ago."

"We might as well look at that island first, since that's the way they headed. By the way, I should tell you, the harbormaster says the locals call it the 'island of lost souls' because nobody that has gone into the island has ever come back out."

"Sounds like retirement heaven or it's dangerous," said Sali. "I could use a nice retirement spot. Shall we investigate?"

"Well, I've come this far," said Masen. "No sense turning back now."

Chapter Twenty-Three
Dark Island

Jason decided he'd had enough riding the seas of the Caribbean for a while and agreed to pay for a nice place to stay the night in Saba. They stayed at the Queen's Garden Resort and Spa, up in the mountainous region close to Mount Scenery, and enjoyed a nice swim in the pool, many cold beers, long hot showers and a gorgeous sunset: a beautiful ending for a thirteen-hour day. The next morning, a little before sunrise at five-thirty, they begrudgingly boarded the *Booty* again and headed off in pursuit of the *Garnet Lady*, hopefully somewhere near Dark Island, and it wasn't long before they came upon it.

It was basically a mountain in the middle of the ocean surrounded on the ground by a dense, tall forest inland, but circled by thick mangroves along the coast. As they neared it, they could see why its local name was Dark Island. The trees and underbrush were so thick, you couldn't see but a few feet into the forest. No wonder it was labeled uninhabited—it would be a monumental effort to build a road or a passage into the interior, and why would anyone want to do that? There was no timber value in the mangroves and trees, it appeared, compared to what it would take to get it out of there.

They approached the island slowly and began to circumnavigate it. They saw an ancient, heavily weathered pier coming out of the island on the north side, with an old Chris Craft tied up to it, yet they could see no road leading up to the pier, which had heavy growth around it anyway. Nothing but jungle all around it.

Masen said: "Why on earth is that boat there? It looks like nobody even lives around here."

They kept on moving, and at last they came to the area the harbormaster mentioned—a small river coming out of the forest on the south side. It moved slowly and the water was crystal clear.

Sali looked over the side and into the water. "Man, it's deep here—I can't see the bottom even though we're so close to shore."

There was a channel where the river came out and it was deep enough for them to enter.

"This feels like a waste of time," said Sali. "There's barely enough room for us to fit in, never mind the size of the *Garnet Lady*."

They nudged carefully past the first overhanging branches of thick mangroves, then entered a cleared space that because of the tallness of the overhanging trees, gave the impression of entering a tunnel through the trees which was certainly wide enough for their boat or the *Garnet Lady*.

"Wow! No wonder the old man's map doesn't show the river—you couldn't possibly see it from the air."

Inside the giant cathedral of high trees and vines, the gentle lap of waves before their entry gave way to a cacophony of birds, monkeys and other animals, as though scolding their entrance and telling them to go back. The gentle chug of the *Booty's* engine seemed but the heartbeat of a new, stranger and larger swamp-dweller as it moved silently through the trees and up the river toward its source, wherever that might be.

"If they're up there, we've either just been announced, or they can't tell we're here over all the animal chatter."

"And if they're not up there, nobody will likely ever find us if we can't turn around for whatever reason."

They continued to chug slowly and easily through the jungle, which had now reduced its volume by at least half.

Sali, who was on the bow again, keeping an eye out for sunken rocks or trees that might puncture the hull, suddenly called out: "Wait! Stop!"

Masen dutifully changed gears to reverse, then neutral, so that their progress forward stopped almost immediately.

"Look," said Sali, pointing to a particularly thick knot of mangrove roots.

It took a while for Masen and Jason to discern what caused Sali's alarm, but there it was: the grotesque, twisted corpse of a woman, pale as alabaster and covered with small crabs, flies, and algae accumulated from the changing of the tide. Strangely, the smell of death had not yet reached them, and the men stared, horrified, as they noticed the unmistakable round bullet hole in the middle of her forehead. Her long blond hair was splayed across the mangrove roots, and her legs, covered by a long colorful green dress, were twisted at odd angles. Her sightless eyes stared upward toward the tops of the trees which shielded her from discovery from above.

Sali said, "Well, that certainly saves on burial costs—just dump them in the swamp and let the crabs have their fill."

"Jeezus, Sali, have some respect for the dead," said Jason.

Masen was vomiting off the other side of the boat.

Jason swallowed hard. "So, is this the work of the Garnet Lady, I wonder?"

"I didn't hear a shot," said Sali. "Then again, I don't know how close we are to them, or even if they're ahead of us, or anywhere on this island at all, for that matter."

Masen returned from his sickness and said, "That looks to me like a pretty effective 'No Trespassing' sign."

They all looked around for any sign of others.

"I don't see any sign of humans except this poor girl."

"What should we do?" said Masen.

"We'll have to tell the authorities about this when we return; otherwise, if we tell them now, whoever killed her may hear our transmission and will know we're here."

Sali said, "Do we turn around?"

"We can't," said Jason, "No room. We have to go further and find a place to turn around. Or else back out, which would not be at all easy. And besides, I still think this is where the Garnet Lady went. That body has been there too long to have been from their boat, but they were heading this way, and I think we have to check it out. If we can't move further up river, we'll just have to try and leave in reverse, no matter how difficult."

"If they are up there," said Sali, "we'd better make an escape contingency. Standard military protocol."

"Right," said Jason, and thought for a moment. "What do you say we go upstream a little further and set some munitions to topple a tree as a blockade, if we need it?"

"Sounds like a plan to me. We have two packets of C4."

They traveled along down the river, through Calabash trees, umbrella trees, Bignonia vines, beautiful pink flowering tabebuia trees, gumbo limbo trees, and mangrove trees. Beautiful red and green todie birds flitted about among the trees, while palmchats nested in the many species of palms. Silence, but for the occasional animal sounds, finally covered the jungle like a blanket. The jungle had adopted them.

Finally, at a big fig tree near the bank of the river, Jason and Sali set the C4 explosive with a blasting cap and a long trip wire so that if they came back the same way they went in, they could easily swing close to the wire and yank on it with their long-handled gaff—just don't get too close! The C4 would explode at the base of the big fig tree and fall across the river and make it difficult or impossible to get around by a pursuing boat. The tension on the wire was set so that only a significant pull would detonate the explosive, and not some small wild animal.

"Let's just remember to dismantle it on the way out, if we're not being followed."

A short while later, after they had gone further through the dark jungle and up the slow flowing river, they saw the sun shining into a clearing ahead.

"Uh oh," said Sali. "If they're actually ahead of us and in the clearing, they'll see us, and it looked to me earlier like they had more firepower than we do."

Jason thought for a minute then said, "Are you afraid of snakes?"

"What? Well, no, so long as they're dead."

"I think there are only a few non-poisonous snakes out in the Eastern Caribbean, but there might be some caimans or crocs. Let's wade up to the edge of the clearing and see if anybody's up there. Bring the field glasses and a radio. Masen, if we get into any trouble, try to back out and trigger the exit bomb and call Jamie. But don't do anything until one of us radios you."

Jason and Sali strapped on their Mark 23s, canteens and radios and tightened their boot laces. Finally, they sat on the gunwale, ready to slide into the murky swamp.

"You didn't ask me about leeches," said Sali.

"Bitch, bitch, bitch," said Jason and they both slid into the black water.

Chapter Twenty-Four
Rubicon Mountain

It was around noon when Jason and Sali waded soundlessly along the side of the river up to the small clearing which was more of a small lake at the foot of Rubicon Mountain. As they neared the lake, the river widened slightly and the water was more clear and they could see fish darting around their legs and in the small river. Shafts of brilliant sunlight broke through the occasional opening in the jungle canopy and nurtured the miasma of fetid air. They stopped just before reaching the edge of the lake and using their field glasses surveyed the tree-lined border. Directly across from them, about a half-mile away, was the foot of the mountain.

"No sign of the Garnet Lady," said Sali.

Just then a wadded-up Camel cigarette package floated up to them and moved slowly past and toward the *Booty* behind them. Jason waded over, picked it up and smelled it.

"That's fresh," said Jason. "But where in the hell did it come from? I don't see anybody or anything."

"It's a Camel pack. That's what Reznik was smoking back at Lyford."

They scanned the shoreline again through their field glasses.

"Aha!" said Sali. "Look again at the base of the mountain. I just saw a couple birds flying and they looked like they disappeared into the mountain, but actually there's a big piece of the mountain, or a big rock, that looks just like the side of the mountain, but actually, set off from it. I think there might be another part of the river or the lake that flows behind that rock. It's sort of an optical illusion."

They both trained their glasses for a long minute on the big rock.

Jason picked up his radio and spoke to Masen. "Bring the boat up. It looks clear up here."

Minutes later the *Booty* arrived and Jason and Sali climbed back aboard.

Jason filled in Masen about the cigarette wrapper and showed it to him.

"I think they're definitely ahead of us. Reznik smokes Camels, and you can still smell the tobacco in it."

"We're thinking the river continues on the other side of the lake," said Jason, "behind a big rock that looks like a piece of the mountain." Jason pointed it out. "Let's go check it out."

They watched warily as the *Booty* approached the edge of the lake.

They slowed as they approached the rock.

"It's deeper to the port side," said Sali who was on the bow looking down into the clear water. Jason continued scanning the bank of the lake with his field glasses while Masen steered a proper course.

As they rounded the big rock, they saw that the river did indeed flow behind it, but it also widened and entered a large cavern they could not have seen previously.

"Wow!"

"Holy shit!"

"Jeezus!"

"It looks like there's plenty of room in there for the Garnet Lady," said Sali as he shone a flashlight into the water and along the walls of the cavern.

Masen put the *Booty* in neutral and said, "Wait a second, gents. There's obviously somebody ahead of us, probably them, judging from the cigarette wrapper; so, what happens if we run into the bad guys, I mean if they are the bad guys? It could easily turn into a shootout, and I don't like our chances, especially considering that woman's body back in the swamp."

"He's right," said Jason.

"Let's continue on foot," said Sali. "It looks like there's plenty of room on the banks to walk ahead. We can radio back to Masen as long as we get reception. We might even be able to float notes in a bottle or something downstream if we need to."

"Brilliant suggestion," said Masen, "and I've got just the bottles that will work—those Grolsch beer bottles with a Quillfeldt top—they're also called swing-tops."

"Quillfeldt?"

"Named after the guy who invented them—Charles de Quillfeldt. I got curious about them once…"

"Right. Okay, hold on while I call Jamie and give her an update." Jason grabbed the satellite phone and dialed her number. No answer, but he got her voice mail.

"Jamie, it's me, Jason. We're somewhere south of Saba on a small island called Dark Island, and we're at the base of Rubicon Mountain. We don't know for sure yet, but we think the Garnet Lady may have gone into this tunnel that leads inside the mountain. We're about to check it out now, but we will likely lose radio and sat-phone reception once we get in there. Don't call us, we'll call you. Later."

Masen returned with a couple of the Grolsch bottles. "I knew these would come in handy," he said, and handed them to Sali. He pulled up a drawer on the map desk and also gave him a pencil and a few sheets of small notebook paper.

"We still don't know if the Garnet Lady is up there," said Sali to Jason, "so what say we play it safe? How about if we have Masen back the Booty out and anchor just in front of the big rock so if he sees anything floating downstream—like our bottle with a message—then he can nab it and read it. Meanwhile, we move ahead on foot up the cave."

"Sounds like a plan to me," said Jason. "Let's stock up on some food and weapons and change into some dry clothes and hiking boots. Masen, here's a radio and the sat-phone. We'll call you 'Booty Man' and I'll be 'Apache'." He tossed a radio to Sali, "We'll call you 'Stinkfinger' on account of those stinky cigarettes you're always smoking."

* * *

"Are you ready for this?" said Jason.

"Always," said Sali.

Masen pulled the *Booty* up close to one of the big shoreline rocks on the port side and Jason and Sali climbed out. Sali gave the *Booty* a gentle shove to get her away from the rocks, then Masen backed her away gently, then while still in reverse, pulled the boat back through the entrance and out into the lake. He turned the *Booty* around so it was facing back the way it came in, then backed it gently to a spot behind the big rock in front of the cave so that it was mostly hidden from the lake, but ready to leave in a hurry, if necessary. He dropped anchor, then moved toward the bow, which was barely visible from the lake, so that he could see anybody approaching from the cave, but also from the lake.

Jason and Sali scrambled up onto the rocks which lined the river which in turn flowed gently from further up into the cave. As they moved inward along the shoreline, they noticed it was lighter inside than near the opening of the cave.

"Look," said Jason pointing upward. There were openings at the top of the cave to the outside. They weren't very big, but they were big enough to let little shafts of light shine down as though they were small spotlights illuminating the course of the river as it crept ever deeper into the silent cave.

Sali pointed his flashlight above to the ceiling of the cave. At first, it seemed like the ceiling was covered in black velvet, but there was the occasional movement from the massive black covering.

"Oh, jeezus. They're bats," he said "Millions of them!"

"Well stop shining the light on them or you'll wake them up!"

They climbed onward quietly, stopping occasionally to listen for sounds or to see any sign of movement ahead.

Abruptly, Jason held up his hand to indicate a stop.

It was barely perceptible at first, but before long, they could perceive the unmistakable sound of a small waterfall, and as they approached further, the sound of a babbling brook.

The sunlight shining through the top of the cavern now came from a greater height, affording the effect of long shafts of soft yellow light shining down upon the low waterfall and the cascading water as it ran downhill at a low incline and into the river they had been traversing. The increased amount of light now provided for the growth of lush green ferns alongside the riverbank where before there had been none. The verdancy was suffused with a powerful new lush and leafy aroma and the water was so clear that the sunlight beaming down from the rocky ceiling made the water seem non-existent and made the rock bottom appear closer at hand than it was.

Jason and Sali gazed in awe at the peaceful scene for long moments and froze in place as they looked cautiously around the enlarged cavern area.

In the middle of the large cavernous area, lit by the holes allowing sunlight through, was an incongruous pile of small rocks rising about ten feet in the middle of a pond about fifty feet wide, and a spring spilling out of the top making the gentle susurration of the waterfall that they had heard earlier. The water made a pleasing splash as it hit the pond which served as the source of two rivers: one was the gently babbling brook as it grew larger back the way they had come, while another separate river formed from the far side of the small pond and flowed the opposite direction. The raised fountain was the source of two small rivers flowing in opposite directions. The clear water surrounding the fountain was approximately twenty feet deep—deep enough for the *Garnet Lady*. The newly formed river leading away from them was also wide enough to accommodate the craft, which was nowhere to be seen.

"Where the hell is the boat?" whispered Sali.

"Let's follow that other river downstream. Maybe it's down there."

They continued their trek up past the spring and into the new river flowing in the opposite direction as before.

After traveling only about a hundred yards, Jason suddenly held up his hand for them to stop.

Ahead of them the light dimmed: there were fewer shafts of light from above, and there were no more ferns or other vegetation lining the banks of the river.

They hadn't gone far when they came to a turn in the river and saw the *Garnet Lady* tied up to a dock at a place where the river had widened to form another small lake, and traveled further inward into the mountain, and apparently found its way outside the mountain and back out into the jungle at another point of egress somewhere further downstream.

The *Garnet Lady* was quiet, the diesel engine shut off, and apparently nobody onboard. There were torches lit along the dock which was shaped like a T, with the boat tied up along the upper part of the T, and the lower part serving as a walkway to the shore. From there, there was an entrance about ten feet high that opened into a smaller cave, the obvious place where the crew and passengers had gone.

Jason took off his backpack, pulled out his radio and tried calling Masen quietly.

"Booty Man, this is Apache, come back."

No response. He repeated the call. Still no response.

"Let's try the message-in-the-bottle trick," said Sali as he unshouldered his backpack. He retrieved the thick Grolsch beer bottle with the swing-top that Masen had given him, as well as the pencil and note paper.

"What do you want me to say?" said Sali.

"Well let's think about this a minute," said Jason. "If he stays where he is, another boat coming along is going to see him and it could be trouble. He's not going to like this, but let's ask him to try to hide the Zodiac up in the mangroves near the beginning of the cave, in case we need it to get the hell out of here, then have him take the Booty back out through the river in the mangroves and anchor, if he can, somewhere out over one of the reefs in the ocean, if he can find one. He can pretend he's fishing or something in case somebody comes by and talks to him. When we get back to the Zodiac, we can call him on the radio and tell him we're coming. Ask him to call Jamie and tell her we've found the Garnet Lady and where we are. Ask her to send us some help."

"All that on this little piece of paper?"

"Write small."

"Yeah…"

Sali spent several minutes hurriedly scribbling down the message, read it aloud to Jason, then put it into the bottle and snapped the cap closed.

"I'm going to have to walk it back up this river to the spring so it will go down the other river, but I'll be right back."

"Right. Get on it and I'll wait right here for you and see if anything happens. Be careful."

"Always," and with that, Sali was on his way back to the spring.

A half hour later Sali arrived at the spring and walked over to the headwaters where the river they had come in on was, and began its course back to where Masen sat not-so-patiently in the *Booty*. He waded into the middle of the stream and gave the bottle a gentle push to send it on its way.

Chapter Twenty-Five
Masen Reports

Masen kept his eyes trained upon the slowly flowing river, awaiting any kind of word on what Jason and Sali had found.

Finally, there it was—one of the bottles he had given Sali to pass a message to him. He grabbed the long-handled net he used for pulling in angled fish and quickly scooped it up and pulled it aboard. He popped the cap of the bottle and gingerly tapped the rolled-up message out of the bottle. He unrolled it and read the message.

"Shit," he grumbled, then set to work on the plan.

* * *

Masen couldn't stop swearing out loud at himself, Jason and Sali as he chopped his way into a thicket of mangroves and found a place to hide the Zodiac and cover it with the chopped foliage. It was not easy to see from the lake, but if Jason and Sali looked really close they should be able to see it. It was the best he could do.

Finally getting back to the *Booty*, he started the engine and turned back to the direction from which they had come and made his way back into the river through the mangroves. As he passed it, he looked closely to make sure the C4 charge and tripwire were still intact and connected to the base of the tree, and they were.

Once he escaped the river and was back out on the ocean, he was relieved to see there were no other boats in the area. As instructed, he found an area about half a mile away from the entrance to the river and dropped anchor at a shallow spot that rose up from the deep bottom like a miniature guyot. He rigged a fishing pole and stuck it off the stern so it looked like he had just stopped to do a little bottom fishing.

It was a gorgeous day with not a cloud in the sky and with a gentle breeze and the water clear as Russian vodka all the way to the bottom where he could see the fish ignoring his bait. He retrieved the satellite phone and called Jamie.

"Hello, is this Jamie Horgood?"

"Who is this?" Jamie recognized the incoming phone number, but it wasn't Jason's voice.

"This is Masen Williams. I'm working for Jason Stouter—I believe he's told you about me."

"Go on, please," she said warily.

"So, Jason called you earlier and told you where we were just passing Saba to Dark Island. Long story short, Jason and Sali have gone inside this large cave in the side of the only mountain on the island, called Rubicon Mountain. They sent me a note via a floating bottle…"

"What!"

"…and they found the Garnet Lady inside the cave…"

"Inside the cave? So, there's a river that goes inside the cave?"

"Yes."

"What else?"

"They said send help."

"That might be a little difficult. The President's daughter has also just been kidnapped, and there are a lot of people looking for her and the kidnappers. I will try to reach the closest FBI Legal Attaché and see what he might be able to do. I can't promise anything right now, though. What do they want you to do now?"

"Just wait and do what you or they want me to do. I'm anchored offshore with a fishing pole trying to look inconspicuous, in case anybody comes by. I stashed a Zodiac in the mangroves so when they leave they can come back out to meet me."

"Okay, I'll call you back when I find out more."

"Roger that."

Masen hung up the phone and plugged it into the charger. He decided it was probably time to make sure his Smith & Wesson M&P 9mm pistol was in working shape and loaded. He belted the gun and a holster on his hip and pocketed some extra ammunition, then checked the fishing pole to see if he had any dinner on the line.

No such luck.

Chapter Twenty-Six
Mountain Resort

Hours earlier, the *Garnet Lady* had pulled up alongside the T-shaped dock inside the mountain and the crew tied her off at the cleats.

Marek walked slowly up to the vessel before anyone had disembarked and said to Reznik, "Any problems?"

"No, not really. We thought the hurricane was going to hit us, but as you probably saw, it went southwest of us."

Captain Chet stepped off the boat and walked toward Marek and Reznik.

"This is the famous captain I told you about," said Reznik. "He had no problems getting us here, and we went through some pretty stormy seas."

Marek held out his hand and shook Captain Chet's. "Your fame precedes you. Thank you for your help. Here's your payment," he said as he handed him an envelope, "and we'll give you some more upon completion of your return voyage."

"Thank you, sir," said Captain Chet amicably. "And where might we be going?"

"We'll tell you that later when I've found out," replied Marek.

Just then Julene, Colorado, and Naieema came on deck, followed by Nadav, and walked out on the pier toward Marek.

"Michael! What the fuck?" screamed Julene. "Why have you brought us here? Why did you kidnap us? And where the hell are we? I feel like I'm in some horror movie. Bats. A woman somebody murdered back there in the mangroves. And these cretins pointing guns at us the whole way. What…?"

"Julene," said Marek, "Shut the fuck up and do as you're told. And by the way, you might as well know now, my real name isn't Michael, it's Marek."

Marek said to Nadav: "Take them all to the holding cell and give them a good meal and let them take showers."

Julene started screaming at Marek again so he smacked her hard across the face with his open hand. "I said shut the fuck up! Now follow Nadav and don't say another word."

The three women were paraded down the pier and along a path to a small cavern with a door made of steel bars so they could not escape. Julene was crying and holding her cheek where Marek had slapped her while the other women followed along in stunned silence.

Captain Chet put the money in his back pocket and for the first time wondered if he was going to make it out of this mountain alive. He didn't know, but he had suspected that he was part of some kidnapping enterprise. He'd dealt with evil men before and he knew when to keep his mouth shut. He'd have to escape this thing as soon as he could without getting shot.

* * *

Inside the cavern, where Julene and the other women now found themselves, they all stood there stunned, soaking in the reality that they were no longer captive on a luxurious yacht, but in a dark, dingy jail with nothing but five cots with blankets and pillows, but at least a private room for a bathroom with a shower. Each of the women sat on a cot they felt comfortable at and said nothing for a long spell while the enormity of their new life sank in.

Finally, Colorado said, "We know our ransom has been paid in jewelry, so why haven't they released us? Do you think they're going to kill us anyway?"

"Unlike you girls," said Naieema, "so far as I know, nobody asked for or paid any ransom in jewels or money for me, so I don't know why they took me. I'm not even beautiful, or talented like you. What good am I to them as a hostage if I don't have any money and no rich husband? That's what I don't get."

Nobody could answer that question, and they all descended back into their gloom.

Finally, Julene spoke up. "Well, I know the asshole who slapped me. When we first started dating he told me his name was Michael Fieldstone. Now he says his name is Marek, or something like that. He let me stay in his condo in Fort Lauderdale and I was his sex partner whenever he came into town, but he never really told me exactly what he did—he would just say 'international trade,' and I never went anywhere with him when he was doing his work. We'd go to boat races and parties when he was in town and I'd be there for sex—all kinds of sex parties, you name it, but I never knew and still don't know what he does for a living."

They fell silent for a moment, then Colorado said, "Well, we may not all have a lot of money…"

"Shit," said Julene quietly, "I ain't got any."

"…but one thing we all do have in common, you've got to admit, is we're all pretty attractive and in pretty good shape, and that includes you, Naieema. We take good care of ourselves."

"Thank God for that."

"So, what does that mean for us?"

"Well," said Naieema, "If we were all even moderately attractive, and nobody was asked to pay ransom, and we were young, this operation would smack of a classic human trafficking operation."

"Oh no."

"They wouldn't…"

"I'm just saying," she continued, "that's what it looks like."

"How in the hell would they expect to get away with trafficking a famous country western music star? That would never work."

Just then they heard the sound of men approaching their jail cell.

Reznik stuck the key into the lock of the iron-gated door, unlocked and swung the door open and said, "Make room for company, ladies."

A young woman was thrust into the middle of the room so quickly that her hair covered her face as she stumbled forward.

The new young woman flipped her hair back with both hands and screamed, "You bastards!"

The room became dead silent, then everybody gasped in unison with the recognition of who she was.

"Oh my God!" exclaimed Naieema. "It's the President's daughter, Charise Pearl!"

* * *

Charise turned back toward her abductors as she screamed through the jail cell bars, "Don't you know who I am you stupid bastards? The whole might of the United States military and intelligence services is going to find me and rescue me and you will all go to prison or be killed!"

The guards walked away saying nothing, save the one who stood outside the jail as guard. "Shut your trap," he said quietly.

The women surrounded her and hugged her. "Hang in there," they said. "Be strong."

Privately, they all felt more assured of their safety. Surely help would now be on the way.

"How did you get here?" said Colorado.

"I was unconscious most of the time," Charise said, "but not the last twenty-four hours or so. I was in a small submarine that finally surfaced inside this cave just a little while ago. I don't remember getting on to the sub, and I have no idea where we are."

"We're somewhere in the Caribbean, is all I can figure," said Naieema. "We headed east out of Fort Lauderdale a few days ago, but they knocked us out with something in our food or drink, and I really don't know how much time has passed."

"Why are we here?" asked Charise.

"We don't know yet."

"Okay, you know who I am," said Charise, "but we're all important to somebody, so we're all going to get out of here together."

Somehow, instinctively, the ladies had left open the best cot in the room. Charise put what few things she had on the cot and continued.

"We have to agree that we're all in together, or nothing. We all go together, no matter what," said Charise.

The ladies all nodded eagerly.

"Good, now how the fuck do we get out of here?"

Despite their predicament, they laughed uproariously—the tension had been released.

The guard peeked into the cell from outside to see what was so damn funny, but then turned away and spit.

With the slight privacy they thought they might enjoy in the cell, they asked Charise how she got there—how did she arrive?

"I woke up in almost complete blackness except for some blue and green LED lights up on the dashboard of some machine I happened to be on. It was a damn submarine! I mean I was tied up, but I saw in front of me this big windshield and fish swimming by! There were big headlights off to the side so we could see better where we were going, but I didn't see anything until about twenty minutes before we left the water. We came up just a short way from here, judging by the short walk. It was like a huge jacuzzi surrounded by a cavern with lights all around it. There was a dock there and they tied up, then they brought me straight over here."

"So, you were at the same level in the cavern as us?"

"Yes."

"Well, we came in by yacht, and it's got plenty of room for us to leave in."

"Or, the submarine."

"Are you shittin' me?" said Julene. "Who's going to drive that damn thing?"

The question hung in the air for a moment.

"Me, I guess?" said Charise.

Chapter Twenty-Seven
Nice Guys

Sali snuck up so quietly behind Jason, who was stealthily watching the guard on the pier where the *Garnet Lady* was tied up, that Jason didn't even hear him.

"Been getting any lately?" Sali whispered just inches from his ear.

Jason flattened himself immediately against the rock wall of the cave and whispered hoarsely, "Jesus Sali, I wish you wouldn't do that! You scared the shit out of me! It's embarrassing, considering I'm part Apache."

"What's happening?" replied Sali.

"There are three captive women, including Julene and the redhead, Colorado. The other one is small, younger looking. I couldn't hear their conversation, but there was one guy apparently in charge who was Julene's boyfriend, or ex-boyfriend, whatever. She was yelling something at him until he slapped her and said something to our guy Bluto—Reznik—who led them all off the pier and through that entrance to that cavern." Jason pointed it out. "The captain went back aboard the boat and belowdecks. Since then, it's just been that one guy on the pier."

They both looked at the guard on the pier who was smoking a cigarette and gazing in the other direction.

"I haven't seen any other movement on the boat," said Jason. "I don't know if there's anybody else besides the captain left onboard."

"So, what's the plan?"

"I don't see any cameras. These have got to be the same guys that tried to kill us back in Fort Lauderdale, so let's not play nice, and let's be very quiet. Let's take this guy out with no gunfire, then explore wherever that cavern goes. Let's swim up to that diving platform off the stern. Get your knife ready to stick him, and I'll be ready to shoot him if I have to, but I'd rather not make any noise or the whole group of assholes will come running. If you get him,

I'll sneak onboard and see if anybody is still in the boat. If you don't, shit, I don't know, I guess I'll have to shoot him after all. If anybody's onboard, we'll try to get information off them, or kill them if we have to. We'll see what we can find out when we get on the boat."

"Okay, let's do it," said Sali, then they both entered the water silently and swam breaststroke to the transom platform at the stern of the *Garnet Lady*.

The guard continued smoking, apparently lost in thought.

Jason pointed his Mark 23 at the guard steadily while Sali silently climbed onto the transom. Sali pulled his combat knife from its sheath and began to very slowly and quietly creep toward the guard.

The guard finished his cigarette and turned to flick it into the water. Just then he saw Sali and reached to grab his Uzi at the same instant Sali ran quickly toward him.

Sali reached him an instant before the guard could get his finger to the trigger and stabbed him straight up from under the chin and into the brain to keep him from yelling any warning. They fell backward but all the guard could do was stare violently at Sali as he stabbed him a second time in the heart. He retrieved the guard's gun and radio, then lowered the body over into the water so as not to make a splash.

Jason watched; his gun now trained on the entrance to the cavern.

When Sali was done, he ran quietly over to Jason, placed the guard's gun and radio quietly on the transom, then both turned to enter the boat from the stern. Jason held up his index finger to his lips to indicate silence. After about a minute, they moved toward the wheelhouse.

Jason stepped quietly down the companionway stairs leading to the main cabin and first noticed the legs of a man stretched out from a seat on to a low table in the main cabin. The man had not heard them enter the boat and was sound asleep, judging by the snore. Jason looked quickly around to see if there were others then motioned Sali past him to check out the remainder of the boat.

Sali, gun drawn, quietly returned as Jason continued to hold his gun on the captain, then shook his head to indicate nobody else was onboard. Jason pointed at Sali's knife and gave him the "give it to me" signal, which Sali did. Jason holstered his gun, then leaned over to the captain, pointing his knife at the captain's throat.

"Hey," said Jason to the captain.

No response.

"Hey," Jason said again, this time a little louder, and this time he tapped him on the shoulder.

The captain awoke out of a deep sleep to see the knife inches from his face, and quickly sat up straighter and looked beyond Jason to see Sali pointing his gun right at him.

"One word," whispered Jason, "and I slit your throat. Do you understand?"

Sweat immediately broke out on Captain Chet's forehead and he slowly raised his hands above his head. "Yes! Yes! Please don't hurt me. I'm just the captain." Then it dawned on him. "Oh my God! You're the guys from the bar at Lyford's!"

"Shhh. Keep your voice down. I'm going to ask you some questions. If I think you're lying, I'm going to quietly kill you and throw you overboard. Do you understand?"

"Yes! Yes! Please don't hurt me! I have a family!"

"Keep your voice down! Just answer my questions and we won't hurt you or your family."

The captain nodded and kept his hands raised.

"Okay, put your hands down. First question. What's your name?"

"Chester Edwards. They call me Captain Chet."

"Who are those guys you're traveling with?"

"I don't know them. They hired me in the Berry Islands."

"Why you?"

"Because I'm a very experienced captain and I know these waters. Been all around the Caribbean all my life. Everybody knows me. I've piloted everything from an inner tube to a cargo freighter."

"Who are the women?"

"I don't know. They were onboard already when I took over, and they've mostly been locked in their rooms. They don't even get much of a chance to talk to each other."

"Where are the men from?"

"They didn't say. They haven't said much of anything except in some kind of middle eastern sounding language. They know English well enough, though. They talk to me about the route we've been taking—stuff like that."

"Didn't you suspect kidnapping with all those guns and the women trapped in their rooms? In fact, this is obviously human trafficking somehow, and you're part of it. Did you know all of this before you took the job?"

"No! I swear! They misled me. They said they were going to a vacation spot in the windward islands with hookers, but I recognized one of them, that country western singer Colorado Jacquette, and I knew she was married to another country singer, but I kept my mouth shut. But that's when I knew their story was bogus and I started asking questions, but they told me to mind my own business, and that I was getting paid a lot of money and to keep my mouth shut."

"How much are they paying you?"

"Two hundred fifty thousand. Half at the start, half when done. Trip is to last one month."

"That's a hell of a lot of money for a boat ride around the Caribbean. Did it occur to you that they just might shoot you dead when you got here?"

The captain gulped. "Yes, but that was a lot of money and I needed it for my family."

"Have you been to this place before?"

"Never, except to pass by it. I had no idea about the caves, the river and all this. I don't think anybody knows about this, or at least I've never heard mention of it."

"Do you know what they plan to do with the women?"

"No. Just guessing they're going to be asking for ransom money."

"Do you know what their plan is after this stop?"

"Absolutely no clue."

"What's the range on this when the tank is full?"

"About five hundred nautical miles."

"What are you supposed to be doing right now?"

"I wait for the guard on the dock to tell me to get the boat ready to move."

"That guard won't be telling you anything. He's dead."

The captain gulped. "Well, I guess the others will be coming for him sooner or later then."

"Does your VHF radio work?"

"Not inside this mountain. Same with the cell phones. But I'm guessing the guy they met here is the guy they were talking to on the way over, so they must have a transmitter here somewhere outside the mountain."

"So, you don't know what's at the end of this dock, or where they took those women?"

"No sir. No idea whatsoever."

"You realize that if you're lying to me, you're dead, or you spend the rest of your life in prison."

"I'll take your word for it. I swear I haven't told you a single lie."

"Okay, listen, when they come back they'll be looking for the guard. Just tell them you've been sleeping and you don't have any idea where he went."

"Oh, man, what if they don't believe me?"

"We'll be watching. Don't worry."

"Shit. I knew this job was too good to be true."

Chapter Twenty-Eight
Wired to Blow

In the North Atlantic the superyacht *Turquoise Lament* was beginning to encounter very large seas forming as a result of yet another tropical storm brewing off the west coast of Africa, just days after the storm that tossed the *Garnet Lady* around like a floaty toy in a bathtub. This ship, however, plunged through the tremendous waves far more easily than any other yacht might have, due to its streamline shape, as well as its large size and weight. The *Turquoise Lament* had traveled in all the major oceans and through the roughest seas at the direction of the cold and ruthless Captain Andrei Yahontov, who was captain for the yacht's owner, Kostya Chugunkin, and who knew the proper passages for navigation the world over. He was fearless and calm because he had been through the worst of rough seas, as well as served in combat in the Balkan wars of the nineties. He was a captain of extreme skill, but also of a mercenary drive to accomplish the task before him: deliver a cargo of beautiful women from Ukraine destined for human trafficking in Mexico, Colombia, Venezuela, and the United States through their partner Zoran Marek. Together, Kostya Chugunkin, Andrei Yahontov, and Zoran Marek were purveyors of sexual servitude, enslavement and misery, an illegal business that is the fastest growing and second (after drugs) or third (after counterfeiting) largest criminal industry in the world.

"The storm helps to cover our tracks," Captain Yahontov said to Kostya, though transponders on the ship, required by international law, would register his passage if he had decided to keep them turned on, which he now decided not to do.

"Turn the transponders off for now," he ordered his second mate. "They won't know where we are or where we've been until we cruise near Saba."

Mountainous seas blocked what little moonlight marked the horizon as they plunged headlong toward the island. The air was mixed with the froth of ocean spray as the helmsman nevertheless steered the ship toward their destination, his eyes focused acutely on the seas and the horizon in front of him. At his side, the captain ordered his first mate to go below and check on their cargo.

"Aye aye, captain," the first mate replied, and followed the passageway down two decks to their ostensible cargo.

The first mate opened up the watertight door into the corridor for the "cargo," and walked in. Before him was a long corridor with cabins on either side so that each had a porthole overlooking the ocean. The first mate knocked on each door, then unlocked it to see how the prisoners were doing, and to inform them that dinner would soon be served, if they could even eat in such seas.

"When do we get to America?" said Nostya.

"Soon," he replied "Just rest until we get through this stormy weather. Dinner will be served soon, if you can eat."

"Why can't we go beyond this deck?"

"It would be unsafe," he said. He closed and locked the door.

He went to each room and answered most of their questions with non-answers: replies which really told them nothing new.

When he returned to the bridge, he told the captain that the cook was almost finished and that their dinners would be served soon.

The captain said, "We'll soon be at the rendezvous site. Call Marek when we get in range and tell him we'll be there by morning."

"Will do."

Kostya turned to Captain Yahontov as the second mate left the cabin. "You will remember that just before we left The Canaries that we brought on board a large orange crate. I want you and your men to open the crate and remove the contents. It's C4 wiring and fuses. Since you're the demolition expert, I want you to wire the entire hull so that if we get visited by the authorities, we can escape on a tender and blow the whole ship by radio control so the boat sinks rapidly and we leave no evidence."

The first mate knew what that meant: all souls still onboard would go down with the ship within minutes. He looked into the captain's eyes.

"Would you rather spend the rest of our life in Guantanamo?" said Kostya.

"Yes sir, I'll get right on it."

"Naturally I'd rather see this all go smoothly and we all get paid by Marek, but just in case something goes wrong we'll meet him over about three thousand feet of water. Not only am I thinking of the authorities, but in case Marek tries any kind of double-cross, he doesn't get his girls."

Chapter Twenty-Nine
Interrogation

Within minutes Jason and Sali heard someone coming to check on the guard.

"Vlad!" The voice was still far down a side cavern leading to the boat dock. He repeated it, only louder: "Hey, Vlad!"

Inside the yacht Jason whispered to the captain, "Remember, don't say anything. Let him come on the boat to find you asleep."

Soon they could hear the footsteps of the guard walking down the pier, this time saying the name in a normal, but insistent voice, "Vlad."

All three men could feel the yacht roll very slightly as the man stepped aboard and walked down the companionway to the galley, where the guard saw the captain turned on his side on the couch, apparently sleeping.

Sali came from behind him and stuck his gun in the man's back just as Jason stepped out of the head and pointed his gun at the man and said calmly, "Drop the gun and don't say a word or you're dead."

The man did as he was told, and the captain returned to a sitting position. "I didn't have anything to do with this," he said to the guard.

Sali pushed the man forward. "Sit," he commanded the guard, after which he tied him up.

"What do you want?" said the guard. "You'll never get out of here alive."

"Where are the women you brought here?" said Jason.

The man didn't say anything, then Sali slapped him on the top of his head with his gun.

The guard screamed. "Ow! Shit, that hurt!"

"Of course it did. Talk."

"Follow the dock to the tunnel," the man grumbled, as he rubbed the top of his head to ease the pain, "then keep walking until you see them in a holding cell on the right."

"Is there another way out of here?"

"You could keep going straight down this creek instead of turning around. Eventually you'll get back to the ocean."

"How many of your guys are here?"

The man didn't speak. Sali cracked him on the head again with his Mark 23. "The man's asking you a question, asshole."

"You bastard, I'll get you for that."

"Keep talking."

"I'm guessing about a dozen. I don't know them all."

"What were you planning on doing with the women?"

"You'd have to ask the boss man—I just follow orders."

"So, who's the boss man?"

"His name is Marek, and it doesn't matter that you know that, 'cause you're never leaving here alive."

"You said that already," said Sali.

"So, what does this guy Marek intend to do with the women," asked Jason.

"I don't know. All I know is that we delivered a shitload of jewels to him along with the women. I caught a glimpse of them when Reznik opened the box to put some more in after we got the latest women."

"Who's Reznik?"

"He's Marek's number one man, his half-brother."

"Did all those jewels belong to the kidnapped women?"

"Well, that's the crazy part," said the guard, as though he was in a dinner table conversation. "Those jewels were supposed to be the ransom payment, but instead, Reznik took the jewels, kept the women, then left. I don't know why he didn't just kill the husbands or boyfriends. He just said, 'Don't worry, we'll be in touch and you can have your wench back.'"

Sali said, "Maybe he was planning on using them as hostages until he got away from the exchange spot."

"Who fucking knows…"

"What did Reznik do with all the jewels he got for the ransom payments?" said Jason.

"He gave them to Marek when we got here. Marek said he was going to put them in the safe with the others. Marek must have so many by now he's got millions in jewels in that safe, wherever it is. At least that's my guess, unless he's sending them somewhere or buying something with them."

Jason and Sali looked briefly at each other as though they couldn't believe what they just heard.

"How many of these kidnapping trips have you been on with Reznik if you know so much about the jewels?"

The guard looked up at him and then resigned himself to his fate. "About a dozen, mostly in Colombia, Venezuela, Haiti and Brazil. This is the first Stateside snatch, so to speak." He chuckled at his wit, but Sali slapped him on the head again.

"You're a fuckin' riot. Cut with the comedy. Go on."

"Word gets around among the crew about the jewels, but we rarely see the exchange, and nobody knows where his safe is. Hey, I've told you guys all this shit, I hope you'll go easier on me if we get arrested."

"When you get arrested," said Jason, then he nodded at Sali, and Sali hit the man in the head again, just behind the ear, at just the right place to knock him out immediately.

"Tie him up and gag him and stash him below. He may be useful."

* * *

They tied both of the guard's hands onto one of the forward bunks allowing him only very limited movement, taped his mouth shut, then returned to the galley where the captain dutifully sat without moving.

"I guess we're going to have to find the women ourselves," said Jason.

"Or, if Masen got word to Jamie maybe the cavalry is on the way," said Sali.

"They seemed to be in a hurry," said the captain. "I think I know which one is Marek, and I heard him say: 'Hurry up, we haven't got much time.'"

Jason thought for a moment, then said, "Let's go follow that tunnel and see if we can find them. Sali, tie the captain up, too, so it looks good and he can deny everything if he's caught, and also so he doesn't take off on us."

Jason turned to the captain: "Captain, if you take off or say anything to them, I will hunt you down and find you, and it won't be a pretty sight when I do."

"Shit," said the captain as Sali began tying him up. "Remind me to have my head examined after this is all over. Don't worry—I'm not saying anything."

"I'm counting on your knowledge to get us out of here, so keep your cool, do you understand?"

"Aye, aye," said Captain Chet, ruefully. "Indeed, I do."

After the captain had been tied up, Jason and Sali moved up to the main deck to discuss their next moves.

Chapter Thirty
A Knave's Ransom

Sali left Jason, the captain and the captured guard on the *Garnet Lady* and took his radio with him. He remembered that it had taken them about an hour from the mouth of the cave to the dock inside Rubicon Mountain where Jason awaited his return, so he knew he had a ways to go before sundown which would make the return all that more difficult, since there would be no more daylight coming through the ceiling of the cave's holes. His return trip, though, was much quicker than he thought it would be and soon he was at the mouth of the cave where, after carefully reconnoitering the scene and finding no bad guys on alert, he called Masen.

"Booty Man, this is Stinkfinger, come in."

"Stinkfinger!" responded Masen gleefully "Glad to hear you're still with us. What's the latest?"

"I'll fill you in completely, but since our fearless leader is still in there, can you come pick me up at the mouth of the cave so I don't have to use the Zodiac?"

Masen looked at the skies above and surveyed all around the boat, and replied, "Roger, that. Looks safe. I'll get there as soon as I can, over and out."

Sali rang off and took another close look at all the mangroves around him and muttered to himself, "If I'm not sucked dry by the mosquitoes by then."

* * *

Masen reeled in the two fishing lines he had off the stern, then started the engine and left it in neutral. He scurried forward to raise the bow anchor, then aft to raise the stern anchor, then he ran back to the wheel and he was off.

The puttering of the diesel soon picked up its cadence as Masen put the gear shift in forward, opened the throttle and aimed back to the obscure entrance to the mangroves.

Thirty minutes later he saw Sali waving at him as he steered toward the entrance to the cave. He maneuvered close to the rock in front of the cave, then turned to come abreast of it so Sali could jump aboard.

Sali jumped in, then Masen quickly swung the boat around to head back through the Mangroves. Sali walked back to the stern where Masen was steering and shook his hand.

"Everything okay?" said Sali.

"All good by me, how about you?"

"Yeah, I'm okay. How're we doing?"

"All good. I called Jamie and told her what we knew and she said she'd try and get some help. She said the President's daughter has been kidnapped, so everybody's scrambling trying to find her. She said she'd do what she could. So, what happened to Jason?"

They broke through the mangroves and headed back out onto the ocean. Sali asked for the sat-phone to call Jamie, and said, "Both of you'll find out at the same time."

Sali dialed the phone. "Jamie, this is Sali. Listen up."

Masen eased up on the throttle as they reached the mangroves.

"So, I guess Masen told you about the cave and how and where we split up. Jason and I followed upstream and we came across the Garnet Lady tied up at a pier. We captured the captain and a guard without the others knowing, but all total we originally saw six guards on the dock, but there might be as many as two dozen or more inside the mountain. The captain will do what we say. My take is that he was just a chartered captain and doesn't really know much of what's going on. The guard didn't want to talk but I used a little persuasion. He was on the boat when it came in and said they took the women to a cell further inside the cave. I don't know who the women were except the two we saw before—Julene and Colorado—plus a younger, shorter woman."

"Well that lets out the President's daughter—I was beginning to wonder."

Sali looked over at Masen as he continued to talk to Jamie. "Oh yeah," he said, "the guard said that the kidnappers kept all the jewels paid as ransom for the women. He said they had told the husbands they'll give their wives back, but they needed to keep them a little longer to help them for safe passage. In other words, it was a double-cross, if you ask me. They never intended to give the women back and they kept the jewels."

Masen was totally transfixed by the mention of the word "jewels," but kept a keen eye while steering through the mangroves as the sun dropped further on the horizon.

On the other end of the line Jamie said, "So, they've kidnapped four American citizens, including Amber, whom they damn near murdered at the Boatyard, and they've got a small army protecting them, and at least one of the women that we know of is a world-famous country western singer. Have I got that right?"

"Pretty much, except there's one more little detail."

"Little detail?"

"Yeah, the guard said the box of jewels that Masen saw is nothing compared to what the head guy has. His name is Marek and he has a safe full of jewels. The guard said the stash is worth millions."

Masen's eyes swelled as he held his mouth agape.

Jamie said, "Did you say millions?"

"Millions," repeated Sali, as he stared back at Masen, "Or more. And I think I know just the guy who can steal them back, no matter how much it is."

"Oh, my," said Jamie. "Oh my goodness. Well, look, forget the jewels for now. I'm going to try and get a rescue team to meet you and go in there, even though Saba belongs to the Netherlands. That could be complicated, if Dark Island is part of Saba territory. I can't find the damn place on the map."

"Well, Jamie, I can't just leave Jason in there. I'm going to have to go back in there and tell Jason what's going on so he doesn't try to capture the whole group or something dumb."

"Okay, go in there and bring him out if you can and wait for the SEALS or the Rangers. If I can't get them, I'll get somebody."

"Yes, ma'am, over and out."

Click.

"Bullshit," said Sali. "We're not going to wait on the SEALs, or the Rangers, or the Second Battalion of the Fifth Marines. I know any of them will get here fast, but things are moving inside that mountain and if we can get those women out now, I think we should."

"I'm going in with you. I want a shot at cracking that safe."

"If we can find it. If we get that close to the safe, we might be dead." Sali stopped and looked back out over the ocean. "Masen, on second thought, nobody figured you'd get this deep in shit with us. Maybe you'd better stay with the boat and wait for Jason and me, and hopefully the women, and then we can talk about it."

"My ass in your face! I'm going in with you!"

Sali could only slowly shake his head as he faced reality. He knew Masen was the perfect man to get the loot away from Marek, as well as the only soul available to help him get Jason out. "You dumb shit. Okay, let's move."

Chapter Thirty-One
Ticket to Ride

The minute Sali had taken off from the *Garnet Lady* to go see Masen, Jason got restless. He couldn't just sit there and wait for Sali, he had to find the women and see if he could get them out, or he had to go deeper inside and capture Marek to stand trial for human trafficking, as well as the others, but he couldn't do it all by himself. At least he could reconnoiter and find out where they were being held. The guard had said they were just a little way down the corridor and on the right.

He double-checked that the captain and the guard were tied tight, then took off. He jumped off the boat, softly as a cheetah, and ran down the deck to the end. He stopped for a moment to listen, but heard nothing. He squatted low with his Mark 23 ready and proceeded to walk toward the tunnel.

The tunnel was easily high and wide enough that two people could walk through it. Jason began walking quietly down the tunnel which was only dimly lit. Just twenty yards down the tunnel, Jason came across the cell on the right, where the women had been held, but the door to the cell was wide open and there was nobody inside. He looked around in the cell and found an almost empty vial of lipstick and a hairbrush. This was the right place.

"They've taken them somewhere," he mumbled under his breath, then hastily left the cell and turned right heading farther into the middle of Rubicon Mountain.

It wasn't but a minute or two before he could hear one of the guards talking on a radio. Jason eased forward carefully and saw him looking the other way. He holstered his Mark 23 and removed his knife. He waited for the guard to finish his radio transmission, then ran as fast and as quietly as he could up to the guard, stabbed him from the back at the base of the skull and up into his brain, freezing and killing the man instantly while he held him up with his left arm. He dragged the man back to the cell where the women had been held captive, then shoved him into the shower stall. He searched his pockets and retrieved a set of keys, then went back to where he had encountered the guard.

Only forty yards more down the tunnel he heard a sound that froze him and made the hair on the back of his neck stand up. The sound was a multitude of kids—children crying and wailing and murmuring to themselves. As Jason walked up to gaze upon them, they each became quiet and looked up at him, no doubt wondering who this new man was and what his intentions were.

Jason was awestruck. He squatted down and said very quietly, "Do any of you speak English?"

A tall girl, maybe fourteen or fifteen, stepped forward and said with a heavy Cuban accent, "I do. I speak English. I learned it in school. I got all A's."

"What is your name, sweetheart?" said Jason.

"Maria."

Jason took the keys he had retrieved from the guard and held them up for Maria to see.

"Now listen carefully. I'm going to open this door, then I want you all to be as quiet as you possibly can, and follow me. Tell them."

Jason waited while she translated his instructions, and she noticed that others had translated what she said into other languages.

"Okay, here we go," he said very quietly. "Be very, very quiet and follow me." He looked around, listening intently.

He opened up the cell, then motioned for them to follow him, holding his finger to his lips to make sure they were completely silent. He walked them all back to the dock where the *Garnet Lady* was tied up, then stopped and waited for all the kids to finally arrive on the dock.

Jason turned to the young translator. "Okay, Maria, this is very important. I'm going to give you my radio."

He handed her the radio and briefly showed her how to operate it. "Do you understand?"

"Yes," she replied, nodding her head in the affirmative.

"Okay, good. Now I want you to have all your friends here follow that river bank on foot," he said pointing to the little river in which they came, and using the walking motion with his fingers, "until you leave this cave. As soon as you get to the beginning of the cave you will see a lake and some mangroves. When you get there, I want you to turn on the radio like this…" He showed her the on-button and how to push the Send button to talk. "Send a message to my friend who is outside the cave. His name is Sali. I want you to say, 'Sali, Jason asked me to call you. My name is Maria and I have a lot of kids with me. Please use your boat to pick us up, then come meet Jason. Please hurry.' Okay, now repeat that to me."

She hesitated. "I can't remember all of that."

"Well you get the idea right? My name is Jason. Jason. Ask for Sali and tell him to come get you. Try it again."

Maria repeated a couple of times to Jason until she got it close enough.

Jason continued as he looked back from where they had come, hoping none of the scumbags would show up. "Good girl. Now ask your friends if they know how to drive a sailboat with a diesel engine."

Maria did as she was asked, and two elder teenage boys raised their hands.

"Be sure to point those two boys out when my friend Sali picks you up, okay?"

She nodded her head enthusiastically and said, "Yes, I will."

"Okay, then," he said, "let's get started!" He pointed toward the direction of the little river. "Go!" He whispered loudly after them: "Be careful! And hurry!"

* * *

The liberated kids exited the cave an hour later as the day was nearing dusk and they could see the *Booty* as it was approaching them. Maria turned on the radio and called Sali as instructed.

Sali and Masen both heard the call from the children. Sali raised the field glasses as they neared the big rock in front of the cave. Sure enough, the bank was lined with a bunch of kids, mostly young girls, teens and pre-teens.

"Holy shit," said Sali. He answered the radio: "This is Sali. Raise your hand and wave."

Maria did so.

"Holy crap," said Masen. "Now what are we going to do?"

"Go pick them up like Jason says, I guess."

Masen pulled up to the mouth of the cave.

"Are you Maria?" asked Sali.

"Yes," she replied.

"What are all of you doing here?"

"We've been taken against our will. We think they intend to make us into sex slaves."

Sali turned to Masen. "Oh my God, a full-blown human trafficking operation, including kids. It's not just the three women."

Maria said, "Your friend Jason told me to tell you that these two boys know how to pilot your boat." She pointed out the two teenage boys. "He wants you to let the boys—he is Jaimito and he is Julio—use the boat to take us away from here, then you go join Jason inside the cave. Jaimito also speaks English."

The two young boys held up their hands and Maria motioned them to step forward.

"Jesus, Sali," said Masen, "am I supposed to just hand over my boat to all these kids?"

"Well, look at it this way, Masen. Do you want a safe full of jewels worth millions, or do you want to keep the boat and strand these kids on this island with a bunch of human traffickers?"

"Or do I want to live or die trying to even find the safe, and then crack it? And even if I do find all the jewels, am I supposed to give them back?"

Sali thought for a moment. "Hell, I won't tell anybody if you don't."

Masen looked at all the children, who had obviously been mistreated and were scared as hell, staring back at him with big fearful eyes while Sali stood quietly waiting for Masen's answer.

"Ah hell," he finally said and waved the kids aboard. "Come aboard, kids. I never could resist a locked safe anyway."

The kids cheered loudly and clambered aboard while some hugged Masen and Sali as they came aboard.

"Okay, okay," said Masen, then spoke to the boys through Maria's translations. "Let me show you how to run this thing, then I want you to go back through the mangroves, over there—you'll see the entrance—then when you get back out in the ocean, I want you to go east to the port at Basseterre in St. Kitts & Nevis, which you'll probably see on the horizon before too long."

After Maria translated, the boys got busy exploring the boat and making ready to leave. Masen explained to the boys about the C-4 in the mangroves and how to disarm it if they had to.

"Okay, just hold on a second," said Sali to Maria. "We're going to grab a few things then get off the boat to go meet Jason." Sali went into the cabin and grabbed extra ammunition, two Mark 23s, the sat-phone, and the radio Jason had given Maria. They now had all three radios.

"He said he'd wait for two hours," said Maria, "and if you're not there by then, he'll move along without you."

"How long ago did he say that."

"Ummm…" she looked down as she guessed. "Maybe an hour ago?"

"Okay, then, let's get moving, Masen. You got your second-floor robbery shoes?"

"Very funny. Hold on, I'll be right back." He went below and opened his secret safe and retrieved the stones he had stolen from Marek's condo back in Fort Lauderdale. He placed them in his backpack and went back up on deck. "Okay, let's go."

They both jumped out of the boat onto the shore and motioned the new young helmsman to pull away as the other boy coiled some line. They stood for just a few moments as they watched the *Booty* depart into the setting sun, then Sali called Jamie on the sat-phone.

"Jamie, Sali here. I have a surprise. Masen's boat, the Booty, is heading to Basseterre on St. Kitts with a boatload of trafficked teenagers that Jason somehow liberated, including a couple of kids from the States. I need you to have the proper authorities meet them there and take care of them, please. Masen and I are going back in to get Jason."

"Holy shit. Why didn't he come out with them?"

"I don't know, but probably to try and retrieve the three women."

"Masen, too? Who's driving the boat to Basseterre?"

"The teenagers."

"Oh my God! Okay, I'll get somebody to meet them. By the way, SEAL Team Five officials have been alerted and they are mustering as we speak."

"Well, that's good news, but we're not going to wait. We're going in now." Sali ended the transmission.

"Some of the kids are from the States?" said Masen? "I don't remember that."

"I made that part up so we'd be sure to get the SEALs and not some local wanna be cops fouling things up."

"Good move," said Masen, and started to move toward the cave entrance, but Sali said, "Wait a minute. What if the bad guys find out the kids have escaped and come after them in the Garnet Lady?"

Masen stopped and thought for a second. "Well, for one thing, if that happens soon, we're going to be caught right in the middle and in a world of shit."

"Let's get the Zodiac out of the mangroves and go back and set the tripwire on the C4. Even if they get us, they'll get blown to bits if they go after the kids."

"Sold."

A half hour later they were in the Zodiac and heading toward where they had earlier stashed the C4 and tripwire. Instead of setting it so they could trip it with the boat hook, they set it so that anybody crossing the watery passage would get blown to bits.

As Sali finished setting the tripwire across the waterway to the outside ocean, he said, "I just hope nobody else comes through here. We have to remember to fix this later when we get the chance, I mean if it doesn't blow." "If we get the chance," said Masen. "Now let's get the hell out of here. We can stash the Zodiac where it was before, just in case."

Chapter Thirty-Two
Blue Lagoon

Jason had just seen the last of the kids make their way down the shoreline and toward the mouth of the cave on their way to meet Sali and Masen. Now he had to go find Julene and the other ladies. He stepped aboard the *Garnet Lady* and inspected the bonds of the captain and the captured guard, then turned to go find the captured women.

He retraced the steps he had taken before when he killed the guard and found the trafficked kids. The light was still dim but bright enough for navigating the winding hallways. Trouble was, if he came across any of the hostiles, there were few places to hide.

After a short while he came across a faint glow from the tunnel beyond so he approached cautiously, keeping as low a profile as he could. He slowed his pace considerably, his ears straining for the smallest possible sound. Miraculously, he heard the sounds of bubbling water, and as he approached the lighted area, it became brighter until he came upon a great chamber within the cave which had a deep blue lagoon, lit from below with underwater lights about twenty feet down. He looked down into the deep blue pool and saw a submersible—it looked like one of those small research subs deployed from ships. He looked up and could see the crane that was used for pulling the sub out of the water as necessary, with a catwalk leading up to it. On the other side of the lagoon he could see there was a little shop with walls lined with tools next to it.

The little submarine surfaced and he could see a hatch opening for the inhabitants to exit.

He scurried quietly back the way he had come—he would await the arrival of Sali and Masen, if they were coming at all.

Sooner or later, somebody would miss the guard Jason had tied up and the one he had killed, and the one Sali had killed, or they were likely going to take off on the *Garnet Lady* again.

He had ten minutes before the time he had left word with Maria that he would meet Masen and Sali. He stepped lively in his return to the *Garnet Lady*.

Chapter Thirty-Three
Interrogation

Jason was waiting impatiently aboard the *Garnet Lady* for Sali and Masen, looking back and forth from the cabin where the captain and the guard were tied up, and back to where he and Sali had originally come. He had the guard's gun and his few extra magazines, as well as his own Mark 23 and knife.

The guard and the captain were just sitting immobile, waiting.

Jason heard a small splash, then looked over and saw Sali and Masen walking up the rocky shoreline, each with a Mark 23 and a sheath knife. Sali waved briefly and Jason waived impatiently for him to come ahead.

* * *

"Had to stop for coffee and donuts," Sali said, as he handed Jason's radio and sat-phone back to him. "Sorry we're a little late."

"Did you get the kids off safely?"

"Yes. That one kid I have a lot of confidence in," said Masen. "He seems to know what he's doing."

"What did Jamie say?"

"She said to go back outside and stay put and wait for the SEALs to arrive," said Sali.

"To hell with that," said Jason. "We're going in there and getting those women out."

"Hell, yeah. I want a shot at that safe full of jewels, too," said Masen.

"I walked a little way down the tunnel," said Jason, "and could see where the women were kept, but they've moved them somewhere. I walked a little further down and found a lagoon with a submersible in it. The hatch to the submersible was starting to open, so I left before they could see me. There was nobody else there."

Jason continued and described the chamber that held the lagoon, including a staircase that went up to another room.

"At the top of the stairs you could see the entrance to another tunnel. That has to be where they went."

"I wish I knew more about where that tunnel takes us," said Sali. "Maybe our guard friend knows."

"Never hurts to ask," said Masen.

The three of them stepped down into the cabin. Jason unwrapped the gag over the guard's mouth.

"Where does that tunnel above the lagoon lead?" said Jason.

"Why should I tell you anything?"

"Because my friend here likes to hurt bad guys. Tell us how this all works."

The guard scowled at Sali who was smiling broadly at him. Sali stepped forward and kicked him in the balls.

Shortly, the guard recovered. "The tunnel leads to many different rooms: barracks for the crew, the boss's private quarters and his office, and the telecommunications room."

"Is there any other way into those rooms?" said Jason.

The guard glanced at Sali, who was smiling, and thought a moment. He had apparently given up all resistance. "Well, yes, there is one way, but it's not easy. If you continue to follow this little river all the way down to where it meets the sea on the other side of the mountain, there's a small trail, right where the river meets the sea. It is hard to see at first, but it winds its way up to Marek's bedroom. His room has a short balcony, but it's hard to see from out in the ocean. The big window into his room doesn't even look like a window from the ocean, it just looks like a flattened part of the cliff. He likes to go out on his balcony and look out over the ocean."

"Why isn't it easy to get there?" said Jason.

"Well, for one thing, it's a very steep trail and there are parts of the trail that are difficult to cross. I tried it once."

Masen smiled. "Let me go," he said to Jason. "If it looks like I can get in without being discovered, I'll check it out then come back here and meet you, unless I meet you somewhere in the middle. And don't worry, I'll be extremely careful. After all, this is what I do best."

"Okay," said Jason, "but if you get in, see if you can find any sign of a telecommunications room."

"Where's the safe with the jewels?" Masen said to the guard.

"If you give me a cut, I'll tell you."

Sali said, "Yeah, let's give him a cut." He pulled his knife out of its sheath and cut him across the forehead. The guard screamed. "Hey, keep your voice down. I can give you a bigger cut, if you'd like, but I'll have to stick a rag in your hole."

Jason threw Sali a wet rag to wipe the blood off the guard's forehead. "Clean him up a little."

"Like I told you before, I've never seen the safe," the guard grumbled, "so it must be in his bedroom, because I've been all over this mountain except into his bedroom."

"Beautiful," said Masen, "I'm on my way."

"Wait. One thing you should know before you do that." The guard was being a little more cooperative, for some reason.

"Marek will soon be contacting a ship bringing in more cargo—probably women from Ukraine or Russia. They're due tonight. A boat brings them over from the ship during the night so nobody, including satellites, can see them. He has radar in the bedroom, too, so he can see when other boats and ships are in the area. We bring them in on that side of the island, so he'll probably be stepping out onto his balcony with his binoculars and looking for them."

Masen asked the guard, "Why does he ask for jewels instead of money for ransom?"

"Jewels are easier to smuggle across borders, and they don't show up as a currency or cryptocurrency exchange on the Internet. The Feds can track all of those cryptocurrencies now. But a lady with a beautiful diamond bracelet can walk through customs no questions asked, even if she declares a low value, so long as it's not ridiculously low. Marek pays the couriers in diamonds or gemstones, same as he pays us. None of us gets cold cash. How we fence it after that, we have to check through Marek before we do it. He's super cautious."

"How come he didn't return the women for the ransom jewels the husbands gave him?" asked Masen.

"Because he's greedy. It was a double-cross, pure and simple. He's already got a buyer for the women."

"A buyer?" said Jason. "What the hell?"

"I don't know what he's got in mind or who these other buyers are, I really don't."

Sali pulled his knife out of the sheath again.

"I swear!" the guard protested. "I have no idea what his plan is."

"Okay, one more thing," said Sali. "Where did they take the three women?"

"Four now," said the guard with a faint smile.

"Four? Who is this fourth woman?"

The guard chuckled and didn't say anything.

Sali retrieved some brass knuckles from his back pocket. "Been wanting to use these," he said, looking at Jason, then smashed the guard in the mouth. "You know, I really don't like your attitude."

The guard straightened up, his mouth bleeding badly. He spat out a tooth. "The President's daughter," he said.

Complete silence.

"Which President?" said Jason.

"Your President," said the guard, smiling, blood covering his teeth and running down the side of his mouth. "Charise Pearl."

Jason and Sali looked at each other. "Oh, fuck," said Sali.

"Oh, shit oh dear," said Jason.

"No pressure here," said Masen under his breath.

"I doubt the President knows she's here, or the place would be crawling with special forces," said Sali. "We're going to have to find her and rescue her ourselves."

"And the others, too," said Jason.

The guard scoffed. "You haven't got a chance. There are about a dozen of us all total."

"That's all?" said Sali.

"The more people you have, the greater the chance of loose lips. So long as we all know how to keep a secret, and get paid well, and the threat that we'll be killed slowly, and our family, too, if the word gets out, the safer this place will be from being discovered. Or at least that's how it was explained to us."

"So, if we fail, you're fucked," said Sali.

"Pretty much. That's why I'm telling you this stuff. I pray you catch him, now that I've told you all this, or he'll kill my whole family, and he'll do it slowly. I know him well enough to know that."

All was quiet for a moment, then Jason said, "Masen, take this idiot with you and tie him up to a tree or something when you get to the ocean. He may come in handy." He tossed him a short line of rope that was coiled by the table.

"Here," said Jason, "Take his gun. It's fully loaded."

"I'm gone," said Masen, kicking the guard to get moving.

* * *

"Let's get going," Jason said to Sali and Captain Chet.

"When I was in the blue lagoon area," said Jason, "I saw a staircase that led up the side of the wall to another tunnel that I could see was lit inside. I didn't see any other way in or out of there, except of course by the mini-sub. That tunnel has to be the passage to where they took the women."

Minutes later, as they approached the blue lagoon area Jason motioned for them to stop; he held his finger to his lips for silence. Around the corner in the tunnel they could hear the sounds of men working.

Jason stepped forward carefully until he could peek around the bend in the tunnel. He could see that the crane had moved the submarine out of the water and over to a working area that had a workbench with tools fastened to a pegboard on the wall. The miniature submarine was suspended over the working area and two men were working on the underside of the sub. Jason screwed on his Mark 23 suppressor, aimed carefully, and shot both of them in the head, leaving them no time to react. They collapsed in sudden death beneath the suspended sub.

"Jesus," said Captain Chet quietly.

"Get used to it, captain," said Jason. "I need you to get inside that sub and figure out how to use it. We may need it to get out of here."

The three men moved quickly to where the dead workmen lay below the sub and began taking stock of the tools and the bottom of the craft.

Jason looked to the top of the stairs that led to a tunnel at the top of the blue lagoon cavern. He spoke in a low voice to Sali, "Let's dump these guys in the lagoon, quietly." He turned to the captain. "Captain, get that bucket over there and wash down this blood."

"All right," said Jason after the deeds were done. "Let me go up first. Captain, you stay here and keep going over the sub until you know how it works."

"What happens if I get caught?"

"Tell them you got kicked off the boat when they took the kids, and you were trying to find a way out of here. Or fake it."

"Oh great. Thanks a lot."

"Hey, man," said Sali, "the President's daughter's life is at stake. Think positive."

Jason turned and moved up the stairs slowly and quietly, his gun pointed to the top of the stairs. Sali followed after he got to the top.

Captain Chet made himself busy studying the underside of the craft and attending to the crane to lower the sub into the water.

Chapter Thirty-Four
Celebrity Marketplace

Jason and Sali started up the steps slowly, crouching slightly, guns raised.

The corridor in the tunnel was a long one and inclined upward slightly; its walls were lit dimly.

Finally, they could hear voices ahead, men speaking casually. They crawled up to an overlook of the scene below. Marek was inspecting a large white screen, apparently just made from bedsheets or some other white material. Marek's bodyguard, Gorsh, was in back of him, fiddling with a digital camera on a tripod. To Marek's right was Reznik, standing in front of another hallway that led somewhere into a dark space behind him.

"Gorsh, is the camera ready?" said Marek.

"Almost ready," answered Gorsh as he finished his tinkering.

"Fine." He turned to Reznik. "Bring me the three women from Fort Lauderdale," Marek said to Reznik. "Just those three."

"You want Julene, too?" said Reznik, surprised.

"I said all three of them, didn't I?" Marek replied irritably.

Reznik just grinned, bowed slightly, then turned to go down the dark hallway.

Above all of them, Jason eased further forward to the edge of the top of the wall, barely peeking over the edge.

Marek was pacing back and forth. Gorsh, the cameraman, stood ready to film an area in front of the big white screen backdrop.

In the distance Jason could hear the women complaining as the voices got louder. Julene's was the loudest.

"Stop pushing me!" she complained. "I get the idea!"

Jason motioned Sali to crawl forward so he, too, could witness the scene. They inched forward and carefully looked down at the scene below them.

Sali touched Jason on the shoulder to get his attention, then pointed to Jason's right. The short ledge that they were on led to steps which led downward to the video room below. The video room was otherwise four straight walls leading up to the rocky roof about twenty feet above them.

Seconds later a queue of the three women from Fort Lauderdale, all with their hands tied behind their backs, came into the room, Julene bringing up the rear.

"All right," said Marek, "line up along the screen in front of the camera."

"You bastard, Michael!" shouted Julene.

"I told you, it's Marek. Now shut up and line up."

Marek waited for the women to line up, then positioned himself off to one side, facing the camera. There was nothing Jason and Sali could do but watch for now. Gorsh arranged a few cables and checked the positioning and focus of the camera, then finally stopped and waited for Marek's word.

"Okay," said Marek, "Let's get started."

Gorsh moved the camera to point at Marek.

"Greetings, Kostya, my friend," began Marek. "As promised, I'm delivering to you some remarkable assets. But first let me show you a special one—my own former bitch, Julene."

The camera moved to show the three women standing and looking at the camera or at Marek.

"Julene is the best-looking woman I've ever had the pleasure of enjoying, although she's a bit feisty today."

"Fuck you, Michael, or Marek, or whatever the fuck your name is," shouted Julene to Marek.

"Gorsh," Marek said to the cameraman, "show the gentleman her magnificent assets."

"With pleasure," said Gorsh. He walked up behind her and yanked down her tube top.

"Now Julene isn't famous, but as you can see, she's got one hell of a nice figure and she knows how to use it better than any other woman I've ever known."

"You fucker," said Julene looking straight at Marek, her face turning bright red.

"Alas," said Marek, "I'm done with her. But enough!" said Marek and he motioned Gorsh to pull her tube top back up over her breasts.

"And," continued Marek, "as I promised, I've brought one of the ladies of your choice, plus one other. My friend, behold Colorado Jacquette."

The camera zoomed in on Colorado Jacquette who was not smiling and said to the camera, "Fuck you."

"And," continued Marek, "I've brought one other who is a bit special. You may remember me telling you about one of my customers who gave me synthesized diamonds instead of the genuine stones, then disappeared. Well I can't let that go or everybody would be trying to screw me like that. So I took his daughter, who doesn't even know that her Dad also trades in beautiful women. Her name is Naieema."

Naieema looked at Marek and her mouth dropped. "What? That's not true! My father doesn't do that!"

"Oh, but he does, and I can prove it when he finds out you are gone. I haven't told him yet because I want the image of you to be part of the surprise when I call him."

Once again, the camera zoomed in on the face and body of Naieema, who looked to her side and closed her eyes, but said to no one in particular, "I hope you all rot in hell for eternity."

Marek continued talking to the camera. "It's the same arrangement we discussed, of course: loose stones for the girls. You can fuck the hell out of them, you can make them sing for you—hell, you can make them wash your dishes and scrub your toilet for you for all I care."

The women turned white, and Naieema started to cry.

"Okay, cut!" yelled Marek. Gorsh dutifully stopped the video of the three women.

Jason and Sali looked at each other.

Sali whispered, "Where's the President's daughter?"

* * *

"Now, move those women out and bring on the star attraction."

"You're a rotten fucker, Marek," said Julene as she was being led out, "you'll burn in hell for this."

"And where would I be now if I believed in heaven and hell? What counts is the right here and now and money I can spend on whatever I want and whenever I want. Now move!"

Jason tensed all over, his hands turning into fists.

"Easy," whispered Sali. "We'll get the rotten prick."

The women left, the guard holding a gun at their back, then minutes later the President's daughter came in, her head raised high in defiance.

"Step this way, please," said Marek.

Charise saw what the situation was and walked over to the white sheet, turned and faced the camera.

"Take your clothes off and put this on," said Marek. He tossed her a sheer negligee.

"Right here?" said the indignant first daughter.

"Yes."

She could see that if she gave them a hard time, they'd beat her, so she turned her back to the camera, then took off all her clothes except her bra and panties.

"Those, too," said Marek.

"You bastard!"

"Yeah, just do it."

She did and quickly put on the negligee, which left little to the imagination.

"Now stand up straight and turn around slowly when I say so."

Marek said to Gorsh, "Now just do a tight frame of my face, then when I point to Charise, turn the camera over to point at her. Ms. Pearl, you do the three-sixty turn like I asked you to when he does that."

Marek told Gorsh to get ready, then he put on a big smile and began to speak. "Okay, go," he said to Gorsh.

"Surprise!" said Marek with a big smile. "I'll bet you thought I was unable to deliver on your other choice!" He pointed over at Charise and the camera moved to point at her. Her face was a mask of anger as she turned three-sixty, as instructed, then Marek motioned Gorsh to stop.

"Okay, finish it up," said Marek, "then give the memory chip to me. I'll edit the video and put in some other footage about priority of stones, then I'll give it back to you to send encrypted as soon as possible. He's on his way here and I want to let him see it before he gets here."

Gorsh packed up his camera gear, gave Marek the memory chip with the videos of the women, then left.

"All right, get dressed and Reznik will show you to my room, in case I need you to talk to Daddy President."

He turned to Reznik. "Lock her in the other cell for now."

But Reznik didn't move. He stared into Marek's face.

"Marek, please, let me just skull-fuck her once, huh? I mean whoever gets a chance to get head from the President's daughter?"

"You do and you're dead. I need her as a hostage, just in case. Now get busy."

Reznik growled in complaint, then shoved Charise ahead of him as they left.

Marek paced a few steps, then left through the same door as Charise and Reznik.

"Holy fuck," whispered Sali. "Now what are we going to do?"

"I don't know yet, but one thing is certain, sooner or later they're going to miss the guards we nailed and those kids, and then there is going to be an all-out search for them and us."

"But what the hell is he planning?" said Sali.

"Obviously he plans to sell the women to someone other than their husbands, and for a hell of a lot of jewels."

"Speaking of jewels, I wonder how Masen is doing."

Chapter Thirty-Five
Down the River and Through the Woods

Masen started out with the guard from the *Garnet Lady*, down the river bank and towards the ocean. It was late to mid-afternoon. He had no idea how far away it was or how long the little river was, but he had a small knapsack with some water, cheese and his safe-cracking tools, his Smith & Wesson, and a small powerful LED flashlight with fresh batteries to guide his way. The river ran slowly and had a gentle rippling sound that followed them as they sloshed forward. As they walked on the left bank, Masen could see to his right and with his light that the river was just deep enough to accommodate the *Garnet Lady's* draft, if they decided to come this way.

About an hour later they saw faint sunlight ahead. It was mid-afternoon, so Masen knew he had to step up his pace if he was going to make it up the side of the mountain in time to see Marek's bedroom. Though he'd been quiet so as not to attract any attention, he picked up their pace with loud splashes as they sprinted toward the daylight. Fortunately, there were no guards in this part of the mountain.

They finally arrived at the end of the river where it merged gently into the sea. After being in so much darkness in the cavern, the sun was blinding, but the brightness and warmth of the afternoon sun were welcome and nurturing against the dark and damp cave and tunnels. He could see the old Chris Craft they'd seen on their first approach to the island, but there were no signs of recent use.

"Okay, where's the path?" Masen said to the guard.

The guard pointed to a spot in the tall vegetation. "Head over that way, you'll find it."

He couldn't find it at first and began cursing at the guard out loud for lying to him. But there! He saw where the tall weeds and grass had been trampled in the past, and as he looked around, he found the more heavily traveled hard, sandy path. He looked up toward the top of the mountain, but could only see the peak: it was going to be a steep climb.

He went back to the guard and tied him to the first pylon on the pier and gave him a drink from his canteen. "I'll be back, I hope."

"Yeah, fuck you," said the guard.

Masen took off and increased his pace. Soon the trail began to steepen and his breathing and pulse started to quicken.

He came to a little valley that was thick with hardwood trees and the terrain flattened out for a short distance. Then he came to yet another river, and this one was flowing treacherously fast, yet he could see the trail continue on the other side, so he knew others had crossed, and so should he. It was difficult to fight the current, but he made it.

Twenty minutes later, walking up the trail as it grew steeper and steeper, he finally saw the big window to the bedroom and the edge of the balcony. He immediately crouched down in the weeds and listened carefully. He could hear no one.

A short while later he was just beneath the balcony which was made of wooden slats and which allowed him to look up through the bottom, yet it was unlikely anyone would look downward at him through the slats when there was such a magnificent view from the balcony. He sat there for a few minutes listening.

He heard footsteps approaching, then a door close, and soon, a voice apparently talking on a phone.

Masen then knew he had to use that phone to call Jamie because Jason had the sat-phone. He had to tell her that the President's daughter was here, and to somehow get help to interdict Marek's men and keep them from recapturing the kids, just in case the C4 trap didn't work.

* * *

"Get me Kostya," said Marek.

When Kostya finally got on the phone, Marek said, "I'm sending you the encrypted videos in about twenty minutes. The unlock code is the same as before. Nobody should be able to intercept and decode it." He hung up without waiting for an answer, then went to the computer on his desk, inserted the chip, played the video and edited it to his liking, then sent the file to Kostya via an encrypted email application.

When he was finished he left his office and closed the door just loud enough so that Masen could hear it.

* * *

Masen concluded that Marek had left his office.

Gingerly, he stepped out from under the balcony and climbed up on it. He held his pistol ready and froze for a second, waiting for anybody to come after him. No alarm, no reaction from inside. Again, he remembered how people in condominiums rarely locked their sliding glass doors, and tried the handle. Sure enough, it was unlocked. He shook his head and uttered "Amazing."

He entered Marek's bedroom, which obviously also served as his office, judging by the computer and desk, filing cabinets, a fax machine, and the phone. He didn't know Jamie's direct line, but through a series of operators and his statements of a "life or death" situation, he finally got through.

"This is Jamie Horgood. How may I help you?"

"Jamie," he whispered loudly, "it's me, Masen Williams, with Jason and Sali, and I don't have much time and I can't speak up. The President's daughter Charise is captive here at Dark Island, south of Saba. I'm sorry, but I can't explain more—I have to go before I'm caught. Do not call back to this number or they'll know I've been here."

He hung up quickly and listened carefully. Nothing. He turned around and looked carefully at everything in the room before starting his search for the safe. He saw none of the obvious places you might see in a condo or house. The walls were made of wood and too flimsy to hold a safe. He looked inside every drawer in the filing cabinet and found nothing resembling a hidden safe; nor did any of the papers appear to hold anything of value in discovering his trafficking customers—that was probably in his computer. He picked up the fax machine and inspected it, as well as looked under it. There was a small couch, as well as a bed, but there was nothing under either one, or inside them, that he could tell, that could hold treasures of any weight. He stood in the middle of the room, perplexed, and wondering if the guard had been right, that the safe must be in Marek's bedroom. Maybe it was in fact in the telecommunications room, which nobody had seen yet, and which, by the way, was used for what, since he had a telephone. He deduced that the phone must use Inmarsat or some other satellite-based telephone system. He stood for another minute, then it dawned on him as he stood in the middle of a big circular rug—it must be under the rug!

He stepped off the rug and rolled it up. Sure enough, there it was—a floor safe! He recognized the model. It was actually a rather old model that was considered one of the best, but they didn't call him the best safe-cracker in the U.S. for nothing. He opened his knapsack and pulled out his stethoscope which had the sound amplifier on it to increase and define the subtle sounds of the combination lock as he spun the dial slowly. He didn't come fully prepared—most safe-cracking attempts could require an arsenal of hundreds of pounds of different types of gear—but the good old stethoscope worked for him on a majority of jobs where the safes were simple and the job was a small breaking-and-entering burglary.

Unfortunately, he was unable to get it opened and cursed under his breath as he tried again and again. Then he stopped—he heard footsteps approaching again. He quickly replaced the rug over the floor safe and looked around quickly to make sure everything was as it should be.

The footsteps were getting closer and he didn't have time to go back out the door to the balcony, so he dove under the bed.

Marek entered, slammed the door, then answered his radio.

"What!" said Marek, and he waited for the news. "They what! How did this happen?"

Marek waited while the other party on the line explained.

"They must not be allowed to reach their destination. Sink the boat if you have to, and search the mountain. They could not have escaped on their own. Muster the men and I'll meet you at the dock!"

Marek threw the radio onto the desk. It was obvious to Masen they had just discovered the escape of the kids and now they were going to go after them. Now he was glad he and Sali had set the C4 and the tripwire.

Chapter Thirty-Six
A Tough Choice

The Director of the Secret Service, Nathan Kale, knocked lightly on the assistant to the President's door. The President's aid answered the door. "He's very busy, sir, can you come back later?"

"I'm afraid not, Nancy, I need to see him right away." He held a package in a manila envelope in his right hand.

Nancy stepped over to the Oval Office, tapped the door lightly, then opened the door and announced Mr. Kale's request. "Excuse me, Mr. President, but Director Kale needs to speak to you right away."

"Okay, thank you Nancy, please show him in." He finished drafting an Executive Order to establish The Caribbean Coral Reef Ecosystem Protection Act, then said sternly, "Hello, Nathan, please come in."

Nancy stepped out of the Oval Office and went back to her desk.

The President stood. He had lost weight since his daughter's disappearance, and his face looked a bit gaunt. His eyes appeared to be slightly red now, rather than clear and full of interest, as was usual for him. He no longer slept well and his laughter and wit were completely gone.

He walked slowly around his desk and extended his hand, slightly shaking, to the Director. They shook hands and sat down at the chairs in front of the President's desk.

"What's the latest news, Nathan?"

"Sir, I'm afraid we've received a rather troubling video, and as much as I hate to do this, I'm afraid I need to show it to you right away. It's about your daughter."

The President stood immediately. "Oh my God. Is she alive?"

"Yes sir, she is," said Kale, now standing also, "but you won't like the circumstances."

"I don't like them anyway. What do you mean?" the President commanded.

"It's best if I just play the video file. Can we just step into the viewing room and chase everybody out except you and me?"

"Yes," the President said, his voice trembling slightly. He stepped over to his phone and called Nancy.

"Nancy, can you please contact the operator at the White House Family Theater and tell him Director Kale and I will be there in a few minutes? I don't want anybody else there except the projectionist, and I don't even want him to see the video. Can you set that up?"

"Yes sir, I'll get on it right away."

The President and Director Kale walked over to the East Wing and the theater. The projectionist was there to meet them.

"Good afternoon, Mr. President," the projectionist said politely.

"Good afternoon, George. We need to see the video the Director has here in private. Can you set that up?"

"Certainly, sir. Both of you please have a seat wherever you'd like and I'll set it up, then I'll come down and show you the remote controls."

Minutes later the projectionist came down the aisle to see the President, who stood to meet him.

George said, "I'll step outside, then turn this knob and the lights will go down slowly. Push this button and the video will start. Push it again and the video will pause; push it again to restart. Push this button to stop the video. Let me know when you're finished and I will retrieve the video for you."

The projectionist left, then the President used the remote to turn the lights down, then pushed the "Play" button.

The video started off with the moving image of his daughter Pearl wearing nothing but a nearly transparent negligee, and slowly turning in a circle.

"Hello, Mr. President," came the voice offstage from the video. "It's your old friend Kostya Chugunkin. Let me get right to the point. You and your cabinet blocked my account in Antigua. I want it back. In fact, I demand it."

"Damn him!" the President yelled into the empty theater, standing as he did and pausing the video. "He knows damn well I can't reverse a decision to block his Antigua accounts without raising questions. I'd have to funnel illegal funds, which I'm not going to do, and I sure as hell don't have that kind of money myself."

The Director continued to sit quietly. "There's more, I'm afraid."

The President pushed the remote button again to restart the video.

Kostya continued. "I have something that I think will make you cooperate. Please hold for one minute while I switch video to an entirely different location."

The picture switched back to Kostya's stern face. "So, which do you prefer, Mr. President: having your daughter returned, or returning to me my Bahamas accounts? Of course, if you refuse, we have other plans for your vivacious daughter."

The video feed switched this time to a woman who looked similar to Charise, in the same negligee, getting gang-raped by two big ugly thugs who were laughing loudly as the woman struggled to get free, and who could not speak because her mouth was full of one of the men.

The President screamed. Then in a raging, shaky voice he said to Director Kale, "He just brought our entire armed forces to his doorstep, wherever he is. They will bring him to the U.S. and he will pay for this."

"Don't even think about trying to capture me, Mr. President," Kostya's voice continued, as though he could hear the President. "For one thing, you have no idea where I am. You have twenty-four hours to make your decision, and if you decide in my favor, I will return her to you. Eventually. If you try to follow up with any sort of unpleasantness—let's say, an attack by your CIA or military—then we'll just have to eliminate this unhappy group of kids—and this is just the first group." He smiled, then the video feed switched again to a brightly lit cave showing hundreds of children, with guards flanking them on all sides. "And by the way, I must say, these young people, besides being sex partners for my clients, bring the highest prices for their hearts, lungs and kidneys—what you call organ trafficking. Hmmm…you know, actually, I'd prefer to keep your daughter for my own pleasure. But no, it's your choice, Mr. President, a deal is a deal." said Kostya, "You've got twenty-four hours," then the screen went blank.

The President turned off the movie and brought the lights back up. Director Kale looked at the President and could see that the President's eyes were red and tears beginning to form. He looked down, to save the President from embarrassment, and said, "I am so sorry, Mr. President. What do you want me to do?"

The President dropped the remote control to the floor and just placed his head in his hand, his elbows on his knees, and just kept shaking his head, saying quietly, "Oh Charise, Charise, I am so sorry…"

Chapter Thirty-Seven
Escape From Blue Lagoon

After witnessing the filming of the women, Jason and Sali turned to go back the way they came.

"We've got the keys to the cells—after they take the women back, we can let them out," said Jason.

"Yeah, then what?" said Sali.

"We take them out in the Garnet Lady."

Just then they heard shouting and men running.

"The children have escaped!" yelled Reznik. "Go get the Garnet Lady and go after them! Everybody, get your ass in gear!"

Jason and Sali were in the only passageway.

"Quick!" said Jason. He motioned to a door with a sign reading, "Storage Room."

They both dove through the door quickly and blocked the door in case anybody tried to get in. They heard the men run by, then no sound, and nobody tried to get in the door.

"How many men do you figure that was?" asked Sali.

"I don't know, but I'd say at most a dozen, maybe less."

They waited a bit longer, listening closely, but no more men ran by.

"Well, I guess that means good news, bad news," said Sali.

"Yeah?"

"The good news is they're probably taking the Garnet Lady, which means we can't use it."

"That's the good news?"

"Yeah. They've got to go right through our C-4 trap, and that should blow them all to hell, or at least slow them down."

"Okay, what's the bad news?"

"We don't have a way out of here."

Jason thought for a second. "Yeah we do—the sub."

Sali blinked at him for a moment. "You really think we can all fit in there?"

"We're going to have to—there's no other way, unless you want to walk out, which doesn't sound like too good of an option to me right now."

"All right, then, let's see if we can even get out of this room without getting caught, then let's find the women and take them to the sub and hope the captain has figured it out and hasn't left us behind."

* * *

Marek closed the door to his room, leaving Masen still hiding under the bed, and said to Gorsh, "We're going to have to walk the stream bed north until we get to the pier and take the Chris Craft. We'll meet Kostya at his yacht, then we can bring his girls back here."

"What happened to the captain of the Garnet Lady?" said Gorsh.

"Either the captain and the guard took off somewhere, or somebody's helping them. You start looking everywhere to see if you can find them. I can't believe that the guard released those kids and the women by himself—somebody had to have made him do it."

* * *

It wasn't as difficult as Jason and Sali thought it might be, getting to the women's cell, since it seemed like all the guards had headed for the *Garnet Lady* to chase the escaped kids.

They got to the women's cell and the women looked at them wide-eyed, wondering who these guys could be unlocking the door to their jail, except, of course, Julene.

"Jason! What the hell? Jason? What the hell are you doing here?"

Jason reached into his pocket and retrieved the locket she had dropped back at Alder's Cay in the Berry Islands.

"I believe you dropped this," he said. "Thought I'd return it…"

Her eyes opened wide as silver dollars and tears began to form.

She was speechless for a moment, then Colorado said, "Oh my God! You've been following us all this time!" She inhaled, hand to her chest, and held her breath for a moment.

"Oh, Jason," said Julene, tears now dripping from her eyes. "Oh, Jason..." She stepped forward and gently grasped the locket then hugged him.

Sali stepped forward, "If the soap opera is over, can we please get the holy living horseshit out of this fucking joint?"

"Wait a minute! Where's the President's daughter, Charise?"

"She wasn't with us when they took a video of us," said Colorado, "and she wasn't here when we came back. They must have moved her."

"Damn it," said Jason. "Well, we've got to go anyway. We can't wait around, at least not here. Let's just hope we can get out of here so we can tell Jamie she's here. We may have to think of a way to come back and get her."

"Who's Jamie?" said Julene.

"She's my contact with Homeland Security. Wait, don't ask—I'll tell you later."

He grabbed Julene by the hand and said, "Let's go," then led them all down the passageway back to the blue lagoon.

Within seconds they were at the lagoon. Sali stepped onto the half-submerged sub and banged at the entrance hatch with his pistol.

"Hey, Captain Chet, it's me, Sali."

Almost immediately the hatch opened and Captain Chet stuck his head out.

"Thank God, it's you," said the captain. "I thought for sure somebody was going to come looking for those two guys we killed."

"Captain," said Sali, "We're in a bit of a hurry, and now there's five of us. We've got to get all six of us out of here as quickly as we can. Will this thing hold six people?"

"Precisely so," said Captain Chet, as he looked back down into the sub. "This particular model of a personal submarine, the Triton 1650/7, holds up to seven people and according to the documentation can stay down for eighteen hours, although it only travels at three knots. But I think I can handle it. If you're ready to go, then let's get the hell out of here. This place gives me the creeps."

"After you, ladies," said Jason, pointing to the entryway of the sub. "Sali, you operate the crane and I'll operate the release, then come on over and hop on."

With all seven of them finally in the sub, the captain began operating the controls, although it was obvious he was a bit uncertain on some of them.

The captain gently pushed the descent lever down and the sub responded immediately and they began to sink into the deep blue hole.

* * *

Not one minute later, Marek and Gorsh came to the lagoon and saw the submarine descending below the surface. They ran to the lagoon's edge and started shooting at it as it dropped deeper.

* * *

Inside the sub, they all heard a "blink" sound, and then another one, and they looked upward. They could just make out Marek and Gorsh firing shots down into the water, but the water was dramatically effective at slowing down the shots so that the speed was more like small rocks hitting the side of the sub, making the many "blink" sounds as the sub sank deeper with no damage to the hull.

* * *

"Damn it!" screamed Marek. "Whoever they are, there's no way to stop them, at least not now. We'll have to call Kostya as soon as we get outside of the mountain and use one of his boats and his radar to look for them when they come up for air."

They ran past the open doors of the jails that had held the three women from Fort Lauderdale, as well as the children and came to the dock where the *Garnet Lady* had been docked. Nobody was around—Reznik had already left with all his men to go capture the escaping children.

"Damn it!" said Marek. "Go get the President's daughter. We're going to have to walk down to the Chris Craft and take her with us."

Three minutes later Gorsh came back to the dock, pulling Charise, who had her hands tied behind her.

Marek grabbed the flashlight that was attached to a holster on his belt and led the way north along the stream and out of Rubicon Mountain.

* * *

The sub sank straight down to about thirty feet into a well-lit large chamber that had just one tunnel leading in and leading out. The captain maneuvered the sub in the direction of the tunnel and slowly increased speed, although top speed was only a few knots. Captain Chet stretched overhead to a toggle switch and turned on the outside lights so that they could see what lay before them. Schools of yellowtail snapper moved in-and-out of their direction of progress, and one very large spiny lobster looked at them as they passed by, with his very long antennae twitching about as they poked outside of his little hole in the rock wall of the tunnel. Ahead, they could see where the faint sunlight was beaming down at the end of the tunnel—it wasn't much further at all until they'd be leaving their mountainous dungeon. What they would do after that, nobody had a clue, except to come back to the surface at some point. Captain Chet had said they may have as much as eighteen hours underwater, but did that take into account seven people? It didn't seem so, in such a small, confined space.

"Once we get through the end of the tunnel," said Jason, "let's go a bit deeper and keep moving, at least for a while, then let's just stop and hover, if we can, until it starts to get dark. There may be somebody on the mountain ready to take potshots at us, but we don't want to go too far out since we have no idea where we're going."

"Aye, aye," said Captain Chet. "Steady as she goes…"

Chapter Thirty-Eight
Dead End

Reznik's men had rushed to the *Garnet Lady* in pursuit of the escaped children.

Reznik yelled at the *Garnet Lady* ahead of the men, "Captain! Let's move! We've got to turn this thing around now!"

Reznik and his men jumped onto the *Garnet Lady* and began to untie the bow and stern lines. Reznik jumped into the cabin. "Captain!" he yelled.

He clambered further down and around the inside the main and forward cabins. "Fuck! Where did he go!" he screamed at no one in particular. He grabbed his radio and called Marek. "The captain has disappeared. No sign of what happened to him or the guard on the pier."

Marek responded, "Can you drive the damn thing yourself?"

"Yes, but I'll be a few minutes turning it around."

Reznik shouted at his crew, "We're going without the captain—I'm driving. Make ready the lines and let's get out of here! Vostya," he said to one of his men, "you stay at the dock in case we need your help back here. Keep your eyes open."

As he struggled to turn the yacht, he mumbled to himself, "If those kids reach Basseterre we're busted."

Soon they were out of Rubicon Mountain and Reznik checked the radar to see if he could find them. It was late in the afternoon, and soon the *Booty* would have to turn its running lights on.

"There they are," he said to Nadav, pointing at a blip on the radar.

"Once we get out of the mangroves we can catch them before they get to Basseterre."

He shoved the throttle down and the *Garnet Lady* slowly began to pick up speed.

"Shouldn't we reduce speed before the mangroves?" said Nadav.

Reznik shouted above the engine, "We'll plough our way through."

The *Garnet Lady* picked up speed across the lake, heading straight for the restricted passage through the mangroves. The magnificent yacht entered the mangroves and immediately they heard the scraping sounds of the mangrove branches against the hull as Reznik misguided the *Garnet Lady* against the few tight turns that were required to pass through safely. The yacht slowed its forward speed as it was slowed by the mangroves, but continued to press forward.

The *Garnet Lady* finally reached the tripwire for the C-4 explosives, but because Reznik was mainly plowing his own new path through the mangroves, they missed it. The *Garnet Lady* pushed forward, its crew unaware they had just escaped near certain death.

Finally, they broke through the mangroves and Reznik pushed the throttle to wide-open. He peered at the radar and saw that the *Booty* still had quite a way to go before they reached Basseterre. Reznik calculated that they would catch them minutes before the kids could reach their destination.

Reznik bellowed: "Stand ready to pull alongside and take them!"

Reznik called Marek, but got no answer—Marek was still inside the mountain with no radio reception.

Suddenly, off the port side, a Zodiac appeared and was heading straight for them.

"Who the fuck is that?" barked Reznik to Nadav.

Nadav grabbed the long-barreled Zeiss binoculars and focused on the approaching Zodiac. "Oh, shit," he said.

"What do you mean, 'Oh shit'? Who are they?"

"I don't know, but there are six of them and they don't look friendly. They're covered in black and they all have guns."

"Shit!" screamed Reznik. "Get ready!"

The *Garnet Lady* pulled alongside the *Booty* and Reznik shouted, "Grab the kids and use them as hostages when those guys get here!"

One of the crew looked back at Reznik: "What kids? There's nobody on deck!"

Reznik was not aware that an hour before he and his men had broken through the mangroves, six U.S. Navy SEALS had already boarded the *Booty* and had the children move belowdecks out of harm's way. Now the SEALs were lying in wait for Reznik and his men. As soon as the first of Reznik's men jumped onto the deck of the *Booty*, the team of six SEALs clambered out of hiding and pointed their guns at Reznik's men and shouted, "Drop your weapons!"

Reznik's men froze trying to make a decision: *Can we outshoot these guys?*

Just then the Zodiac with the other six SEAL members of the team arrived, with guns pointing at Reznik and his men from the other side of the boat.

"Game over, Captain!" shouted the Captain of SEAL Team E-8, the officer in charge in the Zodiac. "Put your guns down and your hands up!"

Reznik and his men froze in a moment of indecision.

"There's more of us than them," said one of Reznik's men, then opened fire. With that, everybody opened fire.

Reznik and all of his men were killed with no SEALs killed in a matter of seconds.

* * *

While the SEALs checked the bodies of Reznik and his men for signs of life and documents they may be carrying, the SEAL Team E-8 leader squatted and spoke to the young man who had been piloting the *Booty* and who had come on deck to see if he could help.

"What's your name, son?"

"Jaimito."

"Who were these guys? Where did they come from?"

"They were bad men who kept us in a cage and were going to sell us. I do not know where they came from, but we were all kept inside Rubicon Mountain." He pointed to the island.

"What do you mean 'inside the mountain'? You mean like a cave?"

"Yes. They drove us in on a boat up a river that runs from inside the mountain. There are many rooms inside the mountain. They must have made them themselves. They even have a room with a big generator that makes the electricity."

"Did they feed you well and take care of you?"

"Yes. We had plenty to eat and there was a doctor who visited now and then and who took care of us, but I haven't seen him in a long time."

"How long have you been in there? How did you end up there?"

"I have been in and out of there about a month. My parents could not afford to take care of me anymore, so they sold me to a guy who said he would take care of me. After he bought me, he said I would have to pay him back. I owe him for my passport, too. I come from Venezuela."

"What is that man's name, Jaimito?"

"They call him Kostya, but Marek is the man who controls the mountain. Kostya has a very big boat. He brought us to the mountain. The man you killed, over there," he pointed, "that was Marek's brother."

"Jaimito, you don't have to answer this next question if you don't want to, okay?"

"Okay," Jaimito said as he gazed at the deck of the boat.

"What kind of work did they make you do?"

Jaimito continued to gaze at the deck and did not answer at first. Then he said, "I don't want to tell you all of it, but I heard they usually sell the girls for sex, just like the women that come through here; and they also take kidneys out of some of us and sell them, but at least they sew us back up."

"Thank you very much, Jaimito. That's enough. We will help you to find your parents or a better place to live, okay?"

"Okay. Thank you Mr. Soldier."

The SEAL Team E-8 Captain stood and walked over to a quieter part of the boat while his men attended to covering up the bodies and going through the *Booty* to compile evidence. He made a call on his radio.

"Sir, this is Captain Lorenzo. It appears the Homeland Security contact was right. We have uncovered a human and organ trafficking operation. Boys and girls. We still have a lot of interviewing to do, but we stopped them before they got to Basseterre."

He listened for a moment, then said, "Roger that. Let me know when they're airborne so we can meet with them and help out."

The Captain rang off and looked into the faces of the boys and girls who had been through horrendous days and nights in their short lives, and now they had witnessed the aftermath of this mass killing of their tormentors. You'd think they should be cheering, but they just stared at the scene where the soldiers were moving the dead.

Chapter Thirty-Nine
Finders Keepers

Masen had waited a few minutes to make sure Marek and Gorsh were not returning to Marek's room, then crawled out from under the bed and went to the rug covering the safe of jewels and peeled it back. Once again he worked methodically to determine the combination to Marek's safe.

It took longer than he thought—Masen had broken open this model of safe before, but this one was giving him problems. It just took a methodical approach and he knew where to start, but he had to keep starting over again because his method wasn't working as it usually did. Finally, he opened the door to the safe and found a collection of bulging bags and a couple of small boxes. He grabbed the biggest bag and spilled some of the contents onto the floor of the room to inspect the contents.

The radiant sparkle of gemstones glistened like bright sunlight through stained glass windows. The wealth equaled some countries' gross national product, yet it was wrought through the innumerable souls lost, and those still held in abeyance, by human traffickers.

"Ho. Lee. Shit." he exclaimed to himself. But time was flying by, so he put the cache of riches back into the bag and pulled the bags and boxes out of the safe, closed the safe, and rolled the rug back over it. He stepped over to Marek's bed and removed two pillowcases from the pillows and put his new collection of plunder into them and stepped quietly back out onto the balcony.

As the door closed behind him he looked out over the magnificent view of the ocean. He saw a superyacht stationary about a mile offshore, just beyond where there appeared to be a drop off from the coral reefs to a deep blue ocean. He looked down and could see the Chris Craft at the end of the pier and reasoned that it might be going out to visit the superyacht, since it was sitting stationary out there for no apparent reason.

He suddenly realized that he had heard no explosion from the C-4 charge yet, but perhaps it could not be heard from this end of the island.

He abandoned those thoughts and hastily stepped through the railing of the balcony and headed back down the trail from whence he had come.

* * *

Marek, Gorsh and Charise exited the cave and walked down the stream to the shoreline of the north Atlantic Ocean. In front of them was the old, long pier that had somehow withstood years of hurricanes and punishing seas. The thirty-foot Chris Craft was tied up at the end of the pier. On the shoreline side they saw their guard who had been guarding the *Garnet Lady* tied to the first pylon of the pier with a gag in his mouth. Gorsh ran up and ungagged and untied him and the guard immediately said, "He went up the trail to your cabin about an hour or more ago! He may be on his way back by now."

"Who? Who went up the trail?"

"A guy they call Masen."

"Who is he?"

"I don't know. All I know is that they are here to free the women. I don't know who they are or where they came from."

Marek looked at Gorsh. "They must be the same ones who escaped in the sub." He twitched his head toward the trail.

Gorsh responded: "I'll find him." He headed up the trail toward Marek's room at the top of the mountain trail.

Marek turned to the guard. "What else?"

"I've only seen three of them, two plus the one who brought me here. The other two took my keys and went to free the women, but I guess they also found the children and let them go, too."

Marek retrieved his pistol from his holster and fired a single shot into the guard's forehead. "You fucked up," he said to the falling corpse.

Gorsh turned toward the shot just as he was entering the trail, saw the execution, then continued up the trail.

Marek took the radio off his belt and tried calling his brother Reznik.

"Reznik," he said loudly into the radio. No response. "Reznik!" he shouted. Again, no response.

* * *

Gorsh bulldozed his way up the small trail which was made for men of a much smaller stature.

Far above him on the trail Masen was stumbling with his two stuffed pillow cases full of jewels and whatever else was in the boxes he had not opened when he was in Marek's room.

Gorsh thundered ahead, unheedful of what may be ahead of him, but Masen heard him thrashing his way up the trail and knew it had to be someone coming after him. He found a landmark along the trail—a large boulder half again as big as himself—and he forced his way through the underbrush, taking care to move the bushes and twigs back to their normal position as he moved his way off the trail to hide from whomever was coming after him. One thing for sure, he could not be caught with the two big pillow cases full of plunder, so he began to look for a hiding place for the two bags before he might be captured.

He came upon a collection of boulders along the side of the mountain and discovered a void between the rocks that was just wide enough for him to hide the two bags. Thinking they would fall just a short way down the hole, he dropped them and listened for their fall to the bottom. He also dropped the stash of jewels he had stolen from Julene's backpack back at Marek's condo in Ft. Lauderdale. Surprisingly, the fall was a long one and the drops took much longer than he thought—he would have to eventually crawl way down into the hole to retrieve the two bags—but at least they were well hidden.

Just as the last bag dropped, he heard the person traveling up the path come abreast of him. He froze, praying his pursuer would not have seen his entrance into the underbrush. Thank heavens, the pursuer kept going up the trail and Masen made his way slowly back to trod down the trail.

* * *

As Masen got to the bottom of the trail he could see that the guard had been murdered, and that Marek was talking to someone through the radio as he stood at the end of the pier next to where the old Chris Craft was tied up. So now he knew the guard had told them he had gone up the trail, and died because of it. He had his radio, but either of the two guys might hear him if he tried to use it right now. All he could do for now was hide until he could get away, maybe at nightfall, or until they left in the Chris Craft.

* * *

Later, the early evening sun fell in the west on a cloudless night on a perfectly flat ocean, sinking in a transitioning color of brilliant orange to a fierce scarlet until it looked as if the horizon itself were on fire. As sundown met the encroaching night, the air temperature dropped steadily by several degrees.

Just then Gorsh came crashing down the trail. "I couldn't find him. If he went into your room, there's no sign that he did."

Marek tried calling Reznik again on his radio, but again, no response. "I don't like this," he muttered. "His battery must have gone dead, the idiot."

Marek started to ask Gorsh about the safe, but nobody knew the location of the safe, and he wanted to keep it that way, so he said nothing.

"Well, where the hell do you think he went?" Marek said crossly.

"He must have gone through your room and into the mountain, because I didn't see him on the trail. Or, he took some other route around the mountain, except that's some pretty heavy brush to do that."

"All right," said Marek. "Let's go get the boat ready to visit Kostya and bring the new women back. Let's just hope Reznik catches up to the kids, and that group in the sub sinks. They can't stay down forever, so keep your eyes open, and I'll alert Kostya and his men to do the same."

But the sun had set, and the clouds before an approaching storm were beginning to gather. Seeing anything with no lights out on the ocean would be almost impossible.

Chapter Forty
Freefall

Their initial excitement on leaving the underwater grotto of Rubicon Mountain gave way to anxiety as the Triton submarine entered the wondrous coral-encircled realm at sixty feet deep and onward to a precipice of an underwater cliff that was hundreds of feet deep. They were quite literally in a twilight zone of reduced light at such a depth, and it was gradually getting darker as the sun above dwindled in brilliance as dusk approached.

Naieema began to shudder and cry. "I'm scared. I'm sorry. I can't help it. I'm claustrophobic and I've never even been snorkeling in my entire life."

Colorado wrapped her arms around her and hugged her. "Hang in there girl. They don't make unsafe multimillion dollar subs anymore."

"She's right, Naieema, and we can start moving up now toward the surface," said Jason. "It won't be long now. Just hang in there."

Jason turned to Captain Chet. "Let's start moving slowly to the surface so we can get our bearings. Stay just below the surface until the sun goes down, then rise slowly to the surface."

The captain tried tugging at the ascent/descent control, but it wouldn't budge. "Uh oh."

The black silence within the sub dumbfounded them all for long seconds as they continued to gently fall through the sea past bioluminescent fish and other animals reflected by the headlights of the sub.

"What do you mean 'Uh oh'?" uttered Jason as they continued to descend.

"I mean the stick is frozen. I can't get it to move one way or the other. It was working fine when we left, but it just now froze, for some reason."

Naieema started to wail louder.

"Is that the only control for ascent and descent?"

"It's the only one I've seen."

Nobody said anything as Captain Chet continued struggling with the control and the sub picked up speed as it continued to fall toward the bottom of the ocean.

Suddenly they could see the bottom approaching. Jason and Captain Chet both looked at the depth meter at the same time. They had just crossed three hundred feet deep.

"Everybody brace yourself!" shouted Jason.

Naieema was sobbing uncontrollably. Colorado's eyes were opened wide and her lips were trembling as she and Julene held tight to Naieema. Sali and Jason both pulled the straps tight on their seatbelts.

They all watched the bottom drawing closer. Captain Chet kept pulling on the stick. "Ooh shit!"

They landed on the ocean floor sending up a great cloud of brilliant white sand billowing around them. It was a soft landing compared to what it might have been, owing to the depth of the sand. Nothing was broken, no leaks. Nothing but silence, and the headlights still shone out into the darkness as various strange-looking fish swam by or sea stars or other critters crept along the bottom.

Soon, however, after the sand cloud settled, they noticed that they were on a slope near the edge of a cliff and they could see nothing but deep blue-black reflecting back at them from the lights of the vessel.

Jason said, "Is everybody okay?"

Naieema whimpered, "I don't want to die!" Everybody else nodded their heads that they were okay.

Captain Chet finally gave up on the stick and started looking around the inside of the vessel for any clues as to other ways to move the submersible.

Julene scolded nobody in particular: "Hey, did anybody read the fucking manual? There's got to be a way to get this thing moving."

Captain Chet, Sali and Jason started looking all over the sub for the documentation or any other clues as to how to get the sub moving.

Just then the sub began sliding down the sandy incline, heading for the edge of the underwater cliff.

"Oh, shit, oh dear," said Julene quietly.

Captain Chet tried pulling up on the stick again. Nothing. It was frozen. The sub continued to slide. Jason and Sali, undaunted by the passenger's apparent slide into oblivion, kept looking around the sub for documentation on the operation of the sub.

"Oh my God," said Colorado. "This is it. We're all going to die down here and nobody is ever going to find us."

"Shut up," said Julene, "You're only making matters worse."

The next moment the sub fell over the precipice of the great underwater cliff, orienting completely vertical and now at over five hundred feet deep and free-falling more, yet at a slower pace than before. Captain Chet was able to steer it back to horizontal, but there was no longer a bottom with swimming organisms to give them any sense of perspective as to how fast and how far they were falling; but they all knew they were indeed falling because the tiny particulate matter was flying upward in the lights as they plunged deeper and deeper.

"How much air do we have left?" asked Jason softly.

"About six hours," answered Captain Chet.

Nobody said anything as the sub continued to descend slowly, and they all just sat there for the moment, wondering what might happen next, if anything, while Naieema continued with a sob muffled by her folded arm over her mouth.

*   *   *

Jason tried to think of all possible ways he might help them get out of this mess, but at this depth—hundreds of feet deep, and counting—even if they could get out of the sub, there was no way they'd make it to the surface, not to mention what the pressure would do to their bodies. The sub had a telecommunication system, but who could possibly be listening up top? His mind ran out of possibilities and he began to feel that horrible dread of no-way-out. And it wasn't just himself this time; now he had endangered all these other people, all of them good people, and it looked like they were going to die down here—alone and unknown by anybody that they were even in the sub and on their way out of the mountain. His remorse was monstrous and his regret found no rationalization in having escaped into this deep, dark hole in the ocean. He should have thought of another way and asked for feedback from Sali and the others. This had been an incredibly stupid move, and now they would all pay with their lives. He closed his eyes and fought back tears of sadness at having doomed all these good souls. He had to do something that could bring hope, though there seemed to be nothing.

He reached for the specialized telecommunications microphone, even though if the ship heard them and rescued them it would likely mean certain death upon capture.

"Hello, can anybody hear us? Mayday, mayday, mayday. Please somebody answer, can you hear us?"

He waited. No answer. He repeated several times, and finally gave up and said to the group, "Maybe we can try again in a little while." But he knew it was fruitless, and so, probably, did they. Who could possibly be listening, and even if they were, what could they do?

They all sat there in their own little world of ruin, each with their own thoughts of their lives unexpectedly coming to an end at the bottom of the ocean.

Chapter Forty-One
The Arisen

"Wait!" said Sali, who had been feeling around under his seat. "What's this?" A fairly thick document had been under the very seat he was sitting in. He pulled it out and the inside light shone on the cover as everybody except the cowering Naieema leaned over to read the document's title: Operating Manual for the Triton 1650/7.

"Fuck!" shouted Julene. "Figure it out, quick!"

Feverishly, Sali looked quickly over the Table of Contents until he saw, "Controlling Ascent and Descent." He quickly turned to the proper section and scanned over the pages.

Meanwhile, the sub was still falling and picking up speed and was coming up quickly to another hard surface.

Captain Chet yelled, "Brace yourself!"

This time the sub made a hard landing and partial roll onto hard rock and the whole sub shook like a giant pit-bull had shaken it. But no leaks, nothing apparently broken.

Sali continued reading as though nothing had happened.

"Captain," said Sali, "that control stick is what brings water in and out of the ballast tanks, but there are two other ways to ascend. The first one is to pump air into the ballast tanks. You do that here." He pointed to a small shaft on the far side of the console and not so readily apparent.

Captain Chet reached over and pushed the shaft gently forward. Nothing. He pushed it some more and a very quiet whisper of a sound pervaded the sub, and the craft began to move ever so slightly upward. Jason peeked at the depth gauge. They hadn't gone as far as they had thought, but it was still deep and it was total darkness outside. The Captain pushed the shaft a little further and they began to ascend only slightly faster.

"Oh, jeez," said Julene, "I almost pissed myself."

Finally, after what seemed like an hour, they could see twilight above as they approached the surface.

Captain Chet adjusted the control and watched the gauge indicating depth display shallower and shallower.

"Stop at twenty feet for now," said Jason, "and turn off the lights."

"Aye-aye," exhaled Captain Chet loudly. "Damn, that was close."

The lights went out and the sub rose very slowly with the dying sunlight, just as the ocean's plankton do every night. They could have been a humpback whale, waiting for the evening meal.

The impending darkness was now overwhelming for Naieema and she just froze, her eyes wide and all her attention on watching and listening.

"Hang in there, Honey," said Julene, "we're going to make it," as she, too, joined the hug with Colorado. "Just close your eyes and pretend you're taking a nap."

Minutes later the underwater light faded to total blackness and all that could be seen was the bioluminescence of the underwater denizens.

"Okay," said Jason, "bring her up real slow, but be ready to dive immediately."

"Roger that, but hopefully not. Been there, done that."

"What's our air supply look like?" asked Sali.

Captain Chet turned to one of the gauges. "If I'm reading it correctly, we still have about four hours."

The Triton sub surfaced and the whole sky was covered with clouds, yet they could still see moonlight through a break in the clouds through the glass globe that covered half the vessel.

Jason exclaimed, "Look, there's a yacht! And a damn big one, at that."

"Yeah, but look over there," said Sali.

They could see Rubicon Mountain on their left, and a long pier with the Chris Craft at the end of the pier, just as they had seen it when they first circled the island.

Jason said, "Hand me those field glasses." The captain took the glasses and handed them to Jason.

Jason took a close look at the boat that was just being boarded.

"It's Marek and the big guy he calls Gorsh…and Charise! They've got her!" He watched them for a few seconds more. "Looks like they're heading for the yacht all right."

Jason turned the glasses toward the magnificent yacht. "It has a tender garage on the stern where Marek's Chris Craft can just drive right in. Amazing. That's one hell of a yacht."

Jason pulled out his satellite phone and tried calling Jamie.

No one answered, so he left a voicemail: "Jamie, the President's daughter is onboard the superyacht Turquoise Lament idling northwest of Rubicon Mountain. Approach with extreme caution. We're about to attempt a rescue before they take her off or do harm to her. Obviously we need backup asap."

He shut off the phone and put it on his belt clip. He turned to Sali and Julene.

"Are you just about finished with your social calls?" complained Sali. "Don't you want to check your Facebook messages, too?"

"Very funny. Are you guys ready?"

"Fucking-A," said Julene. "Let's get the show on the road for Christ's sake!"

"What's the plan?" asked Sali.

I'm going to try to call Masen. He held up his radio and clicked the Send button, "Masen, can you read me?"

* * *

At that very moment Masen had gotten as close to the pier as he could, without being seen, but he had turned his radio off in case Jason or Sali tried to call him, thus giving away his position.

* * *

"Masen, do you read, over?" He waited a few moments.

"Well, I don't see the guard on the pier. Masen could be hidden with the guard, or just by himself, or maybe he's in the mountain or the radio's dead. At any rate, we can't expect any help shoreside at the moment."

Sali said, "Even if you could reach him, the guy on the yacht, or Marek, might hear the call and be after us, or take off, and the President's daughter is in the wind."

"We can't go far in this sub. We can take you ladies back to the shore, but I don't know what your chances would be with them on the island—probably not good, but Masen is there somewhere, I hope."

"One thing I know for sure, though, Sali—I have to try to rescue Charise. So, you can go with us, or we'll drop you off."

Naieema said, "I know I've been scared to death coming out here in this thing, but I'd rather die than be sold as some sex slave."

They all agreed in one voice.

"Okay, then," said Jason. "We can try to get as close as possible, and Sali and I can get on there and try to somehow either take over the ship, which is highly doubtful, or just get Charise off the boat and into the sub and go underwater and get as far away as possible. When we start to run out of air, we'll have to surface and try our luck with the radio."

"I'm going with you!" shouted Julene. "I don't know how, but I want to ruin that miserable fuck Marek's plans."

"Julene, this is too dangerous," said Jason.

"Too dangerous? What do you call sitting on the bottom of the fucking ocean for an hour? I'm going!"

Jason and Sali looked at each other and shrugged. "Okay," said Jason, "but please try to stay behind us and out of the way until we need you. And be quiet!"

"I will. Just let me go with you."

"Okay, Captain Chet, take a compass heading toward the yacht's stern, and descend to about twenty feet. No lights, and let's hope there are no obstacles between here and there. You got an approximate range?"

"Yeah, I'm pretty good at that over open ocean."

"Okay, then, let's do it!"

Chapter Forty-Two
The Superyacht

Charise was still whimpering and crying moments after Gorsh had kicked the guard Marek murdered off the pier and into the ocean.

"All right, button your lip," said Marek as he holstered his pistol. "Let's go for a boat ride."

Gorsh firmly grabbed the arm of Charise and began to lead her down the pier.

"Ow!" she complained. "You're hurting me!"

"Then move it," said Gorsh.

The three of them walked briskly down the old wooden pier. The old bleached-out wooden planks clacked under their steps and the occasional squeak of a nail meant the old wood planks were about to come loose through years of hurricanes and tropical storms and intense heat, saltwater, and sunlight.

At the end of the pier the beautifully restored 1976 thirty-foot Chris Craft Tournament Fisherman, *Bloodstone*, was tied up. Within the wooden pylons close by were motion detectors, hidden cameras, and a loud alarm that Marek shut off with a security keypad three pylons before they got to the craft.

The three stepped onto the *Bloodstone* and Marek took the wheel. He inserted a key into the ignition and started the two T/454 Crusader engines, turned on the running lights, and finally turned on the inside cabin lights. She was a beautiful boat designed to sleep a family of five, but could hold more people if needed.

He revved the engines a couple of times to make sure they were running smoothly, then motioned to Gorsh to untie the bow and stern lines.

Gorsh did so, then gave the boat a hefty push away from the pier.

Marek told Charise to sit down, then headed for the superyacht a mile offshore. The old Chris Craft had surprisingly good speed and performed with a very smooth ride.

Before long they were nearing the *Turquoise Lament*, which had four decks plus a roomy flying bridge. Marek slowed and aimed for the tender garage opening at the stern of the yacht.

All along the outline of the yacht, underwater lights shone every few feet making for a spectacular outline of the boat from high above, or below.

Marek carefully pulled the *Bloodstone* into the tender garage of the *Turquoise Lament*. Inside the superyacht, one side of the tender garage was a bar, with Emile the bartender shaking a drink for Kostya, who sat at the bar waiting for Marek. On the left was a lounge area where guests could sit and enjoy their drinks and chat.

As Marek pulled in, two crew members closed the opening to the tender garage to form a walkway of teak so that you could walk completely around the *Bloodstone*.

"Welcome aboard," said Kostya as he took the first sip of his drink. "I'm having a pisco sour. Would you and your guests care to join me?"

Gorsh was busy tying off the *Bloodstone*, although it didn't really need it, since it was enclosed within the tender. Charise just scowled at Kostya and said nothing.

Marek stepped off the *Bloodstone* onto the *Turquoise Lament* and into the bar where he took a seat next to Kostya and nodded at the bartender to signal that he would indeed like a pisco sour.

"Say, what exactly is a pisco sour, anyway?" said Marek.

"It's the national drink of both Peru and Chile, invented in 1920 by an American bartender named Victor Vaughen Morris in Lima, Peru and improved to its present recipe by his employee, Mario Bruiget. As you can tell, I'm quite a fan of the drink. Peruvian pisco sours have egg white, the Chilean version does not. We're having the Peruvian version."

As the bartender poured the drink, Marek said, "So here she is, I've brought you Charise Pearl. She's all yours for the gemstones we agreed upon. However, I have a bit of a problem."

Kostya looked at him for a full two seconds. "What kind of problem?"

"Three men—I don't know who they are—found their way inside Rubicon Mountain. Their mission was apparently to rescue the three women we brought from Fort Lauderdale. I don't know if they are hired guns or what, but they're good, really good, and they not only left with the three women, but they let all our young assets escape in the boat that brought the three men to the island."

Kostya's face began to turn red and his voice trembled with rage, but it was still quiet. "And how did the three men and three women escape?"

Marek took a short look at his drink, then knocked it down in one gulp. "Two of them and the captain who brought the boat over, plus the three other women, escaped in the Triton sub."

Kostya's face looked like it was going to explode, and this time he screamed, "They escaped in my five-million-dollar submarine?" He slammed his fist down and the pisco glass jumped an inch into the air. "Where are they?"

"Well, they escaped about two hours ago, so they can't be far."

"What about the child assets?"

"Reznik went after them in the boat that he came over in from Fort Lauderdale, but he's not answering his radio. He's bad about remembering to charge it, but I don't see that he could have had any problem—they didn't get that much of a head start."

Kostya motioned to one of his men: "Take the Pearl woman to my stateroom and lock her in." He turned to Marek and Gorsh. "Sooner or later Reznik should call to report in. If he doesn't soon, we'll have to assume he's been captured or killed."

Gorsh climbed off the *Bloodstone* and sat at a table near Kostya and Marek.

Kostya said, "Do you think these men that came to get the three other women know anything about Charise Pearl?"

"I don't see how," replied Marek. "Surely they would have taken her, too, if they had the chance and knew she was there."

"Or maybe," said Kostya, "they knew about her but couldn't find her, or knew they had to get the hell out of there, then called the marines and we're about to get invaded."

"There's no communication to the outside world from inside the mountain, and they sure can't transmit underwater."

"Which means," broke in Kostya, "that we'd better find them fast, or kill the President's daughter and get the hell out of here. But I want that woman. I fucking hate that President, and I want to fuck his daughter till she can't walk for a week, and I want him to see a videotape of it."

"Okay, what next, then?"

"Let's move to the bridge and see if we can find the sub on the radar or the sonar. Maybe they went to the surface since it's night and they won't know where in the hell they are."

Chapter Forty-Three
Kill Everybody

Thirty feet directly below the *Turquoise Lament* the Triton sub hovered while the occupants gazed upward at the monstrous yacht encircled by its halo of underwater lights.

"They won't be able to find us on the radar if we're right under them," said Captain Chet.

"Okay, there's the stern," Jason pointed out, "and there's Marek's boat in the tender garage, so he and his bodyguard and Charise are onboard." The whole tableau was lit up brightly by the halo of lights around the superyacht. "If Kostya hadn't had such a big ego and smarts instead, he would have turned the lights off."

"This is going to be tricky," said Sali. "How do we know where to surface and board the vessel without getting spotted?"

"If we surface near the bow," said the captain, "it might be harder for them to see us, but that would be almost impossible to scale because it's so high from the waterline."

"To me," said Sali, "the best spot would probably be near the stern, since they've already done the business of onboarding Marek and Charise and the big guy, but we don't want to come up right inside the tender garage either, or they'll see us. So, I say let's surface right close to the starboard aft quarter and try to get onto the fantail or however we can, then the captain submerges again and stays directly under the boat."

"Spoken like a true former SEAL," said Jason, "but then what?"

"We kill everybody," said Sali.

"You make it sound so easy," said Julene quietly.

"Except Charise," continued Sali, "and throw a bunch of flotation in the water so the captain can see where to pick us up. Then we jump in the water. I guess."

"You guess? Well, that is a simple enough plan, except the 'kill everybody' part, so we'll have to grab weapons and ammo every chance we get and pray it's a light crew."

"On a ship like this? I doubt that," said Captain Chet. "Superyachts like this one typically have a pretty large crew—could be a dozen to fifty onboard."

"There goes the 'kill everybody' part," said Julene.

"Unless we really have to," said Sali. "You're right about grabbing as many guns and as much ammo as we can, just in case."

"Okay, the primary mission is to rescue Charise, but capture or kill Marek if we can."

"I'll kill him," said Julene enthusiastically. "Oh, *please*," she begged, "let me kill him. I *want* to kill him."

Jason and Sali looked at each other. "We'll do our best to accommodate you," said Jason.

A short silence ensued.

"Okay," said Jason, "check your weapons and your ammo. Julene, are you sure you want to do this? There's an extremely high likelihood that one or all of us will be killed."

"Fuck yeah!" she replied. "Give me a knife, too, so I can slit his throat."

"Here," said Sali. "I always carry two knives. This one's a fixed blade pocket knife—you operate it like this." He showed her how.

"If we kill some bad guys," Jason said to Julene, "I'll give you a gun. Do you know how to shoot?"

"Sure do. My Dad was a marine and made me learn how to shoot fucking almost anything."

"Well, that explains the language," Colorado said coolly.

"On second thought," said Sali, "give me back my knife and I'll give you my Mark 23. It's easier to kill someone by shooting than stabbing."

They made the trade and Julene chambered a round into the Mark 23. "Let's go get that fucker."

"Hold on a second," said Jason. "Let's see if we can check on Masen. Maybe he has some intel or can tell us what's going on. As soon as we open the hatch, let me try to reach Masen first."

"Are you crazy?" said Sali. "If they hear us, we're dead."

"As soon as we surface, we'll just move so the hatch is just above water. I'll pull the antenna on the radio up all the way and just stick that through the opened hatch. I'll try the call just inside the sub, quietly, and see if we get a response. Either way, we carry on and board the vessel."

"I hope it's worth the risk," said Sali doubtfully.

"If they spot us when we peek up for the transmission, we abort that plan and reassess the situation—probably drop down twenty feet. If someone spots us, we close the hatch and dive again. If it's clear, we go for it. Everybody clear on that?"

Everybody nodded their approval.

"Okay, then, head for the surface, Captain Chet. Slowly."

Chapter Forty-Four
Call for Backup

The SEAL Team Commander called Jamie Horgood from their headquarters in Coronado, California.

"You were right," he said. "We captured the boatload of kids and ended up in a gun battle which we tried to avert, but could not, and every one of the perpetrators on board was killed with no losses on our side."

"Well I've got more news that's right down your alley. The President's kidnapped daughter Charise is there somewhere."

"Holy smokes! Somewhere?"

"All I know is she's on the island, or was, just a little while ago. I notified the Secret Service, and I thought they would have contacted you by now."

"Probably hasn't trickled down from the Special Operations Task Force yet. We'll get reorganized on the ground and do a recon asap. I'll keep in touch with you and your team as often as possible. We'll be directing aerial surveillance as soon as we can. Do you know how big this operation is?"

"Not yet. I have three men on the ground there whom I have high confidence in, but I don't know where they are at the moment. They definitely need some help. I'll do what I can to find out where they are and get back to you. Actually, if there's a chance, I'd like to go there, too, and see them myself."

They rang off, and Jamie stared at her phone, trying like hell to will Jason, or Sali, or Masen to call and tell her what the hell was going on over there.

"Jason!" she screamed at the phone. "You're really pissing me off!"

Chapter Forty-Five
Masen in the Mangroves

Masen had not heard from Jason or Sali, and he had just seen Marek and the goon who had tried to find him take off with a woman he didn't recognize from afar on the boat at the end of the pier. He hoped this might be a chance to go back up through the mountain by way of the river again, and cross on over to the other side of the mountain where he could gain access to the Zodiac they had hidden in the mangroves. It could be dangerous if any guards were in the mountain, but he couldn't just sit there—he had to do something. The question in his mind, though, was whether he should take some or all of the jewels with him, and what was he going to do anyway if he did get to the boat? And where were Jason and Sali, anyway?

He held up his radio and called in, "Stinkfinger, this is Booty Man, come in." He repeated several times, trying "Apache," too, but no luck. Either they were in the mountain, out of range, dead, or captured. In any case, he decided to move and leave the jewels and boxes behind, at least for now.

Slowly he moved out of his hiding place in the tall grass and boulders and made his way to the stream that came out of the mountain and led back to Marek's lair. He waded as quickly as he could back into the mountain and only used his light when strictly necessary. The sound of the stream running around him and the occasional squeak and smell of the bats seemed natural and reassuring to him, so he quickened his pace until he got to the pier where the *Garnet Lady* used to be tied up.

So, Marek's men had gone after the kids in the *Garnet Lady*, apparently, just as Marek had ordered, and it appeared as though no one was around. He started to move again, but just then a shot rang out and the rock wall of the cave immediately adjacent to his face exploded in dust and shards. As he jumped to the ground he looked to his left, where the pier ended and the tunnel began, and he saw one of the guards getting ready to shoot again.

Just then a tremendous cloud of shrieking, velvety black bats—alerted by the gunshot—began to leave their peaceful existence clinging to the top of the cave and fly quickly in every direction of the compass and downward toward the stream, bombing everything and everybody with little piles of runny bat dung. The shrieking was deafening and Masen heard the guard scream in terror and turn to run up the tunnel toward the blue lagoon. Masen stuck his whole body underwater, with his gun in hand just above the water, for as long as he could. When he finally ran out of breath and stuck his head above water, the noise had abated somewhat, and most of the bats had gone one way or the other to exit the cave. He quickly washed the blood from his face and found that the wound was minor and would soon heal.

"Holy shit," Masen muttered to himself as he finished washing and cautiously stood. He looked where the guard had disappeared, but there was no movement there. He quickened his pace to a near run to leave the cave, looking behind him often to see if the guard had reappeared, but fortunately, the guard apparently had decided he'd had enough of screaming, crapping bats for the day. Finally, Masen came to the entrance where they had first entered a seeming eternity ago.

The sun had already set, and the sounds of the swamp frogs and other animals had begun their nightly chorus, when far in the distance, toward Basseterre, he faintly heard a mighty gun battle ensuing.

"Oh shit," he murmured, "the C-4 must not have gone off," and he guessed Jamie had gotten through to some local enforcement.

But he didn't know who was winning that gun battle and almost certainly somebody would be coming back this way, and if it was Reznik and his men, he didn't want to be anywhere around.

He ran the rest of the way, as best he could, to the Zodiac hidden in the mangroves. He finally reached it, and like a madman, he tore away the covering leaves and branches and finally pulled the Zodiac out of hiding and on to the lake. The quiet electric motor started right up and Masen took off toward the opening in the mangroves from whence he had come, but when he got to the tree where he remembered they had planted the C-4, he moved slowly, very slowly, then stopped to inspect what had happened. The triggering string had caught on a twig before it could pull the detonating device, and snagged, and it looked like the *Garnet Lady* had plowed through a new path anyway.

"Oh shit," he said. He could hear a boat beginning to approach his location, but something told him this C-4 device might come in handy. Only problem was he didn't know fuck-all about explosives. He remembered what Jason and Sali had told him about arming and disarming the device, so he very carefully leaned over the Zodiac and very slowly started to disarm the device.

"Booty Man! Booty Man!" he heard in a hushed voice over his radio. "Are you there?"

Masen snapped back into the Zodiac and grabbed his radio and answered, "Jesus fucking Christ you scared the shit out of me, right while I was trying to disarm the C-4 and take it with me in the Zodiac. Obviously it didn't trigger. Yet."

"I can't talk right now," Jason whispered into the radio. "Come around the island to that big superyacht, but stay well clear of it, just within sight of it. We're about to board it. Gotta go!"

Masen signed off and said to himself, "Holy fuck, now what have they gotten themselves into?" He leaned over and disarmed the C-4 and took off in the Zodiac, into the black night and the flat seas to the other side of the island.

Chapter Forty-Six
Silent Entry

The engines of the *Turquoise Lament* had been slowly idling as it maintained its position in the sea. Although the noise from the engines and the bubbling from the exhaust pipes had been quiet, it was enough to cover up Jason's voice as he had just talked to Masen.

Jason pushed the hatch all the way open and stood ready to climb on to the fantail at the aft of the *Turquoise Lament* as Captain Chet pulled slowly up to its stern. Jason clambered quietly onto the fantail, keeping his eyes facing forward, looking for any sign of movement by the crew. He saw none and waved Sali and Julene on up to join him. The captain closed the hatch and immediately submerged far enough that he could look up and see the entire outline of the ship, blazingly obvious by the circle of underwater decorative lights surrounding the ship. Both vessels moved slowly.

The *Turquoise Lament* was of course magnificent and had several decks for multiple purposes. They had come aboard right where the fantail opens up to allow the tender garage to open up and allow the entrance of the *Bloodstone*. The *Bloodstone* was floating there, inside the yacht, but nobody was around, except the bartender, where Kostya, Marek, Gorsh and Charise had been sitting less than an hour ago.

The bartender was busy cleaning up the bar and mostly had his head down into the bar, straightening bottles, stacking the refrigerator with beers, and cleaning glasses.

Jason stepped quietly up to the bar and stuck the barrel of his Mark 23 into the temple of the bartender.

The bartender jumped with a start, then all the blood drained from his face.

"Don't say a word," Jason said, "and nobody will hurt you."

The bartender nodded vigorously.

"Now give me two of those bar towels over there so I can tie you up, unless you'd rather I put a bullet through your temple."

The bartender got the towels.

"Where is everybody located?" asked Jason.

"The boss and the people who just came in moved to the stateroom, two decks up those stairs." He pointed to a stairwell on the starboard side. "One of them looked like President Pearl's daughter."

"All the young women," he continued, "are down one deck. They have separate rooms, but they're locked in their rooms. I think the boss was going to move them to the island tonight."

"Wait. You say there are other women on board? How many?"

"Four. Very beautiful women, from Ukraine."

"What's their plan?"

"I don't know, Mister, I'm just the bartender, but every time before, he brings beautiful young women on board, then this guy Marek comes out and brings them to the island, then I never see them again. I don't know what they're doing."

"Sometimes," the bartender continued, "he brings new women—always beautiful women—but they don't come willingly, and we don't always go to this island. The boss takes them in and locks them in their rooms, then lets them out to other superyacht owners, one or two at a time, but always at sea and always at night."

"Let's go," said Julene. "Let's go get those mother fuckers."

"Those 'mother fuckers', as you call them, are surrounded by some very dangerous men with guns," said the bartender.

"Big surprise," said Sali. "Now set down and let me tie you up so you look like you didn't say anything."

Jason said, "Since the women are locked up, I'm guessing they're not guarded too heavily. Let's go down there and see if we can let them out. The plan is to get them on that Chris Craft and get them away from the yacht."

Just then one of the guards came down the stairs and said, "Boss wants two more pisco…"

He stopped in mid-sentence. "Who the fuck…?" He pulled his pistol from his shoulder holster and started shooting at the three of them.

They all dove for cover, but Sali stood like he owned the place and put one bullet through the guy's forehead.

"Holy shit!" screamed Julene.

"Quick," said Jason to Sali, "grab his gun."

As soon as Sali grabbed the gun off the body, they could hear shouts from above and a lot of people running down the stairs.

"Julene!" screamed Jason. "Get down to the deck where the women are and see if you can open their doors. Shoot the locks off if you have to. Sali and I will hold them off until you come back up and get them on the boat."

"Shit, I don't know how to drive that stupid thing!"

"Julene! Shut up and get moving! We'll drive it, if we get that far. If all else fails, jump over the side and hopefully Captain Chet will see you."

"Hopefully…" Julene said as she ran down the stairs. "Yeah, right…"

As soon as she disappeared down the steps, men came running down the other stairs, guns drawn.

Both Jason and Sali opened up with their H&K Mark 23s.

The roar of the guns was thunderous as everybody started shooting.

*　*　*

In the Stateroom, Kostya, Marek, Gorsh and Charise heard the gunfire and froze for a moment. Then Marek told Gorsh, "Go down there and kill whoever it is."

Gorsh pulled the gun from his holster and took off for the stairwell.

"Come with me," said Kostya to the others. He took them to a special den where he kept all his firearms. He unlocked the gun case and took out a small device and put it in his pocket.

"Take your pick," he said to Marek. "You," he said to Charise, "sit down there and don't move or go anywhere." He locked the gun case.

"Follow me," he said to Marek, "then he locked the door to the den behind them."

In the hallway he said to Marek, "As much as I hate the thought of destroying this yacht, I've wired it to blow with this remote." He pulled the device out of his pocket and showed it to Marek.

"We're sitting over a drop-off from Saba Bank that is over three thousand feet deep. If I sink the yacht, everyone and all the evidence of our mutual enterprise will be torn to pieces and sink to the bottom of the ocean. They'll have no evidence to hold us on."

"Let's hope it doesn't come to that. How do we get off of here if you decide to do that?"

"I had planned to take the Triton sub, but now they have it. That means we have to take the Zodiac tied down on top of the bow."

Marek chambered a round. "Let's go do it."

* * *

Masen was speeding around the island and even though the whole North Atlantic was now in front of him, the ocean's swells were barely perceptible and the surface was perfectly smooth—not a ripple as far as he could see. The sound of the quiet electric motor was the only sound in this vast quietude, and his thoughts turned to the fate of his partners. They had just boarded the superyacht, and it seemed like their chances were slim indeed.

Was Charise on board?

Were the women on board?

How did they get out there, anyway?

What would they do next?

Just then he heard gun shots from the superyacht, though he was still about a mile away.

"Shit. The fireworks have started," he said aloud. The only thing he could do was keep going as fast as he could toward the yacht.

Chapter Forty-Seven
Fight or Flight

Julene made it to the lower deck in a hurry and tried the handle on the first door on the left. Locked.

"Hello?" She shouted, "Is anybody in there?"

"Yes! Yes! Help me please!" Said a young woman in broken English.

Julene looked around the corridor for something to knock the door knob off. She didn't want to use the gun because she thought she might need the bullets. There it was: a fire extinguisher. She opened the case with the big red extinguisher and pulled it out: it was heavy.

She put her gun in her pants, grabbed the extinguisher and slammed it down on the door handle. Nothing happened. She tried again and really threw herself into it, and this time it snapped off the handle which went bouncing down the hallway. She stuck her fingers into the hole where the handle had been and finally got the locking mechanism to move and allow the door to open. She pushed the door open and a young Ukrainian girl, maybe twenty-one years old, stared at her wide-eyed, frozen, not knowing what to do next.

"Hey, girl!" said Julene, "Let's get the hell out of here," and she motioned for the girl to leave the room. It was Nyura, and she did so immediately.

Above them they could hear the guns blazing away.

She spoke loudly to her: "How well do you speak English?"

"Speak, not so good. Understand, okay."

Julene spoke slowly and used her hands: "We have to get the other girls free and try to get to the small boat one deck up. Do you understand?"

She nodded eagerly.

"Okay, let's work on these doors."

They set about trying to knock open the doors…

***

Jason and Sali had killed all the guards except Gorsh, who had picked up a machine gun from one of the dead guards. They were all exchanging fire when suddenly new gunfire erupted from the open sides of the tender garage.

It was SEAL Team Five and they were firing at Gorsh. Jamie must have told them what Jason and Sali looked like.

Gorsh backtracked to another staircase away from the SEAL's fusillade and ran up to where Marek and Kostya were and said, "They've got us outnumbered big time."

Kostya said, "Shit. Let's head for the Zodiac at the bow and blow the ship. Follow me."

They ran down a long corridor and came to a watertight door that led to the bow. They unfastened the Zodiac, then Kostya said to Marek and Gorsh, "We'll have to lower it to the sea, then jump in the water and swim to it just before I trip the explosion."

They lowered the Zodiac to the sea, then Gorsh and Marek jumped into the sea and climbed into the boat. Kostya got ready to jump, then tripped the explosion switch, and jumped.

Rather than one massive explosion, a series of small explosions triggered in the lowest deck. Fires began to spread.

***

Jason yelled at Sali: "You go down and get the girls and the bartender onto the Bloodstone! I'm going to go find the President's daughter!"

In the decks below, the explosions rocked the ship, and it wasn't long before fires began to spread around the deck where Julene was still trying to crash open the doors.

Sali came running down the stairs and yelled, "Follow me!" to the girls.

The young women ran up the stairs and Sali took them to the *Bloodstone*. As the women boarded the smaller boat, Sali and one of the SEALs opened the transom to allow the *Bloodstone* to go back out to sea.

"All of our guys aren't here yet. Where's the President's daughter?" said the SEAL at the helm.

"My man Jason's gone to get her!" yelled Sali over the sound of the encroaching flames. "Just get these girls out. I'm going to go help get the rest of them!"

The SEAL took over the *Bloodstone* while the other SEALs made their way to their own boats they had arrived quietly on.

The flames were now almost totally engulfing the *Turquoise Lament*. One of the Ukrainian girls came running up the stairs.

"Where's Julene!" screamed Sali at the girls over the sound of the flames. "The American girl with the blond hair!"

"She would not leave," the girl said. "She said she had one more door to break open. I had to leave—it was just too hot and I couldn't help her."

Suddenly, the whole ship took a violent, big twist to port and began to sink as the flames on the remaining deck grew even larger.

"Let's get out of here," yelled Sali at the top of his lungs. "There's nothing more we can do!"

Sali looked back to where he'd just been, and said in a quiet voice, "So long, Julene, I'm sorry…"

Two decks up Jason found Charise, frozen in fear and surrounded by fire. "Quick! Follow me!" he screamed. He grabbed her arm and pulled her through a hole in the flames and they found themselves near the railing of the great yacht. "Jump!" Jason shouted to Charise. She looked at him in total terror. "Don't worry, I'm coming right behind you!" She jumped, and Jason followed her into the sea as the yacht began to lurch and dip into the sea.

"Swim away from the ship," Jason yelled to Charise, "or you'll be sucked under when it sinks!" They both swam as hard as they could away from the slowly sinking vessel.

The SEAL was still holding the *Bloodstone* for them when Sali and the three other Ukrainian girls jumped aboard. Rapidly, the *Bloodstone* moved in reverse and left the *Turquoise Lament*. The great superyacht then quickly sank and a complete silence surrounded them.

"Help!" It was the last Ukrainian girl who was swimming away from the sinking ship. The SEAL took the *Bloodstone* over to where she was and picked her out of the sea and safely aboard.

"Look!" yelled one of the Ukrainian girls. She pointed over to Jason and Charise swimming toward the *Bloodstone*.

Sali turned to the Ukrainian girl they had just plucked from the sea, "What about the woman who freed you, the blond woman? Did she jump with you?"

"No. She was running after she pulled me out of room."

Just then the sub surfaced near their boat. Captain Chet opened the hatch and stuck his head out. "This must be all the floating debris you were talking about."

Far in the distance they heard two shots, then silence.

Chapter Forty-Eight
A Swift Kick

Masen was running as fast as his little five horsepower propane-powered outboard could take him, which wasn't very fast at all. The *Turquoise Lament* had just sunk and Masen was steering toward the faint lights of the *Bloodstone* he saw in the distance, as well as some other lights, which he couldn't distinguish. Ahead of him he saw a Zodiac with three men that was stalled, yet they didn't appear to hear Masen approaching. The big man he had seen chasing him after he had stolen Marek's jewels had his back to Masen as he was trying in vain to get the outboard started, so these guys were definitely trouble. Masen cut his engine, pulled out his pistol and drifted up next to their Zodiac. Maybe they would tell him what happened and where Jason and Sali were.

But just as Masen pulled alongside, Kostya pulled his pistol out of his holster and aimed it at Masen. Masen fired into the man's brain before he could get off a shot. Marek already had his gun out by that time and aimed it at Masen and pulled the trigger.

Click.

No shot! The gun was empty.

Gorsh turned at the instant of the first shot and began to pull out his gun, but by then, Masen saw it coming and shot Gorsh through the heart, sending him back over the transom and into the ocean. He turned to Marek.

Marek dropped his gun and froze as Masen held the gun on him.

"Hey! Over here!" It was a woman's voice screaming out in the sea.

Masen turned to the voice, but couldn't locate her at first.

"Hey, you dumb bastard, over here!"

"Leave her," said Marek, his eyelids dropping to half-mast.

"Hold on!" said Masen toward the voice. Then to Marek: "Toss me your bowline, and don't do anything dumb or you'll be in for a long swim. Or a bullet."

Marek threw the bowline and Masen tied it to the stern of his Zodiac. He restarted his engine, then yelled out into the black sea, "Where are you?"

"Right here, you dumb fuck!"

She was very close to him, bobbing up and down with a bright orange lifejacket on, waving her arms.

He pulled up alongside Julene and said, "Here, give me your hands and I'll pull you in."

She did so and settled down on the seat and shivered. She didn't look at him. He retrieved a sweater in the knapsack he had brought and tossed it to her. "Here; hopefully this will warm you up."

She took off her life vest and Masen's eyes widened at the sight of her physique. She put the sweater on quickly then said, "I'm sorry for yelling at you like that. Thank you. I guess you just saved my life. Who are you?"

"My name is Masen. I'm with Jason and Sali."

"Elvis," she chuckled under her breath, then louder, "Where are they?" She started to look around.

Just then she noticed that Marek was in the other skiff. She screamed, "Hey! You dirty rotten bastard!"

"Whoa, sit down or you'll fall over. Who are you and who is he?"

"My name is Julene and that son-of-a-bitch is the guy who kidnapped me and is the ringleader of that whole damn human trafficking scheme! The asshole just tried to sell me, and he was my fucking boyfriend!"

She noticed Masen's gun in its holster and reached for it, but Masen stopped her. "Whoa, don't kill him. We might need him as a hostage when we go back to the mountain."

"Go back to the mountain?" screamed Julene. "Are you fucking nuts? That's where he lives! Let's go over to where the yacht just sunk and meet up with Jason."

Masen thought for a second. "We don't know we can meet up with them, and I don't have much fuel left. We'd better take the safe bet and head back to the island."

"But his whole fucking army is back there!"

"Not any more they're not, and I'm not going back inside the mountain anyway. I need to pick up a package near the pier."

He put the engine in idle and turned to Julene. "You tie him up while I hold the gun on him. Whatever you do, don't get between him and me."

Julene stepped over into Marek's skiff and skillfully and with much gusto kicked him hard in the balls.

Marek collapsed in agony, groaning loudly.

"That ought to soften him up," she said, then set about tying him up as best she could.

Chapter Forty-Nine
Prince of Thieves

As the sun rose, the U.S. Navy SEALs and support vessels were all over the area where the *Turquoise Lament* had sunk the night before. There was debris everywhere, but they had spotted a Zodiac floating aimlessly two miles from where the ship had sunk.

Jason and Sali, joined by Jamie now, were aboard the U.S. Coast Guard vessel *Opuhala* as it approached the Zodiac that Marek, Gorsh and Kostya had escaped in. On the bottom of the boat was the dead body of Kostya, with a bullet hole in his forehead. He was sloshing back and forth in a mixture of blood and sea water, and birds of various types were walking quietly around on the gunwale of the boat.

"I wonder who that was," said Jamie.

"I don't know, but I think he was the owner of the yacht that went down. He was with Marek and his bodyguard when I got in a shootout with him right before the whole thing caught fire and sank."

They searched the rest of that day and night for their friends Masen and Julene, as well as Marek, but found no signs of them and assumed they had drowned or were killed.

"Damn," said Jason. "I really liked your friend Masen. We couldn't have done this without him. And Julene," he said, sadly shaking his head. "She was one in a million. I'm really, really going to miss her spirit. Never had a bad word to say about anybody…except Marek, of course. Yeah, I really liked her a lot. Damn."

Sali just took another drag on his Djarum and tossed the butt out into the ocean. "I guess I shouldn't pollute the ocean like that." He shook his head, turned and walked aft on the Coast Guard cutter.

Everyone who had been rescued was alive and well.

* * *

The young ladies from Odesa were given the choice of being extradited to Ukraine, or continuing on to America and apply for citizenship or temporary work permits. All but Nyura decided to move on to America and take their chances. Nyura returned to Odesa and decided to live with her parents until she decided what to do with her life.

Three months after the sinking of the *Turquoise Lament,* in the President's re-election inaugural speech, he declared, "Human trafficking is the most evil form of greed, using a currency of souls stolen from the underprivileged, the destitute, the uneducated, and the unaware. We must make a strong moral stand against this global scourge and fight it with all our might."

Within a month, a bill was passed in the U.S. Congress that quadrupled the resources allotted to Homeland Security Investigations to investigate and combat human trafficking. The funds were utilized to track down hundreds of human traffickers due solely to the damning details found in a book of transactions sent to the State Department from an unknown source with a fake return address.

About the same time, seventeen different reputable anti-trafficking organizations around the world each received briefcases that had five million dollars cash in each.

Masen's boat, the *Booty*, had gone unclaimed, and a local church had taken over the care of it, and a local Captain had joined the effort and helped the church and taught the kids the ways of the sea. It helped that some unknown benefactor had donated over one million dollars to the church for the upkeep of the boat.

Soon after all that, Sali got a custom post card with a picture of Julene and Masen smiling and sitting on the porch of a palatial mansion somewhere in the tropics, having drinks with little umbrellas in them, and their left ring-fingers conspicuously showing wedding rings, each made with a huge diamond, sapphire, and emerald. In the background was Marek, hanged by the neck from a gumbo-limbo tree, hands bound behind him, naked, and with a big sack of coconuts hanging from his scrotum.

There were only these words on the postcard: "Finally got back at that rotten son-of-a-bitch. Love, J & M."

THE END

Epilogue

There is no island named Dark Island, or mountain called Rubicon Mountain, in order to protect the sensibilities of real nations who do in fact facilitate and harbor the international trafficking of sex and other types of slaves; and the Caribbean, South America, and North America are certainly not innocent in this global reach of the second or third most profitable scheme of crime in the world today. This book renders a scene of the sex slave trade in perhaps a new light, but greatly understates the scope of this global scourge. Millions of peoples' souls are stolen every day for the sake of gaining a profit for people who are arguably the most unfathomably evil in the world today. Although there is debate as to whether it ranks second ($120 billion) to drugs ($450 billion) or third (after counterfeiting, $250 billion) in illegal proceeds, there is no doubt that it is a crime of the soul in which people's lives are ruined. For more information, you can start here: https://humantraffickinghotline.org/.

The character Masen Williams is based on a real person, Bill Mason, regarded by many as the most successful cat burglar in American history. So far as I know, he's never had anything to do with catching human traffickers.

CPSIA information can be obtained
at www.ICGtesting.com
Printed in the USA
BVHW051531210423
662800BV00007B/400